BLOODROOT

DANIEL V. MEIER JR.

North Carolina

Published in the United States by BQB Publishing
(an imprint of Boutique of Quality Books Publishing, Inc.)
www.bqbpublishing.com

Printed in the United States of America

978-1-952782-04-6 (p)
978-1-952782-05-3 (e)

Library of Congress Control Number 2021937624

Book design: Robin Krauss, www.bookformatters.com
Cover design: Rebecca Lown, www.rebeccalowndesign.com
First editor: Caleb Guard
Second editor: Andrea Vande Vorde
Map Illustrations: Rosana Kelcher

Praise for *Bloodroot* and Daniel V. Meier, Jr.

"By turns heartbreaking and fascinating. . . . A raw, powerful story.

Meier returns with a stunning story about a man caught in the grip of treachery, passion, and the inescapable flow of history. England 1609. After a minor scuffle with his master, the young Matthew, an apprentice carpenter, finds himself running away from the law, joining his best friend Richard on an excursion to the early British settlement of Jamestown, Virginia. But what begins as a journey to a promising land soon turns into a nightmare of impossible proportions with hunger and savagery testing the limits of humanity. With lust for Richard's wife, Anne, Matthew soon embarks on a path of sin and treachery. But guilt soon takes over, and living becomes a burden.

Meier's eye for detail is immaculate, whether it is the evocation of the rugged, unforgivable landscape of Virginia or the portrayal of the grizzly horrors of a desperate and dying community. He ably interweaves scenes of settlers' everyday life along with the fantastical world of the native American culture and their legends and beliefs into the affecting narrative.

The characters are universally human in their emotion, be it honest, morally upright Richard or troubled Anne. Matthew is a triumph; he has loose morals and integrity is not something he values much, but Meier depicts him with humanity and compassion, making him thoroughly humane.

The narrative moves at a swift pace, building to shocking revelations as fate intertwines and Matthew eventually finds meaning in life. Meier's skillful manipulation of interlocking plot strands, keen insight, and entertaining storytelling make it a page-turner."

– The Prairies Book Review

———•◦•———

"I thoroughly enjoyed yet another book by Daniel V. Meier. In *Bloodroot*, he returns to a familiar theme—the goodness and the brutality of man. Set in the early days of the Jamestown settlement in Virginia, when Matthew and his friend Richard arrive after a dangerous sea journey, they have very different goals. Richard's unfailing belief in the goodness of man does not serve him well in the new rough colony which is run by fear and force. His character is well-drawn and while realizing he is naive in his beliefs, the reader is drawn to him. Matthew's approach is more alert to the brutality of the adventurers, but at heart, he is a kind, fair, and just character.

The conditions of the settlement are so clearly drawn, and take you back four hundred years to suffer, cheer, and weep with the folk in Jamestown. The deprivations during the long, hard winter will make you shiver. The author's descriptions of the ways people fought to stay alive will haunt me for days. The tenacity to cling to life is brilliantly depicted in this story of greed, pride, and superiority so unwisely let loose. In retrospect, it's a miracle anyone survived and thrived. Highly recommended."

– Lucinda E. Clarke for Reader's Favorite

Table of Contents

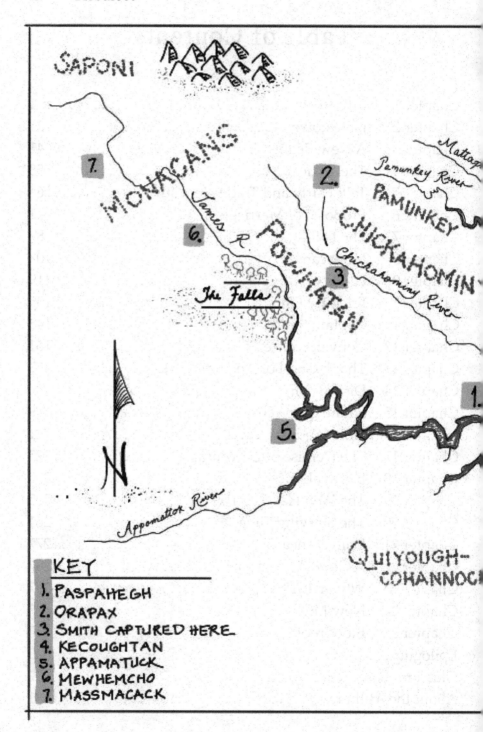

KEY
1. PASPAHEGH
2. ORAPAX
3. SMITH CAPTURED HERE
4. KECOUGHTAN
5. APPAMATUCK
6. MEWHEMCHO
7. MASSMACACK

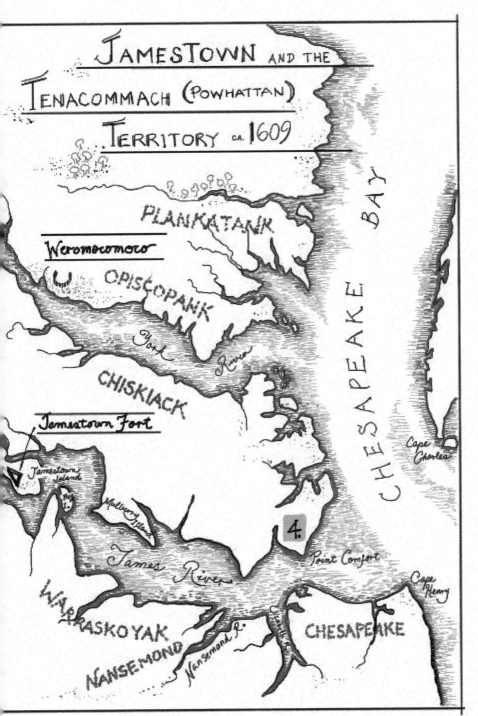

JAMESTOWN AND THE TENACOMMACH (POWHATTAN) TERRITORY ca. 1609

CHESAPEAKE BAY

PLANKATANK
Weromocomoco
OPISCOPANK
York River
CHISKIACK
Jamestown Fort
Jamestown Island
Hog
Mulberry Island
James River
WARRASKOYAK
NANSEMOND
Nansemond R.
Chisiack
CHESAPEAKE
Point Comfort
Cape Charles
Cape Henry
4.

Map Illustrator: Rosana Keleher

This book is dedicated to Elizabeth.

Acknowledgment

Caleb Guard, my editor, for his professionalism and assistance. Teeja Meier for her faith, patience, endurance, suggestions, hard work, and love.

CHAPTER 1

July 1609

I had fought this time more bitterly than before with my master of Exeter. He struck me once too often with his whip and, being a young man of almost twenty years, I was seized with a blind rage. I jerked the whip out of his hand, wrapped it around his shriveled neck, and started to haul him up on one of the crossbeams of his shop, but his choking and gagging brought my senses back, and I let him fall to the floor where he cursed me and swore that he would have me thrown in prison that very hour. My rage returned, and I kicked him until he lay unconscious at my feet like a heap of dirty rags.

I left his shop and the city of Exeter without stopping to gather my few belongings, and started out for the city of Plymouth where I had a friend who would shelter me until I could find new employment.

It was well after dark when I arrived in Plymouth and found my friend, Richard, busy packing his chests. He seemed extremely pleased, not just at my arrival but in what he called his "future prospect" in Virginia.

"How wonderful, how prophetic, that you have arrived at this hour! God himself must have guided you, my friend. I tell you truly, Matthew. It is a new promised land, a new Canaan," he said to me while packing away his books in a smaller chest. "We are the ones chosen to leave this vile and sinful land.

Virginia will be our new Paradise, where men can live the way
their Creator intended: in goodness and charity."

I had always known Richard to be a dreamer, but this, going
to a wilderness like Virginia? I wondered if he had not lost his
senses from too much reading and studying.

"I have heard of this place called Virginia, Richard, and I
have heard that it is inhabited by naked savages who think
nothing of bashing a man's brains out or of eating their own
people. And I have heard that this place is often as cold as it is
here in England and as hot as it is in Spain, and that the air is
filled with many sicknesses."

"Rumors, gossip, exaggerations!" Richard said, pulling a
pamphlet out of his book chest and thrusting it at me. "Read
this," he said, excited. "It was written by one of the London
Company's own members who has himself been to Virginia
many times."

I read through the pamphlet and returned it to him.

"It truly does sound like Paradise, Richard, but perhaps it
sounds too good."

"But it was written and published with the consent of the
London Company. What reason would they have to lie about
it? What profit would there be? Surely, they would be found out
if they were not telling the truth."

"I admit that what you say makes sense, but I don't want
to leave England. I am not the scholar that you are. Vice and
corruption do not offend me the way they do you."

"Then think of it this way. You are in need of employment.
You have broken the terms of your apprenticeship by running
away. You have assaulted your master. Good God, Matthew,
you could go to prison for many years. And if you survive that,
what would you do?"

His reasoning was sound. The very thought of prison

stunned me into silence, and as long as I remained in England, my old master, Dorn, would not rest until he saw me behind bars. I was swept by a feeling of danger. I realized then how important my freedom was to me and how precious was my life. Few survive more than three years in the King's prison.

"Come with me, Matthew. Virginia will be our new kingdom. It will be our chance to begin the world over again, the way it should be, a place full of love and happiness. As for the savages, they are only children in a Garden of Eden, waiting for the light of Christianity. You see, Matthew," he moved closer to my face, his breathing short, his eyes dancing with excitement, "this is our opportunity to do what is right."

I turned away, hoping the gesture would calm his passion.

"Do you have any ale?" I asked.

He stood up at once, erect as if I had slapped him across the face.

"I do not need ale now, Matthew. I have discovered that God's own purest water is enough for me. My only interest now is in food and drink for the spirit."

"Well, if you don't mind, Richard, I would like a tankard of good ale and some food for my body."

"I have some bread and sausage newly purchased today."

"Thank you, my friend, but I would like to find a tavern and think on what you have proposed."

The tavern was crowded with men like myself, on the move, without prospects, men on the watch for opportunity. I spotted a sailor seated with several other men at a corner table. The sailor was using tobacco, as were most of the men in the place, but he was smoking it in an unusual pipe, a short thing made out of dark clay, brightly painted and with a large bird's feather fixed at the end.

I went over to them and asked if I could join their table. The sailor wanted to know for what purpose, and I explained that I was thinking of planting in Virginia and that from the look of his pipe, he was a man who might be acquainted with those parts. He laughed aloud, and I could see in the dim light of the candles that he had only a few teeth, and those were stained and crooked, and that his left eye was as white as marble.

The other two men looked at me suspiciously.

"Aye, lad, sit down," the sailor shouted. He slapped the bench next to him with a gnarled hand. "I will tell you all you wish to know about that heathen land, but me throat be hot and wishes to be cooled by the sweet elixir of this fine tavern's ale."

I waved for the barmaid and ordered four tankards, a deed which would considerably reduce my finances.

"Now," the sailor said, leaning back against the tavern's wall and drawing smoke from his pipe. "Why would a lad such as yourself, a young gentleman, if I'm any judge of men, wish to go to such a place?"

"I am a carpenter, sir," I said, trying to appear older than my years, "and work is not easy to find in England these days. I have heard that certain worthy gentlemen of these parts have set out to build a town in that land and would most likely have need of a man of my trade."

The sailor nodded, and then, seeing the barmaid coming with both of her arms full of tankards, smiled happily. Almost as soon as our maid had sat the tankard before him, he buried his face in it for a long time. The other two men followed his example. I watched their Adam's apples work in unison as they gulped down the ale.

"Aye, yes," the sailor said, finally setting his drink before him and wiping the foam from his beard with the back of his hand. "They do have need of men with your skill in Virginia. They have need of every man they can get."

The sailor laughed heartily and so did the other two men.

"And God knows," he continued, "there is timber enough to build not only a town but a hundred cities the size of London. There is hardly a square yard where a good-sized tree does not grow. But for every man cutting a tree there be four and sometimes six to guard him against the bloody, throat-cutting savages. And often that is not enough, for there must be a hundred savages to every one Englishman. Nay, I say even a thousand savages to one of our men. What is wanting in Virginia is an English army, and not the merchants and gentlemen who are presently there. By God, as much as I despise those popish swine of Spain, I'll say one thing good for them, they know how to plant a colony. None of this cowardly, weak-bellied, hands-off policy toward the savages for them."

The sailor leaned closer to me. "If you want to find your fortune in Virginia, my lad, first learn to fight."

"But that is true enough for any man," said one of the other men.

"Aye, it's true enough, but in Virginia it is always your life you're fighting for. There is scarce any law even among our own men and none among the savages, save the hatchet and the arrow. But for a man who can use a sword and a musket, Virginia is a vast, rich land waiting to be claimed. You could be a king, my lad."

"Or at least a lord," the other man said.

They all laughed good-naturedly, not meaning to offend.

"Sir," said I to the sailor, "you are certainly a fighting man yourself. Why have you not claimed your share of this new land?"

He laughed again, spitting some ale on his beard.

"True enough. I've done my share of fighting, but it was never for myself. It was always some quarrel between princes, and you see how I am rewarded." He pointed to his dead eye. "Fighting is for young men such as yourself. We old men stand aside and pick at the spoils and tell everyone how glorious it all was when it is over."

"Will your ship be taking the planters to Virginia?" I asked.

"Aye, that she will. *Diamond* is her name, and a good ship she is too, the luckiest ship that I ever served on. But I will not be aboard her. The sea has taken her toll of me. I am off to my little cottage in old North Devon, there to live happily among my sheep and cows and look out upon the sea from my window."

There was much laughter at the sailor's table after this. I ordered ale to be brought to our table until I had spent my last shilling. I listened with more than common interest as the sailor told stories of the foreign lands he had seen and the many strange wonders in these far-off places. But my thoughts were on Virginia, which during the course of the evening, began to be more favorable than the punishment and starvation that were sure to be mine if I remained in England.

In the early hours of the morning, I took my leave of the sailor and his friends with much good cheer and happy farewells and walked, half-dazed with ale and thoughts of Virginia, back to Richard's room. I woke him from a sound sleep and said that I would go with him and that he must arrange passage for me.

He wanted to know how much money I had, and I confessed that it was all in the hands of the tavern keeper. Richard opened the chest where he had packed his clothes, dug out his purse and checked its contents.

"There is just enough for passage for us both," he said triumphantly.

"Richard, I'll pay you back as soon as I can."

"Don't worry yourself, Matthew. We will not need money in Virginia. Come," he said, pulling on his shirt and britches. "I am sick of the waiting. The *Diamond* is at the dock now and will be sailing not many hours from now. Help me with my chests, Matthew. We will be the first on the wharf, and I will arrange passage for you with the Captain."

I had never before seen Richard in such a haste. We placed his book chest on top of his clothes chest and together we bore them, with much effort, through the streets of Plymouth to the dock where our ship was still secured. Richard was correct. So far as I could determine, we were the only passengers yet to arrive. There were a few drunken sailors lying around the wharf, some sleeping, some yelling at phantoms in the night. I waited, sitting on a low group of pilings, while Richard went aboard the ship to speak with the Captain.

Except for the few shouting sailors, it was a strangely quiet night. The ship, with her fresh burden of supplies, rode in the still water like a majestic swan, asleep. The city of Plymouth seemed devoid of its human inhabitants and as empty and useless as a beach with no shells. The many scents of spring filled the air, and even dulled the occasional wave of putrefied stench from the harbor.

I lost myself in the sound of the water lapping up against the pilings and, for a terrible few moments, felt the old fears that I had known in childhood filling my breast. The fear that one morning I would wake up and find all those I knew gone, dead perhaps, leaving me completely alone. It was an icy feeling that started from the inside, as though I had drunk cold water too fast.

That fear had come true for me a few years ago, shortly after I had been apprenticed to Master Dorn. It remained for me the clearest memory for many years—the messenger riding up to

Mr. Beanie's shop and informing me that my parents had died in the fire of their house, and that I would be required by the solicitor to sign various papers regarding the remainder of their estate.

While I was about this sad business, I renewed my acquaintance with Richard, who was the only friend from my childhood and who had recently returned from Oxford to seek employment as a tutor. His friendship had guided me through those black moments when I felt that the very world must soon come to an end.

Richard returned from the ship shortly and said that the Captain would like to speak with me before giving his permission.

"What does he want?"

"I don't know," he said; this with a clear note of desperation in his voice. "He seems a fair man. His name is King, Captain William King. He is sailing as vice-Admiral of the fleet. We also have on board the illustrious Captain John Ratcliffe, apparently to resume his position as Governor of the colony and take it away from Captain Smith. We are among experienced men, Matthew. It is surely a good thing. Please go and speak with him. He took the money. He only wants to see you himself, I'm sure."

Richard patted me on the shoulder, and I walked slowly onto the ship and to the Captain's cabin. The door swung open, throwing the dim light of a lamp in my face.

"Enter," the Captain said.

He was a man not as big as I am, but from his eyes and manner I could see that he more than made up for his lack of size by force of character. His beard and mustache were light red, and he walked with a hard step, solidly planting his feet wherever they fell. His voice was strong, having battled with the ocean winds for many years. His clothes were wrinkled from having slept in them too often.

"So, you want to go to Virginia?" he said, and continued without giving me a chance to answer. "Your friend says that you are a carpenter?"

He stopped and looked directly at me, demanding the truth.

"Well, sir, I served four years to a master carpenter of Exeter."

"But you didn't complete your apprenticeship?"

"No, sir, but I know as much as any master about the skill, and—"

"I'm sure you do, lad—quarreled with your master, did you?"

"Yes, sir."

"Did you kill him?"

"No, sir."

"So you ran away?"

"Yes, sir."

The Captain laughed mightily and flopped down in his chair.

"God's wounds! It reminds me of my own youth, when I was apprenticed to a fishmonger of London. What a hard man he was. How I prayed many a time for God or some worthy soul to strike him dead. But, like most hard men, he only grew stronger. The time came when he proposed to beat me, and I hit him beside the face with one of his cold codfish. I liked it so much that I used it like a club and beat him until nothing was left of the cod but bloody strings of meat."

The Captain laughed until his face glowed as red as his beard. He went into a coughing fit, and when that had subsided, he said, "Those fools in Virginia have need of your skill more than they realize. You may sail with us if you like. One more will not make a difference. But take care and do not go near my mariners. They're a base lot, and some had as soon stick a dagger in you as not."

I thanked the Captain for his courtesy and started to leave.

"Since you are here," he said, "you can tell your friend that he can come aboard, but you and he are not to quarter among the stores. The best place is amidships."

I thanked the Captain again and hurried off the ship to tell Richard what had taken place. He was very pleased, and we immediately began loading his belongings aboard the ship.

Coarse, cloth bags stuffed with straw had been provided for our bedding. We found a good place on the first deck, in the middle part of the ship, next to the hull where we would be protected from the weather on all sides. At first the place between the decks seemed so small and cramped that I began to feel a shortness of breath, but as I lay on my rude bedding next to Richard, the whole space appeared to open up and become as vast as the sky itself, and before long I was sound asleep.

———·•◦•·———

It seemed only an instant of time before we heard the tramping of feet over our heads and voices calling out. We crawled over to the hatch and up the ladder to the main deck. It was well into the morning, and the sailors were running about the ship, preparing her for departure. The passengers were crowded on the quay, waiting their turn to walk over the wood planks to the ship. Most had a few possessions stuffed into cloth sacks, which they carried over their shoulders or under their arms. Some, like me, had nothing at all. Still others, mostly gentlemen, had large chests which the sailors handled with contempt, crashing them down on the deck with many curses.

They were mostly city people with the marks of their trades on their hands and faces. Most looked very pale and worn. Some were laborers with hard bodies. They stood together, looking suspiciously at everything and everyone. The gentlemen, in their fine clothes, stood off to one side and chatted among themselves.

I looked to the stern of the ship and saw Captain King pacing like a lion on the high poop deck. Now and then he would go to the rail and shout something to his men.

When all were aboard, the Captain gave the order to cast off from the quay, at which time men in two long boats strained at their oars, pulling the great ship slowly away from our last touch with England. The sight of the wharf moving away from me caused a peculiar pain in my breast. For a moment, if Richard had not been standing beside me, I would have jumped from the ship and swam joyfully back to shore. Instead I waited, not moving, listening to the Captain give the orders to get the ship under sail, soothed somewhat by the chants of the sailors as they went about their work.

We glided gently into Plymouth Sound where the Captain brought her up beside a fleet of ships, six of the larger tonnages and two pinnaces. There we dropped anchor, and within an hour, Captain King, along with Captain Ratcliffe and his rowers, had set out in our ship's long boat to meet Captain Christopher Newport, a well-known privateer and Master of the newly built flagship named the *Sea Venture*.

The Captain had not been gone but a few minutes when a quarrel broke out among some of the passengers as to where their places would be on the ship. One of them pulled a dagger on the other and made as if to stab him with it. But before he could advance two paces, one of the larger sailors jumped in among them, holding a fid in his right hand, and with it he knocked the dagger from the attacker's hand. The attacker, then in a rage, started for the sailor who, without the slightest hesitation, struck him on the side of his head and rendered the man senseless for over a quarter of an hour.

This incident put a quick end to the dispute, and most of the passengers went about preparing their places on the ship in silence. By evening the Captain returned, much flushed with wine and, staggering about the deck, ordered the Master's Mate into his cabin. After a short while, the Master's Mate emerged from the cabin and ordered the sailor on watch to look for a signal from the Sea Venture for getting underway.

We were served a delicious, hot meal of stew, containing much meat and bread and green plants and herbs. It would be our last hot meal for some time. Beer was served liberally, and we drank until we began to feel bloated and sleepy. Richard and I crawled around and over some of the passengers until we reached our beds, and there, fell onto them and slept like two newborn infants.

I was awakened suddenly by a sharp blow to my shoulder, and further aroused from my drowsiness by the cries of those nearest me. The sound of rushing water could be heard clearly against the hull, and my shoulder was pressed hard against the ship's heavy oak frame. Some passengers had slid, with their bedding, against the hull. After overcoming the surprise of it, they made their way back to their former places, crawling and sliding over other passengers like sheep bounding away from a charging wolf. To my surprise, Richard was still asleep and did not seem in any danger of rolling against the hull. I saw no need to wake him, so I made my way out of the ship onto the main deck.

It was growing well light, although the sun was still down. The ship was crashing through the water under full sail, and it seemed that all around, the ships sailing with us were bobbing and leaping over the sea as though all had taken wing and were flying at top speed for Virginia. Behind our fleet lay the rocky coast of Devon, and ahead of us, open green sea.

The wind was blustering and blowing from the southwest, and as we bore away down the channel, the heel of the ship eased, and the pitching became less violent. The ship no longer burst through the waves but seemed to join with them, rising gently as the seas rolled in from our stern and we nestled down into the troughs as they rolled ahead of us.

I walked on unsteady legs to the ship's bulwark and, holding onto the shrouds, watched the shore of England slowly recede. It occurred to me for the first time since I had decided on this adventure that I might never see England again; and though I had certainly suffered more there than necessary, it was still a home where the language and customs were known to me. I had never been abroad before this, not even to France or Holland. Now, through the uncertainty of fate, I found myself truly bound for an unknown land that might as well be one of the spheres of Heaven. I turned away. There was only one direction for me to look now, and that was to the sea.

It was about this time that several passengers came on deck and promptly ran to the bulwark, there to vomit and gasp as though they were dying. They were soon followed by many others until the whole bulwark was lined with people from stem to stern, all heaving and praying to God for relief. This, of course, was an occasion for much fun and joking among the sailors, some of whom added to the passengers' misery by eating hunks of roasted meat or bread.

Richard also took his turn at the bulwark and I, at moments, began to feel a stirring uneasiness in my bowels. But, after a day or so, the uneasiness passed, as it did for most of the passengers, and we all settled down in our own spaces, such as they could be with 150 souls living as close to one another as if they all shared the same bed.

Yet there was little in the way of abuse toward the women. I suppose those who would commit such a crime knew that they had no chance of being undetected and would be instantly punished by being cast overboard. Almost every day a quarrel broke out among the men passengers, but nothing ever came of it—no blows were struck, only harsh words from men being too long in close quarters.

I seldom ever saw the gentlemen of our company since they occupied the cabin under the Captain's cabin, and they seldom ventured out into the sun and salty ocean spray.

Richard spent much time with his books, reading Cicero and Pliny the Younger and making a vain attempt to write the texts into English from the Latin. He worked using the top of his chests as a table. I was concerned for his eyesight and advised him to do his work on deck, but he was afraid that he would be in the way of sailing the vessel, so I went to the Captain and asked if Richard could come on deck with his work. The Captain refused my request but said that he would try to procure a place for him in the gentlemen's cabin where there would be more light.

In a short time, the Captain hailed for me to come to his place of watch next to the binnacle. I did and was told that the gentlemen had no objection so long as Richard pursued his work and did not sleep or eat or remain in their area after he had finished his noble and scholarly endeavors.

I quickly informed Richard of the Captain's arrangements, but he did not seem overly pleased. I told him that it would not be wise to offend the Captain and the other gentlemen on board.

He looked at me strangely and said that he was quite content to do his studying among "these good people. But since you went to such a great deal of trouble for my sake, I will not offend you or the Captain."

I preferred spending as much time on deck as I could, even in foul weather. The sight of those other eight ships sailing in company with us like a gaggle of great birds was always a happy one for me. The sea became a pure, sky blue and contained many strange and unexpected things. Once, a large sea turtle, with crusty barnacles and other sea growth on his back, surfaced near our ship. The sailors tried to capture him with a barbed lance, since turtle meat is considered a tasty delicacy among them, but failed. The turtle was too old and wise to be caught this way.

Late one afternoon we espied a group of whales near the bow of the ship. I could hear their blowing nearly a half a league off and see their water-spouts shooting up into the air, higher than any fountain that I had ever seen. The whales stayed with us well into the night, and their blowing and hissing began to worry the superstitious sailors.

I began to suspect the sailors had reason for their fears when one passenger after another died of the yellow fever and more from an unknown sickness. It was rumored that "The London Plague" was among us, but because I had never seen one of its victims, I could not be sure.

At the end of four or five weeks, we reached a place in the sea where masses of sea growth the color of amber floated together in great fields, sometimes as far as the eye could see. Some of the sailors feared that we would become entangled in this sea growth and remain locked in this place forever, but the Captain, being a knowledgeable man, sailed right through it without the slightest inhibition to our vessel and, indeed, the growth proved to be very thin on the surface and easily broken up.

I hauled some of this growth aboard with a fishing line and discovered that it contained many living creatures—crabs and shrimp, small fish and snails, and others which I had no knowledge of. Besides this, there were many fish floating on the surface, shaped like a piper's bag, only with bodies as clear as a film of soap. The sailors called these Portuguese men-of-war and considered them very poisonous and deadly.

The mariners, seeing that I had an inclination for the sea, let me handle many of the deck lines and instructed me in most of the particulars in their uses. I was on the point of believing that a seafaring life might be a proper calling for me when six or eight days—by the master's reckoning—from Cape Henry, the sky turned to a pale gray and the sea took on a tossed, oily look and the wind had a strange sigh in it.

By nightfall the wind had begun to moan like a lost soul, and the sea waves crashed against the ship with increasing fury. By daybreak—at least by the hourglass—the clouds were so thick and black that night scarcely became day.

The wind became an ever-present roar. The ship pitched and rolled almost beyond control, and every wave that crashed against her sides sent a hideous tremor through her, powerful enough to shake her timbers loose.

Somehow the ship held together, but the passengers had a hard time of it. Most had tied themselves with ropes to some part of the vessel's structure, whether it was a nail sticking out of the deck or a huge crossbeam. Some held on with their hands and some clung to others who were themselves tied down. It was impossible to move about the ship without a fast hold onto something solid. If one ever lost his grip, even for a moment, or tried to jump free-handed to the next handhold, he would be instantly thrown tumbling until he collided with a fixed part of the ship. At one time, a passenger near the forward part of our hold lost his grip and rolled into a group of men and women who were hanging on to a center stanchion. The force knocked them loose, and all went tumbling about the deck like feathers dumped from a pillow.

Most everyone became sick, and there was not a corner or any part of the ship that water did not find its way into. Richard covered his book chest with his bedding and lashed himself there, vowing to me in a voice above the din of the storm and screams of the passengers that he would not release himself until the storm had passed or until he drowned. A shout rose from the hold that we were sinking, and screams erupted all about me, both from men and women. People tore at their clothes in desperation. One man's fear of drowning was so great that he attempted to stab himself but lost his dagger in a severe roll of the ship and watched it tumble into the hold. Knowing that rumor can often be worse than the truth, I made my way over to the hatch and looked down into the hold. Water had filled the bottom of the ship with a black sludge which covered most of our stores. Several sailors were wading in this bilge water with candles in hand, searching with eyes and hands for leaks along the ship's hull. I climbed up to the main deck and asked if I could be of assistance. The boatswain shouted that I could join with his men at the pumps and soon more men came up to take their turn at the pumps. Even the gentlemen did not hesitate to earn a few blisters on their hands when it came to saving the ship.

For days we did nothing but stand to the pumps, each man taking his turn until exhaustion forced him to retire. Still we could gain no headway against the water in the ship. The Captain, who had remained at his station on the poop deck day and night during the storm, ordered all souls aboard who could stand on their feet—men and women—to work at bailing the ship with buckets. This action, 1 know, saved the ship, for the water started to diminish in the holds, and by the sixth day the storm had abated, the sun returned, and the sea—although still swelling and rolling—had spent its fury.

We had lost sight of our companion ships on the second day of the storm, and all wondered what had become of them. Some said that we were blown into an unknown sea where we were doomed to sail forever, never seeing land again. But the Captain took a sighting of the sun and put us at a degree of latitude only a few leagues north of Chesapeake Bay.

We altered course, very cheerful and happy, and made for Cape Charles with all sails billowing out so that we looked like a great cloud moving over the waves. On the morning watch we sighted land, appearing like a flat, white line on the horizon. We ghosted well off this shore, heading to the south until we reached Cape Charles and entered the calm and beautiful waters of the Chesapeake.

There, at the entrance to the King James River, rode four of the ships from our fleet: Blessing, Falcon, Lion, and Unitie. They hailed us with many good cheers and even fired off some of their ordnance. The Captain brought our ship skillfully up to their rode and dropped anchor. Our ship had hardly taken hold of the ground when two long boats came skimming over the water to our side. Most of the ships' captains and a rough-faced captain of the land fort had come to inspect our ship's damage and confer with our captain as to what course of action would be taken.

It was decided to leave the pinnace, with her crew of mariners, at the entrance to the river to await the arrival of

Swallow, Virginia and *Sea Venture* while we, with the remaining ships, would depart for Jamestown on the next flooding tide.

All of the passengers, including me, spent the remainder of the day drying out in the hot sun. We laid all of our bedding and clothes that were wet on every part of the ship exposed to the air. Through a miracle, Richard's books were spared. Not a single drop of water soiled them. The sailors busied themselves with making what repairs they could to the ship. Since I had nothing but the clothes on my back to be concerned with, I helped them where I could, pulling on lines when told to, and generally lending the weight of my shoulders when it was needed.

As soon as the tide changed in our favor, we weighed anchor, hoisted our topsails, and glided in line with the other ships up the river to Jamestown. We arrived there late in the afternoon, and as we were the last in line, dropped anchor. All the other ships found places at the quay that provided enough deep water for their draft.

CHAPTER 2

Jamestown

I don't truly know what I had expected to see. No one on our ship had been to this place before except some few of the sailors. There had been much talk about what we would find, and we all began to have a vision of an English city, much like Plymouth, built in the midst of a tropical garden. What we saw was a rude fort made of palisades and surrounded on most sides by a stinking marsh.

The passengers seemed dumbstruck at this sight and most stood in erect silence, looking as though they had been dazed by terrible news. The sailors soon shook us out of our stupor and started helping us embark onto the longboats to row us ashore. We landed on the beach almost at the fort's gateway and assembled there to wait for our belongings and the remainder of the passengers. When all were safely ashore, we streamed into the fort, lugging whatever we had, and since I had nothing, I helped Richard with his two chests. We assembled in the center of the fort and waited in the heat for almost an hour for the Governor to make his appearance.

It was very hot in the fort and the smell, like rotted flesh, caused some of our company to become sick. A woman standing near Richard fell to the ground, unconscious. The people around her stepped quickly away, forming a cleared circle. There had been talk of plague in the ship and at the fort. Richard, being more enlightened than most of us, rushed to her side and called for water.

"She has only fainted from heat and thirst," he shouted.

An officer pushed his way through the crowd and knelt beside the woman. Richard held her head up gently while the soldier sprinkled some of the water from his flask over her forehead, and in a few minutes she revived. The soldier offered her the flask of water, and she drank it so hungrily that I thought she might faint again.

Soon everyone began to complain of thirst and hunger. Others also fainted and were removed to a place away from the crowd. After a long while, we were given a biscuit made from the flour of ground pagatowr, the Indian corn, and each was allowed one cup of water from a common water barrel. The passengers found pagatowr bread coarse and uneatable and, at first, Richard and I found the food very nauseous, but I convinced him that we should eat it for our strength.

Richard had arranged a seat from his chest for the girl who had first fainted to sit on, and she sat staring as though she was in a trance. Richard talked with her in a low voice and discovered that her name was Anne Breton and that she was a servant to a gentlewoman, Mrs. Fitzsimmons, who had come to live with her husband in Virginia. Mrs. Fitzsimmons had asked her to report what the present governor had to say, if important. But as for her, she would be busy sorting out her belongings and inspecting suitable lodgings.

The crowd surged inward, and people stirred around us in quick eddy currents as though we were all fish in a pond disturbed by a small stone. A path was cleared near us. Captain John Smith, followed by two men in tattered garments, entered our group and walked past us to a raised platform near the church. He walked briskly, carrying himself like a soldier, and looking straight ahead, he mounted the temporary platform that had been made from a few planks and empty barrels.

He looked slowly over the three hundred or so people assembled around him, stopping occasionally to dwell on a particular face. A deep hush settled over the crowd. Their groans, their sighs were all silenced. Even the dust inside the fort seemed to stop still in the air.

One look at Captain Smith and there was no question of him being an able man. His strong beard and long mustache seemed more to burn like the bush of Moses. His eyes, fed with this same fire, shone as bright as jewels. He spoke, and his voice carried to all corners of the fort.

"Welcome, citizens," he said. "Let us first get down upon our knees and give thanks to God for bringing you here in safety."

We knelt down and followed the Captain in a prayer of gratitude. When it was over, we rose to our feet once again and gave our complete attention to Captain Smith.

"My countrymen, most of you have come through the many dangers of sea travel to land here and found a new country. Perhaps you were told that this is a land flowing with milk and honey, that gold lies in every path and roadway, that whatever a man wants he has merely to stretch out his hand and it will be given to him. My countrymen, nothing can be farther from the truth. There is no milk here because there are no cows, and the honey is the food of the savages. There is no gold here or in any parts of the country that I have explored. There is not even a simple pathway or roadway such as you have known in England, and if a man stretches out his hand in this country, a waiting savage will chop it off with his hatchet.

This is what awaits you, my friends, here in Virginia; a journey ten times—nay, a hundred times more hazardous than what you have known upon the sea."

A low moan arose from the crowd.

"If you are to survive in this country, you will have to work until your hands become as the toughest leather, and until you drop from exhaustion. Do not expect to live in luxury for your toil. It will be enough that you can eat and find shelter for yourselves. That is the true condition of life in Virginia.

"All victuals will be kept in a common storehouse; that includes meats, grains, fruits—all that is eaten. There is a common well where all may get water. Each day after prayers you may draw your rations from the storehouse and at no time before or after. No man will be allowed to live off the labor of another. Every man will do his share of work for the common good, for no man will eat who does not work."

At this point, a noise was heard in the crowd, a man shouting.

"Are you saying, sir, that I should have to sow corn and fell trees and slaughter animals?"

The voice was that of one of the gentlemen of our ship, and beside him stood another gentleman dressed as though he would be attending the court.

"Yes, sir, that is what I said."

"Sir, if you expect me to do such things, then you are a fool."

"And you, sir," Captain Smith answered in a stronger voice, "Are a knave."

The gentleman reached for his sword but before he could clear it, Captain Smith drew out his pistol and leveled it straight at the man. The people in front of the gentleman cleared away like smoke blown in the wind.

"Sheathe that sword, sir, or I will put a ball through you as easily as if you were a rabid dog."

The gentleman looked utterly disbelieving. Then, seeing that Captain Smith was sincere, he started to tremble slightly and slowly replaced the sword back into its sheath. After that he turned and, with the other gentleman, pushed his way through the ring of people and out of the fort toward the ships.

"I have assigned a man to the passengers from each ship. He will instruct you as to what should be done in the way of lodging and what work there is to do."

Captain Smith then jumped down from his platform and walked at the head of his escort back to the President's house. One of the men of the fort came to the platform and read out the names of the ships and in what part of the fort they should assemble. Anne was not one of our ship's company and so had to go with her own people, much to Richard's disappointment. She promised, with hesitation, to let him visit after evening prayers.

We assembled with our people at one corner of the fort, under a piece of ordnance mounted on raised earth. Our fort man, a soldier, climbed up on the raised earth and, standing in front of the ordnance, said that all men, excepting gentlemen and those men with wives and families, would sleep out under the stars or under such shelters as they could provide.

"Are there gentlemen among you?" the soldier called out.

"Not unless this be a tavern," a voice answered, followed by much laughter.

"Then all those with wives come with me. The remainder shall await my return."

The soldier jumped down from the gun emplacement, and we watched with considerable envy as the men, with their wives, left our company and walked in a loose group toward the first street of houses. Richard and I sat down on his chests and waited.

"Look around you, Matthew. Surely this is the lost Eden that we have found. Think of it, Matthew, to become as innocent and as loving as little children again, yet to be aware as men."

I glanced around the fort. The trees outside of the palisades were tall and so intensely green they seemed light blue in color. The river flowed peacefully. So many birds were singing that the very air was continually filled with music, and the wind blew cool and refreshing. Perhaps Richard was right.

He suddenly stood up.

"Look!" he said, pointing to a gate near us which opened to the woods.

A company of Indians were walking into the fort, escorted by a few of the fort's soldiers. They were the first Indians that Richard or I, or any of the members of our company, had ever seen. I was amazed at their size. They seemed like giant men. They were a head taller than us, and all carried themselves as nobly as any English Lord.

They were unarmed and completely naked except for a loin covering made of animal skins. At the time they were the strangest men that I, or any of us, had ever seen. Their dark, muscular bodies glistened in the sunlight. The feathers that they wore in their hair gave them an almost haughty air. Behind these men came other men of lower estate, carrying baskets of corn and other victuals.

When all of the Indians had entered the fort, Captain Smith came out to greet them. They made signs of peace to one another, and Captain Smith spoke to them with gestures and a few words of Algonquin.

"Friends, you are welcome in peace."

Then Captain Smith signaled to his men, and two soldiers brought out several baskets containing copper trinkets, hawk's bells, and plates with the images of King James pressed into them. The Indian who was at the head of his company looked at the baskets with contempt, then ordered some of his men to take them. He turned to face Captain Smith and began moving his hands gracefully yet forcefully, conveying his message in a style of sign language that was familiar to both men.

"The great Powhatan, ruler of all the peoples of the Chesapeake, sends his greetings and wishes to know when the mighty Captain Newport, your father, returns from out of the great salt water."

"Tell his majesty, Powhatan, that I do not know the day of my father's return. My father is like a hawk on the wing, and when he returns it will be as the hawk, swift and without warning."

"Captain Newport is a good and generous man and as brave and fearless as his son."

With this, the Indians turned and left the fort. Captain Smith waited until the gates had closed behind them. Then he took off his hat and dashed it to the ground.

He turned to one of his Lieutenants and said, "That goddamn Newport! He has ruined it all for us by promising those damned savages arms for corn and forever ruining our bargaining power by overpaying those devils with copper. Now Powhatan is using him against me. Goddamn, that savage is a clever one. Where is that rogue Newport? Bet that damned fool has gone up the bay to do a little trading on his own. Send to Point Comfort and tell them there's a shilling in it for the first man to spot the *Sea Venture*."

The Lieutenant left the fort immediately with a file of soldiers in a longboat and started downriver. Captain Smith, seeing us standing nearby, signaled for us to follow him.

We waited outside the door of his house until our turn came to go in. Richard went before me and did not stay long. He looked a bit dejected when he came out, and I asked him the reason for it. He shrugged.

"The Captain said that the colony has no need for clerks

and scholars; that unless I learn to use the musket and plow, it would be better for all if I immediately boarded a return ship to England."

When the next man came out, I entered. Captain Smith was sitting behind a table made of rough, hand-sawed boards. The floor was yellow dirt, packed hard, and the small house contained only a single bed, table and chair, and a fireplace.

"Your name?" he commanded.

I told him. His eyes moved up and down the passenger list of our ship. When he found it, he placed a mark beside it. Then his face brightened. "Carpenter? Aye!"

"Only an apprentice, sir."

"And how long were you an apprentice?"

I told him.

"Good. Good!" he said. "The company must not have known your trade or I'm sure they would have sent a gentleman instead."

He laughed loudly and banged the table with his fist.

"Can you use a musket, son?"

"No, sir."

He leaned back, unperturbed.

"That is of no consequence," he said. "Any man of your skills can easily master the art of musketry. I will train you myself. If we are to survive here, my lad, and plant our English nation, we must have men who can serve as soldiers, farmers, tradesmen, and know enough of all occupations to provide for himself and the common good. Come to the church tomorrow after you have breakfasted."

He leaned back over the ship's list and, taking this as my signal of dismissal, I left. Richard was waiting for me. He appeared exceedingly vexed.

"What did he say?" Richard demanded to know.

I told him as easily as I could, not telling him that the Captain thought little of having scholars and thinkers here in Virginia.

"He didn't say anything about sending me back, did he?"

"No. Not a word of that. He only talked about muskets and plows."

"Good God, I can learn to use a musket as well as the next man. And a plow."

"Did he ask you to come to the church tomorrow?"

Richard looked puzzled. "No. What does it mean?"

"Nothing. Come with me tomorrow. Captain Smith probably forgot to mention it to you. He is a man with much on his mind."

———•◦•———

That night we slept on the ground with the other single men of our ship. It could not be said that we truly slept, since the mosquitoes swarmed all over us the moment darkness fell, and sucked our blood throughout the night. Richard and I had some protection from them by sharing his only blanket, but most of the men had no protection except the clothes on their back, and all night we could hear their slapping and cursing.

It seemed to me that the dawn would never come, and at the first glow of daylight I crawled out from under Richard's blanket and hurried to the fire that was being built for our breakfast. I stood as close to the fire as I could get, hoping that this would drive off the mosquitoes, which it did. I could hear them buzzing nearby, but they would not approach the heat. I was later told by one of the cooks that the smoke from a fire also deals roughly with them, and that is why the Indians keep a fire going in their houses even in summer. He also confessed to me that fish oil was a good protection against them but that after trying it once himself, he preferred the mosquitoes.

The sun rose very quickly, evaporating the dew and morning

coolness. The people of the fort began to assemble in large numbers around the cooking pots; some laughing and joking, others solemn and dazed from sleep or lack of sleep.

It was easy to tell the difference between the older inhabitants of the fort and us newcomers. We were plump, well clothed and jovial, in spite of our first miserable night, whereas those of the fort were thin as mongrel dogs. Their clothes were faded and torn, their faces hard and unyielding. I made it a point to stay out of their way, for most of them, even the gentlemen, looked more like common cut-throats.

I would be the first served since I was at the cooking pots early. Richard came toward me, rubbing his eyes.

I asked the cook for two servings. "One for my sick friend," I said, and he filled two earthenware bowls with a thick, brown soup and tore off two hunks of bread from the common loaf for me.

I jostled my way back through the breakfast line to where Richard was standing near the church. He was very pleased to have the victuals. I could see that the journey from Plymouth and our first night here had left him somewhat weak. We ate the soup and the bread, which only reminded us of how hungry we were. When we had wiped the last trace of it from the bowl, we sat down on the ground and leaned against the wall of the church, feeling with pleasure the warming of the sun.

"I don't think I can bear another night such as last night," I said.

"Yes, it was not pleasant. Yet think of it this way. Adam had his snakes while we have our mosquitoes. As long as they are content to prick us for a little drop of our blood, isn't that preferable to the more subtle, though more damning, temptation of forbidden fruit?"

What could I say to this but that I agreed? Yet if some serpent had slithered up to me at that moment and offered to rid the place of mosquitoes for all eternity, I would have gladly fallen into the fires of Hell.

Richard jumped to his feet and waved his hand over his head. Looking in the direction of his attention, I saw Anne Breton leaving the cooking pots with her breakfast in both hands. She saw Richard and smiled.

"Come join us, Anne. Come," Richard shouted.

Anne stopped, looked around for a moment, then started toward us. Richard smoothed a place for her on the grass beside us. He took her burdensome bowl, which looked much too large for her, while she arranged herself on the grass.

"May the Lord please that I never see another mosquito for the rest of my life," she said. "My mistress swore this morning that she would be back on the ship for England the moment that it was ready to sail."

"Will she do that, you think?" Richard asked.

"Her husband managed to dissuade her from it but at a heavy cost to him, which I'm sure he will never be able to pay."

"Where is your mistress now?" I asked.

"Dining with the other gentlewomen. Captain Smith is meeting with many of their husbands and other gentlemen at this very hour. There is some talk among the women of planting settlements at places farther up the river. They say that the land is better there and can be better defended against the savages."

"Oh, Anne," Richard said, with a broad smile across his face.

"You are in an enviable position to know so much. What else do they plan?"

Anne took a large bite from her piece of bread.

"Some of the gentlemen say that they have been ordered by

the London Company to find gold in these parts, and to seek a water route to the South Sea. And they are determined to do it, I believe."

"What does Captain Smith say?" I asked.

"He is against it. He says that there is no gold here and that there is no ocean beyond the mountains. He quarrels much but cannot avail against these gentlemen who are much favored by the company."

"That is too bad," I said. "Captain Smith has been in the country longer than any one of these gentlemen, and he knows the Indians."

"They say that Captain Smith has explored all the country for miles around, all the way to the head of the Bay of the Chesapeake."

"Then he should know," Richard said.

"I fear these gentlemen will make trouble for us even if they do find their gold and South Sea," Anne said.

"Captain Smith has shown himself to be an able man. He will certainly be able to handle any trouble of that sort."

"Maybe so, at least until the Governor arrives," Anne said, finishing her breakfast.

I gathered up all of our bowls and returned to the cooking area. The cook waved me off.

"They are yours to keep. Only take care and don't break them, for you will have to pay for the next one."

I thanked him for his information and advice and returned to my friends. They had begun some happy conversation while I was gone and seemed hesitant to continue it in my presence. I gave no more thought to it but passed on to them what the cook had told me, which pleased them greatly. I suggested to Richard that we return to his chests with our new eating bowls but he refused, saying that he would not leave the church before Captain Smith's arrival.

I conceded. "If that is your desire, I will clean and deposit the bowls safely on my own."

He nodded agreement but would not move from his place.

When I returned, a large group had begun to assemble inside and outside of the church, and shortly we saw the Reverend Mister Albright walking, or more correctly, strutting toward the church, Bible in hand and clerical robes flowing behind him. He looked as thin and drawn as the other first inhabitants of the fort.

Richard declined to enter the church, so I waited outside, together with Arne and Richard. We could hear the strong voice of the reverend through the open window nearest to us.

"We have come to a new land," he said, after the beginning prayers were finished, "by the grace and will of God to bring to the heathen inhabitants of this place the light of Christianity, so that they may walk with us as brothers and sisters in the arms of our sweet Jesus Christ. Go out, my brethren, and spread the word of God. Show to these simple savages the true meaning of our Christian love. Teach them by your own example the saving graces of charity and mercy, for surely that is God's purpose in bringing you safely across the sea. Do not worry about what you shall eat or what you shall put on, for God will provide all of your wants."

At the conclusion of Reverend Albright's sermon, the congregation sang many psalms, and there was a last prayer from Reverend Albright before the service ended. Captain Smith, with his Lieutenants, was the first to leave the church, followed by the rest of the congregation. He came immediately to the place appointed for us to meet. There were twenty or thirty men gathered, all young and lusty fellows, all curious as to what would happen next.

Captain Smith called for order, and we immediately fell quiet. He unshouldered his musket and stood it before him, resting the stock on the ground and holding the weapon by the barrel.

"Lads," he said in his booming voice. "It is my purpose to teach you the use of firearms so that you can properly defend yourselves and these settlements against the savages. I say defend, for you are never to provoke a fight with the savages lest you receive a severe punishment. Yet if the savages assault you or any member of your company or household, you must fight, if necessary, to the last man.

"I have been in this wilderness long enough to know that the savages fear only one thing—not the dark of night, or the forest, or any man now living. The savages fear our weapons. And because they do, they are more inclined toward trading and living at peace with us.

Therefore, if it comes to me that any one of you has disclosed the use of our weapons to a single savage or has traded with them your weapons for corn or any commodity, that man I will slay with my own hand."

The Captain's words had a sobering effect upon all of us. I began to suspect, in earnest, that this colony of Virginia was not the paradise that Richard claimed. Captain Smith's words, however, did not seem to have the same effect on Richard. I was ready to depart the place and take my chances back in England, but Richard gave his full and unwavering attention to Captain Smith's instruction in the loading and firing of a musket.

At the completion of this first part of our instruction, Captain Smith ordered Lieutenant Webster to go and fetch the new arms brought with us from England. Then he turned to our group and, with slow deliberation, walked up to Richard and asked him, in a forthright way, why he had come.

Richard explained that he had come to learn the art of musketry and that he wanted to learn all the skills necessary to deal with the savages, adding that he expected to bring them into the fold at a time in the future.

Captain Smith laughed aloud at this, so much so that his face turned exceedingly red, and he had to wipe the spittle from his beard with his sleeve. When his orgy of laughing ended, he examined Richard's hands and skin.

"Young man," he said, "you have never held a workman's tools in these hands, much less a musket or a pike."

"But I can learn, sir. I am always quick to learn."

"I don't doubt that, my lad, but here a man must know how to use his hands as well as his head."

Having said this, the Captain shoved Richard against the shoulder so hard that he fell backwards upon the ground. There he lay for a while, looking up at Captain Smith with surprise and hurt.

"How do you feel now, my lad? Do you want to strike me? Would you run me through with this sword if you had it?"

Then Captain Smith drew his sword so that it whistled in the air, and thrust it into the ground beside Richard.

Richard was terrified and looked with horror at the weapon swinging in the ground next to his body.

"Well, take it up, lad, and run me through," the Captain yelled.

Beads of perspiration were now running down Richard's face. He reached for the sword's handle, pulled it out of the ground and, after looking at Captain Smith for a long while, let it fall from his hand.

"Go back to England, my lad. Continue your studies, be a schoolmaster or a Divine. There is little you can do here."

Richard bit his lips and, picking the sword up from the ground, again made a half-hearted cut at the Captain, who easily parried the attempt with his musket.

Bending down next to Richard, the Captain gently removed the sword free of his hand. "So be it, then. Lad, you are a fool, but one more fool in this place will matter little."

Richard got to his feet and, although still shaken from his experience with Captain Smith, stood erect and pleased to be a part of the colony.

Muskets with powder and ball were issued to the men. Lieutenant Webster showed us how to stand in ranks and shoulder the weapon. It was the first time that I had ever held a musket. The sheer weight of the piece was heavier than all the carpenter's tools I had ever used. The Lieutenant marched us out of the fort, behind Captain Smith, to a clearing beside the river. There, targets were set up, and we were marched to a distance of about ten to twelve English yards. It was the first time we had been outside the fort since our arrival, and I began to feel a strange uneasiness.

Captain Smith stood in front of us, his musket once again positioned before him. He explained to us how we were to shoot at the targets, our row firing first, then stepping behind the second row to permit them to fire.

"Remember," he added in a quieter voice, "the savages are watching. You can't see them but they are out there, hiding behind every tree and bush. You cannot hear them. They fly through the forest as quietly as birds. But us they will see and hear. So hit the target, lads, and, on the command to fire, make your muskets roar."

I looked quickly around at the forest. It was dark as night

beyond the first trees. Nothing stirred. Captain Smith stepped to the side of the clearing, and the Lieutenant ordered the first rank to load, which we did somewhat clumsily, then to aim and fire.

All of the muskets seemed to explode at once with a thunderous noise which caused my ears to start ringing. Startled flocks of birds burst out of the trees and scattered into the blue overhead. The Lieutenant examined the targets and pointed with a stick to the hits. My aim had been considerably to the right of center, but some had not hit the target altogether.

We exchanged places with the row behind us, Richard taking my place. When the order came for them to fire, Richard was late pulling the trigger. When he did, the back kick of the musket knocked him off his feet. Had I not been there to catch him, he might well have broken part of his body.

We continued firing all that morning until our marks had considerably improved. All except for Richard, who finally could no longer lift his musket to his shoulder. When we had used up all of the powder and ball given to us, the Lieutenant marched us back into the fort and gave us instructions on how to oil and clean our muskets and to keep them by our side at all times. He told us to assemble after prayers in the same place the next morning. Before he had departed for the storehouse, Lieutenant Webster and Captain Smith called Richard aside. I could see them all speaking earnestly to each other. I drew my day's rations and waited for Richard, who came from the store not long after.

"What did they say, Richard?"

He shrugged. "They admonished me to give it up for my own sake as well as that of the colony."

"And are you?"

Richard reached up to his painful shoulder and rubbed it

gently. "I conceded that they had a point. I know that I was never suited for the life of a soldier and if I am to be only a soldier, as those in Europe, I would not hesitate to abandon this infamous weapon at once." He looked at his musket. "But this is not tired old Europe. Here, a man must be a little of every man, as the Captain says." He looked at me questionably. "Do you see what I mean, Matthew?"

I said that I did, but I suspected that he had some deeper meaning which I could not grasp. Nor did I care to at the time, being hungry and thirsty and not giving a whit for philosophical thought.

That night we were quartered with two other men in a small house at the end of the second row of houses on the east side of the fort. The other men, neither of whom we knew since they were from another ship, spent most of the night gambling with dice and drinking a cloudy red wine. So, Richard and I had very little sleep that night.

While these men drank and gambled, they talked of nothing but the gold and silver they would find upriver, and of what they would do with it upon returning to England. Both wanted to be Lords and live in palaces with hundreds of servants, with a beautiful mistress for each bedroom. I later discovered that they were miners from Cornwall and were convinced from their soil deposits they saw in the river that a rich gold field was not far off.

The next day we were instructed in the use of the pistol and sword. Richard, unfortunately, cut his leg with the sword and, during target practice with the pistol, he mistakenly overcharged the piece and the thing exploded in his hand, giving him a serious and very painful wound.

Captain Smith had the surgeon dress Richard's wounds and then angrily ordered him to await his pleasure in the President's

House. The Lieutenant said the Captain's anger was due mostly to the loss of a good pistol which, as he added, was "more useful than a hundred damned scholars."

CHAPTER 3

A New Reality

O ur training in arms continued for two more days. Afterward, I was selected to go out with an armed party under the command of Lieutenant Webster in search of good timber for the building of houses and to lade the ships returning to England so that the London Company could satisfy their expenses. I was to go with the men and select the best trees for cutting, and since my skill at arms had proven more than adequate, I was also to accompany the Lieutenant and a few soldiers on a brief scouting expedition for future timber supplies. Richard would remain at the fort and help in the fields, tending what little crops there were and assisting with repairs to the fort.

Our party of thirty or so men left the fort at first light, after hearing prayers from the Reverend Albright and breakfasting on hot corn meal and fresh fish. Most of the men, like myself, had not been into the forest before. All were silent as we made our way from the trail and into the trees. I could hear the men tramping through the woods but could see only the few that were nearest me. We moved this way like a herd of beasts, crushing small trees and leaves underfoot until the Lieutenant called a halt and summoned me for a counsel.

"It is the Captain's wish," he said, "to clear all of the trees from here back to the fort. Take the cutters and mark all of the best trees along a north-south line to the clearing in front of the fort. Then we will cut along this line, moving back until the area is cleared out. I will arrange my men so that we can protect you from all sides."

Lieutenant Webster handed me a small compass and instructed me on how to use it. I told the cutters what our task would be, and they followed me.

There were many trees that would be good for our wants. By the time I had reached the clearing at the fort, all of the men were busy with saw and ax. The cutting went well, with many sturdy trees of all kinds crashing to the forest floor. By two o'clock of the afternoon, all of the marked trees had been cut, and the Lieutenant set the men to work trimming the branches and cutting the legs into lengths of twenty feet or less. He then posted a close guard around the workmen and, taking three men of his own, led us into the forest.

We pushed our way through thick woods in single file, the Lieutenant leading. I was second in line, the other men behind me. We climbed up and down small hills until we came to a small stream. The water ran clear and bubbly. The forest was colored in a thousand shades of green and spotted with many different flowers, some smaller than a fingernail while others were larger than a man's fist. The air seemed nothing more than a sweet, natural perfume. Perhaps Richard's thoughts on this place were true. It seemed to me at that moment that this land had been preserved by God for Englishmen such as us.

The Lieutenant stopped and signaled for us to remain silent. Then he crept quietly ahead. A few yards on we came to the edge of a small clearing where hung the carcass of a stag on a frame. The animal had been freshly skinned and gutted. His entrails lay in a large earthenware pot nearby. There were also about ten baskets of corn in the center of the clearing, and the remains of a fire. The Lieutenant motioned for us to gather close to him.

"We will enter the clearing," he said, "and take the stores."

"Christopher," he said to one of the men behind me, "you stand guard here. If an Indian looks as though he is to attack us, then shoot. The rest of us will bring the stores from this place as fast as we can."

"But sir," one of the men said, "has not Captain Smith instructed us to first offer to trade with these savages, and not to use force unless we are provoked?"

"Jonathan, you know as well as I the straits our people are in. I would gladly offer to trade with them, but do you see any with which to trade?" The Lieutenant did not wait for the man to answer. "And what would we offer them, our weapons? You know what the penalty is for that. I know full well what Captain Smith has said regarding our communion with these people. And I also know what he has had to say to appease the minds of those fat merchants back in London who know nothing of the true conditions here. Captain Smith well knows what our needs are, and he knows that starving men make poor bargainers."

There was no more said after that. We waited for a long time watching the clearing. Only the birds of the forest seemed to protest what we were about to do.

At Lieutenant Webster's order, we rushed into the clearing and started carrying away the baskets of corn. The Lieutenant took me with him to cut down the stag. We severed the leather lashings with quick sweeps of our knives and were dragging the game toward our hiding place in the woods when Christopher, our guard, screamed at the top of his voice. He fell to the ground, gripping the arrow that stuck from his groin.

The air at that moment seemed to be filled with singing

arrows. I dropped onto the ground next to the dead stag and thought to use his body for protection. The other men huddled around the baskets of corn. More arrows flew overhead, some striking the trees on the other side of the clearing and some sticking into the ground all around us.

I looked up and saw that Lieutenant Webster had sought not the slightest protection but stood facing in the direction of the attack with his musket aimed. He fired, and for a while the arrows stopped. He was reloading when a new flight of arrows came in. One struck his breastplate, making a sound like a hammer striking a nail, and another stuck into the sleeve of his shirt.

He was on the point of raising his musket again when a young Indian jumped into the clearing and drew back his bow. The Lieutenant brought his musket up as quick as a slap from a cat's paw and fired. The ball struck the young Indian in the chest and knocked him on his back.

The attack stopped, and we heard the sounds of rustling leaves as the remainder of the Indians fled into the forest.

"Go after them!" the Lieutenant yelled to his men, "Go after them. Don't let them escape!"

The men leaped up from their hiding places and, with angry yells, dashed after their attackers. I started to run with them, but the Lieutenant grabbed me by the arm and swung me around to face him. Perspiration was pouring from his face and small bubbles of saliva formed at the corners of his mouth. His lips seemed pulled tight over his teeth.

"Help me with this one," he said to me, and swiftly turned toward the downed Indian.

He was a young man of maybe eighteen or twenty years, and he was bleeding a great deal from the chest and mouth when we reached him. He looked up at us with wide, dark eyes.

He moved his lips as if to speak, but no sound came from him.

The Lieutenant knelt down beside the stricken man and examined the bloody wound. He stood up and called for the water bottle, but it was pointless. The young man had already died. His bright, dark eyes had become as dull as stones.

"Sir," I said. "Why do these savages fight us? Don't we come in peace? Haven't we made our peaceful intentions known to them?"

The Lieutenant looked up at me, his face twisted with sorrow. "These people fight with us for the same reasons that we would fight with them if they were to invade our country. We call them savages, but what is more savage than English law that would disembowel a man and then pull his body apart while he yet lives? These people are no more savage than we. We call them savages because they are not Christian, but I tell you most truthfully that there are many in England that are savage and we call them gentlemen.

"The people of Powhatan have their own laws and old customs. They care for their children as we do. They care for one another when they are sick. They do not let the poor among them starve or live in grievous want as we do. Their society is much like ours. Powhatan is the great king over all his land, and he is called Mamanatowick. He has his vassals, his lords, and they are known as Werowances. The Werowance has his warriors. Then there are the women and children. Each has their proper role, and I have heard that they never depart from it. This will go on." The Lieutenant said, looking down at the body of the young Indian. "Men have always fought over the land, and it will not stop until we or they are dead."

The Lieutenant rolled the body over slowly and, seeing nothing that interested him, walked back over to where Christopher lay, groaning. He examined his wound and offered

Christopher a good-sized twig to bite down on. He then worked the arrow from his body. Christopher let out a yell such as I have heard only in a slaughterhouse and promptly fainted.

In a few more minutes our men returned, saying that the Indian had completely vanished and that they turned back for fear of becoming lost. The Lieutenant ordered our strongest man to carry the wounded Christopher on his back while the rest of us were to tie together as many baskets of corn as each man could drag and pull them back along the way we had come.

We reached the fort about dusk and, with many cheering hands, carried our spoils to the storehouse. Christopher was taken to the surgeon, who did all he could for the young man but, in spite of his efforts, Christopher died a few hours later. The Lieutenant asked me to accompany him while he made his report to Captain Smith. Having nothing else to do, I went along.

Captain Smith was seated at his table with the Reverend and many gentlemen, some of whom I recognized from our ship. They all looked at the Lieutenant.

"Your men did well with the timber today. There is enough to lade two returning ships, and the forest is well cleared on the land side of the fort. We will start on the other side in the morning. Lieutenant, I wish you to take charge of loading the ships when the milling is done. Take what men you need, and next Monday we will train thirty more in the use of arms."

I recognized one of the gentlemen sitting there as Captain Ratcliffe, who sailed with us on the *Diamond*.

"Ask him what happened in the forest," he shouted. "Why has he brought back one man dead and the rest as torn, and bloody, as if they had been in a battle?"

"If you don't mind, Ratcliffe," the Captain shouted back, "I am in charge of the forces here now. It was agreed that I take over from young Scrivener and serve until the new governor arrives. I, alone, will hear this man's report and then, if it pleases me, I will tell you of it. If that is not to your liking, then either wait until my term of office has ended or quit this settlement for good."

A tense silence fell on the room.

Then the Captain said, "This meeting has ended," and he slammed his fist down on the table, causing the candles and empty tankards to jump as if alive.

The gentlemen moved out of the room, muttering to each other. When they had gone, the Captain smiled at us, took three tankards from the table, and filled them with cider from a barrel near him. He sat the cider at seats nearest him and asked us to be seated.

"Those fools in London think of nothing but gold and passage to the western ocean, so they send us miners, tradesmen, and knaves the likes of Ratcliffe and Percy. God's wounds! I thought I had rid this colony of them for good, but no—what did they do but give the company in London a false report of the happenings here, and now have returned with their heads full of quick riches and fool's dreams. However, they are not our concern at the moment. Tell me what happened in the forest."

Lieutenant Webster told the story truthfully, occasionally looking to me for agreement. When he had finished, the Captain refilled the Lieutenant's tankard and said that he had done well.

"These gentlemen," he said with the highest contempt, "seem to believe that there is little difference between this place and Covent Garden. Powhatan and his people do not wish or intend to share any part of this land with us. They intend to get rid of us any way they can. These savages aren't so simple as it is believed in London."

The Captain, seeing the Lieutenant's expression, continued. "Yes, I know what you are thinking, that the backers in London want to avoid the Spanish mistake and not settle in a state of continuous war. But I tell you, Powhatan behaves no differently than the Germans would if we were to sail up the Rhine and plant our colony there. Soon it will have to come to a contest of arms. And now that these scoundrels who I once sent away have returned, I can well imagine what they think of me in London."

Captain Smith looked down into his tankard with sadness.

"God knows what will become of us."

He held the tankard up and drank the last drops of cider and then poured more from the barrel, but the liquid stopped running out before filling his tankard.

"Well, here it is. Another empty barrel for Newport's gold sickness, and the last of our cider unless more is brought on the *Sea Venture*."

He looked directly at Lieutenant Webster.

"Has there been any sighting of that vessel yet?"

"No, sir. Not the slightest sign of a sail."

"God's blood! I would gladly give up a year's ration of cider to know if that ship was cast away with all those pompous knaves who were to lead us."

"Shall we proceed with what orders we have, Captain?" the Lieutenant asked.

"Yes. And, by God, endeavor to keep these fools from losing their hair to the savages. Did you know this man you killed?"

"He was one of Powhatan's men, sir."

"That slippery old fox. Let us take care that he never goes to England. With his guile and cunning, he will make himself a guest in the royal chambers."

Captain Smith and the Lieutenant laughed until the Captain's laughter erupted into another fit of coughing, which could only be cured by large draughts of cider. The Lieutenant and I left the Captain after making our bows.

———•—•——

I returned to our house where I found Richard lying on his straw mattress, sick and exhausted from the day's labor. His rations were unprepared and lay where I had stored them that morning. Our housemates had already prepared their meal and sat grimly eating their corn bread and drinking water from an earthenware cup. Neither man looked at me or gave the slightest awareness of my presence.

I took my rations and mixed them with water that I obtained from the common well. I made a batter of them and returned to my house, intending to use the fire. The larger of the two men, John Wilcox, put his foot in my way.

"This is our fire," he said. "If you want to cook that filth, build your own."

I knew that it would be pointless to reason with this man. It was clear he wanted us gone from the house and, seeing as there were two against one, he decided to provoke me. Since civilized discussion was now out of the question, I placed my boot against his shoulder and kicked him from his seat.

He sprawled on the floor, losing his cornbread to the fire. I reached for my musket just as he pulled out his dagger and made a dash for me. I parried his lunge with the barrel of my musket, the force of which sent him tumbling out the door. He remained on his feet, however, and whirled around to face me, the dagger clutched tightly in his hand, his face contorted with rage. He started circling me, kicking up a little dust as he did so. A cheering crowd had gathered and bets began to change hands.

"Ten shillings on the one with the musket," someone shouted.

"My money's on the killer dog with the dagger," another shouted.

Wilcox made a half-hearted lunge at me, but I stood my ground. Then he made a feint. I parried but was too late to block his true lunge at my midsection. I rotated away from him and, thinking he had me on the run, he came at me wildly. I made a motion for his head. He raised his arms for protection, and I brought the butt of my musket up into his stomach. He doubled over, gripping his waist, and pitched forward to the ground.

There were sighs from some of the people gathered around. I heard coins jingling as they went from one hand to another. I removed Wilcox's dagger from where it had fallen next to him and went back into my house.

The other man, a Benjamin Holt, had watched from the doorway, and when he saw me coming back with the dagger and my musket, he feared for his life and begged me to spare him. I told him that I had no intention of harming him or anyone, but that it would be better for us if we shared the same quarters as friends and not as enemies. He agreed. I handed over Wilcox's dagger to him and began cooking the corn batter and thought no more of the incident. When the cornbread was ready, I roused Richard and convinced him to eat as much of it as he could and to drink as much water as he could hold. He struggled to take all of this nourishment, but soon had to leave the house and vomit it up outside.

It was not a pleasant night. I slept little and Wilcox returned at some time close to morning. He had been drinking all night on one of the ships. He swayed several times. I saw his head turned toward me once. Then he fell onto his hay mattress and snored abominably for the remainder of the night.

The next day, it was cooler. The wind blew from the north, stirring up a little chop on the river, and rustling the leaves on the trees. Richard seemed to be faring better and managed to eat his breakfast with no ill effects. I returned to the woods to mark and cut more trees, but Richard was given a different task.

It was the day of the week for fresh meat to be procured for the colony, and Richard was to go with the party over to Hog Island, to kill a number of hogs. He was given a hammer and told to strike the pig chosen for him on the head hard enough to render him unconscious or lifeless. Then the man who was experienced at such things was to cut the beast's throat.

Richard was so upset by this action that when it came his turn to strike his animal, he pulled his blow short, hit the beast on the snout, and sent it squealing and running throughout the entire herd. A wild melee of running pigs and men soon developed, and Richard was quickly banished to the boats to await the completion of the slaughter. He was sick again when I returned, but now sick at heart, he vowed never to touch meat as food again.

Lieutenant Webster had departed on another scouting mission while I was busy with the cutters in the woods. He returned later with two Indian prisoners, bound together at the wrists. Captain Smith came out to talk with them since he, and a few of the soldiers, were the only people who could speak and sign the language. Richard was still as enthralled by the sight of the Indians as at our first arrival. We listened to their strange tongue, which is nothing like any in Europe, as Captain Smith and the Lieutenant spoke with them. The two Indians did not carry themselves as prisoners do in Europe, with heads and eyes cast down, but stood erect and defiant. When the questioning was over, they were led away. Richard told me that he was going to follow them and try to speak to them.

I asked the Lieutenant what was said. He told me briefly that one of the prisoners was the nephew of Powhatan and the other was the son of Opechancanough. That it was he who led the attack against us while we were taking his stores, and that his father and uncle fully intended to cut all of our throats. His people would not rest, he said, as long as he was a prisoner in our town.

I asked what the Captain intended.

"To keep them as hostages. The savages would not dare to attack the fort as long as Powhatan's nephew is within. The Captain will trade them for supplies."

CHAPTER 4

The Lexicon

The women in our settlement marveled greatly at the many strange and varied designs on the bodies of the Powhatans. They were amazed at their smooth, dark skin unblemished by the pox, and that they had no beards or hair on their bodies such as European men have. There was much giggling and whispering among them.

Richard returned while I was preparing the day's rations. Our sullen housemates remained quiet and unfriendly. Richard was in a very excited state and begged me to take him to Captain Smith so that he could seek his permission to learn the Indian's language.

"That's it, lad!" John Wilcox said in a loud voice, from his place at the opposite end of the house. "Learn their language, find out where the savages get their gold, and I'll see to it that you receive a goodly portion. Didn't I say it was a good thing to have a scholar with us, Ben?"

"Aye, that you did, John. They is always good for thinking on new things."

"That I did," John Wilcox said.

"Master Wilcox, it is well known that the Indians here have no gold. When I learn their language, I intend to use it to add to our knowledge of their science and philosophy."

"God's blood! These brutes have no knowledge of that sort.

They are nothing more than animals of the forest. I'll wager that Captain Smith and his cohorts don't allow it. They want all this Indian treasure for themselves."

Richard looked to me.

"Very well," I said and took him to Captain Smith at that same moment.

The Captain was busy eating a biscuit and filling his tankard with ale purchased from the ships. He permitted us to see him, even though he made it plain that he wished us to state our business quickly and leave him to his supper.

"Learn the Indian's language?" he said, letting a few crumbs fall from his mouth, and wiping the ale from his long mustache. "For what purpose? They can tell you nothing. They are pagans without skill in metals or science."

"It is also my plan," Richard added, "to make a lexicon of their language so that all, if they so desire, can learn to speak with them."

Captain Smith let out a belly laugh.

"You are even a bigger fool than I had at first thought. You are not maddened by dreams of gold. Yet," Captain Smith leaned closer to us, "you are a little mad in other ways. So be it then," he said, not giving Richard a chance to defend himself.

"You may write your lexicon of the Indian language, but only after you have completed the day's work."

The Captain wrote his permission on a scrap of paper nearby, and handed it to Richard.

"This will inform the guards of your purpose and require them to cooperate with you. Now, for God's sake, be gone and let me drink my ale in peace."

I went with Richard to the jail, where he showed the guard his pass from Captain Smith.

The guard looked at it suspiciously, then said, "If I was

you, mate, I'd have nothing to do with these heathens—bloody savages."

He turned to unlock the heavy, barred door. Both Indians moved toward the door.

The guard lowered his pistol and screamed, "Get back, you demons from Hell. Get back or I'll blow your fiendish heads off!"

The prisoners moved back against the far wall, and the guard opened the door. Richard stepped in, but before I followed, I whispered to the guard to keep a watch over us and to use his pistol if one of them made as if to attack us. The guard jiggled his weapon in front of my face to show me that he was anxious to use it for that purpose.

I closed the door behind us and heard the lock engage. The two prisoners remained against the wall, both staring at us with their black eyes and waiting for what might happen next.

It was very hot in the jail room with only a small, barred window for air. The stench was almost overpowering. Richard ignored this unpleasantness and, taking a step toward the Indians, pointed to himself and pronounced his name.

The Indians remained unmoving, without the slightest sign of comprehension in their faces. Richard pronounced his name again. The largest Indian's eyes flicked a quick glance at me. Richard pointed to me and pronounced my name. The large Indian then looked at Richard and made an utterance that was close to sounding like his name. Richard smiled happily.

"Yes, yes," he said, and the Indian repeated, "ess, ess."

Richard nodded, then pointed to the large Indian as a sign for him to give his name. The Indian understood and, smiling, said, "Pomatas."

He pointed to the other Indian, and the Indian said,

"Waahtmoca," in a deep voice.

Richard then withdrew two white beads from his pocket and handed one each to the Indians. They thanked him in their own language, expressing regret that they had nothing to offer in exchange. Richard caught the meaning of what they were saying and, smiling, he said in English that the knowledge of their names was gift enough. Of course, the Indians did not understand a word of what he said but seemed content.

At my request, the guard let us out and slammed the door after us. He shouted to the prisoners, "Get back! Get back against the wall, you stinking, dark bastards."

"There is no need to be that harsh with them, sir," Richard said.

The guard wheeled around to face Richard.

"Don't you tell me how to treat these swine. When you've been here as long as I have, lad, and seen a little of what these Godless brutes can do, you'll not be so loving toward them."

"You are right, sir," I said to the guard, seeking to ease this tense situation. "My friend is but a scholar, unused to the ways of the wilderness and, as you know, newly arrived from England."

"Then if he is to live here, he must become a schoolboy again and learn under the most cruel of masters, the forest and the savages."

"That he will, sir, but you well know the way of scholars often being the most stubborn of learners."

The guard nodded, "That is very true, my friend."

He looked at Richard, who avoided his eyes.

"They are often a thick-headed lot."

I laughed heartier than the situation warranted.

"Are you the official keeper here?"

"Not the official one, but it has been my task to guard pris-oners since I injured my leg last year at harvest time, chasing the savages from our fields."

"Then we will see you here when we come?"

The guard nodded and turned toward the barred door. "As long as they are here, I will be here," he said.

I thanked the guard for his vigilance and led Richard away before he destroyed the good relations I had established with the man.

Richard reproached me. "Why did you say those things, Matthew? The man is a simpleton who would as soon kill those men in his keep as not."

"No doubt he had rather kill them than stand guard over them," I said. "But trying to teach him morality or to dissuade him from his hatred is wasted effort and will only succeed in turning him against you. What you must do, Richard, is flatter him, let him feel important. That is what he wants."

"Yes, that and possibly a substantial bribe."

"If you are to advance in this project of yours, Richard, you must have easy access to the Indians. Do you have any money left?"

"Perhaps a little. I don't know."

"An occasional tankard of ale when you can get it may open the doors quicker for you, and without a word of protest."

"I will not do it, Matthew. Look at how we've already be-gun with violence. Are we to add to it bribery and deceit? I appreciate all that you have done for me, but I cannot begin life here in a state of sin."

"Would you have eaten your rations uncooked and let Wilcox throw us out with the flies and mosquitoes?"

"Before I would have struck him, yes."

There seemed little to say after this, and we returned to our house in silence, there to find Anne Breton waiting at the door.

"Master Scott," she said in a formal manner, "My mistress has heard that you are a scholar and learned in Latin and Greek. She wishes you to come to her and bring your books. She would like you to read to her whatever text is to your liking."

Richard said that he would be delighted to go with her to her mistress. He ducked into our house and in a few minutes came out again, carrying several of his books. He had a strange expression on his face, but I thought little of it, my attention having been diverted by some activity in the fort.

When I returned to the house, I found Wilcox bent over Richard's chest, examining its contents. He looked up at me, startled, as I rushed toward him. He leaped back and pulled a pistol out of his belt. My body seemed to freeze in spite of my mind's urging, and I watched as he took aim and fired.

All of this action took place in a matter of seconds, yet it seemed hours to me. It was as though time had become a thick fluid and I watched, like an objective observer, as he slowly withdrew his pistol, aimed, and fired. I believe I could even see the ball flying at me. Perhaps I moved or his aim was bad, for the ball whistled past my ear and lodged in the wall of our house.

Having missed me, he tried to use the pistol as a club to bash my head in. I had, by then, regained my composure and parried the blow with my left arm while sinking my right fist into his midsection. He crumpled to the floor and held up his hand as a sign that he had had enough.

"Your friend is a fool, you know. He came in and saw me going through his belongings and said not a word. How far will he get, huh? Now you're a man who knows the game. Come in with us, make your fortune, and we can all be gone from this place in a year's time."

I couldn't despise Wilcox for the way he felt. Not all men shared Richard's vision, including myself. Wilcox saw this place for what it was, a hard land covered with thick forest and peopled with men who lived little better than the animals they hunted. Virginia was not a garden where men walked with God. Death could come from behind any tree, and all fruits were forbidden. I even felt a little sorry for Wilcox lying there on the floor, desperately trying to protect himself from me. I, in fact, felt hardly superior to him at that moment, and more like the hated Cain, for I truly had it in my heart to kill him. When I realized this, I was deeply ashamed.

"Get up, man," I said to Wilcox, "I will not harm you further. I fear you are right about me, and perhaps you are close to being right about Richard. Let this be the last of our quarrels. It is easy for us to fight, but it will not be easy for us to survive together. As for the wealth that you speak of, Captain Smith assures me that there is no gold or silver in all of Virginia."

Wilcox slowly got to his feet, brushed the dust from his clothes, and replaced his pistol back in his belt.

"Captain Smith may protest all he wants, but the adventurers back in London now believe him to be a liar and a knave. There are many good gentlemen who came out here with the first settlers and who have returned to swear that there is much evidence for gold and other minerals here. If the *Sea Venture* had not been lost, Captain Smith would find himself in chains this very day and waiting ship for England.

"Did you see the *Sea Venture* go down?"

"Nay, but with the fury of that storm it is only good fortune that any of us survived. The *Sea Venture*, new as she was, is rumored to have been launched early. I'll wager my life that the fish are swimming between her ribs at this very moment. The people of our ship knew that Captain Smith's days in the colony were numbered; and it is the worst kind of fate that all of our leaders were in that doomed ship. Now we must contend with that boastful fool who, I believe, has set himself up as King of Virginia."

"How do the adventurers in London and these gentlemen here feel about the colony?"

Wilcox glanced aside at the door and around at the window.

"This settlement is first a business venture in which a great deal of money has been invested. These men must show a good profit, other than what oak planks will bring, or they will withdraw their support. New investors cannot hope to be attracted, and I need not tell you what will happen to the colony then. You see the situation here—what they have to eat, the work that must be done to clear the forest, the savages. Without support from London, this place will wither as surely as fruit bitten by early frost."

I could not deny that what he said made tempting logic. I well knew that men have to eat and shelter themselves from wet and cold and that debts have to be paid. It seemed to me that in order to appease these newly arrived men, Captain Smith should encourage them in their search for profit. If there was no gold, let them find out for themselves.

CHAPTER 5

Talk Fairly and Trade Honestly

That night I slept little, thinking on what Wilcox had said and my own place in this world. I had no family who would welcome me back. I was not even a recognized tradesman. I was in a wilderness far from anything I had ever known, with only the clothes on my back.

I lay for a long time thinking of what it would be like, returning to England a wealthy man with chests of gold and precious gems, a retinue of servants, coaches, country houses, and more fine clothes than I could wear in a lifetime. Wealth would bring respect, honor, and, perhaps, even the love of a beautiful woman.

As much as I respected Richard for his dream of a new paradise, it was becoming clearer to me that the people in this colony were here for what they could get out of it in the way of profit. It occurred to me, with startling clarity, that I who had nothing would end my life with nothing unless I used this opportunity to better my station. Since wealth was the seat of power on earth, I resolved, on rising in the morning, that I would go in quest of it.

My quest did not begin immediately, however, as there was still much work to be done in the way of providing additional shelters to relieve our overcrowded condition, and to provide a sizable store of timber to load the ships with. I spent many hot days that summer laboring out in the forest, cutting and sawing logs into clapboards. In the evening, whenever I could, I went with Richard to visit with the Indian prisoners.

They spoke very courteously but reservedly with Richard, as is their manner, and with many strong gestures. These gestures were an important part of their language, and Richard wrote them down as he did the words. They spoke much about the strength of their various werowances and of the power of their gods. Most of their praise was for their great Mamanatowick, Powhatan, whom they said was Lord over all the peoples of the Chesapeake. Richard asked why Powhatan had not come to free them, and they said that he most certainly would. When the time was proper, he would avenge the wrongs that had been done to them.

They were exceedingly proud men, confident in their own strengths and beliefs, and to me, at that time, they seemed as natural to the forest as the deer they hunted.

On many evenings, after our visit with the prisoners, Richard would excuse himself, saying that he was going to call on Anne Breton, and would I guard his work from our two housemates. I would take this opportunity to read through his lexicon for any hint of where wealth might be found. Wilcox, with his demonic sense, seemed to know what I was about. Occasionally, I would catch him smiling at me like a fellow conspirator, and I would threaten to club him. He knew, with disgusting accuracy, that I was only trying to cover up my own avaricious heart, that I would not admit to myself the sickening truth that I was on his side now.

A week later, while I was working in the forest on the southern end of the peninsula, the alarm sounded from the fort. We dropped our work at once and with axes and muskets raced back to the fort. We arrived there in time to see a great number of Indians, possibly as many as two hundred, coming to the fort.

The men, although not armed, walked in front of the women, who bore in their arms baskets of corn, fish, and venison.

At the head of the group walked Opechancanough himself, with his arms folded across his chest and his head held high. The group stopped at the gate and waited in silence. Not a soul moved so that, in an instant, they all seemed more like brown statues with dust settling to the ground around them.

Captain Smith readied his pistol and checked his sword to make sure nothing bound it. He looked around the fort to see that his soldiers were in place, then ordered the gate opened. I readied my musket and made my way up to the nearest cannon emplacement. I could see most of the interior of the fort and the Indians outside.

Opechancanough spoke with signs and gesture, and intermittent guttural sounds which Captain Smith seemed to understand.

"I have come in peace, Captain Smith. As you can see, my people bear only corn and meat. Why do you greet me in such a manner, with your men of iron and your weapons of fire?" Captain Smith had, without knowing it, placed his hand on the hilt of his sword. Then, realizing what he had done, removed it as though the sword had just been taken out of the fire. The look in his eyes was of a man who did not have an answer, but he quickly recovered and smiled. Then he spoke.

"Because you have come in peace, you and your people may enter, and we can talk of peace and friendship to come."

"Not until your men have put away their weapons. My people will not venture into the fort. They cannot bear the sight of those cruel objects and will not venture forth, not even at my word."

Captain Smith mimicked a posture to show he had taken offence.

"The sly old fox," said one of the soldiers standing next to me. "I'll wager the woods are full of 'em, all with arrows aimed right at the Captain's heart."

I looked out at the forest. "I don't see anything," I said.

"That's because the devils can hide behind a reed no bigger than me finger, but if I was to put a ball over the head of Opechancanough, you would see nothing but arrows coming from them woods."

Behind his back, Captain Smith gave an arranged signal to Lieutenant Webster. He waited for a moment, pretending to be much in thought, while the Lieutenant gathered many soldiers out of sight of the Indians and stationed them in houses along the fort wall. When this had been completed, Captain Smith called out in a loud voice for every man to put away his arms.

The soldiers in the fort, and in clear view, lay their muskets down on the ground. I ran down to our house where I could be closer to what was happening and leaned my musket just inside the door.

In a few minutes, a wide circle was cleared inside the fort and Opechancanough entered, followed by all of his people. He directed the women to place their baskets on the ground and stand back, away from them. The young men—and by the look of them, they were good fighters—he instructed to remain close to him. Captain Smith walked among the baskets, examining them like a careful shopper in an open market, stopping now and then to pick up some of the corn and let it fall through his fingers.

"Opechancanough," he said, after finishing his inspection, "I am right happy that you have come with such good and honorable intentions, and the stores you have brought are of the best quality."

Opechancanough nodded with approval.

"But I know that the great Powhatan does not value his own son or his brave and lusty nephew so little as to bargain with so paltry a sum as this. He well knows the price I have set for his son and nephew who attacked my men without provocation and sought to do them grievous harm. It was almost outside my power to preserve their lives, and this," Captain Smith pointed to the baskets of corn and meat, "is the best that he can offer in gratitude?"

Opechancanough looked stunned but quickly regained his composure. A wave of unrest swept through his young fighters. Some of them quickly placed their hands on their warclubs and stone knives but did not withdraw them.

"This is more than we have to feed ourselves. There is no more to be found. Do you wish us to spend the winter digging in the snow for acorns and eating sour berries? And if you will not accept all that we have, then we must depart this place and, with many tears, leave our sons in your hands."

"Do not play false with me, Opechancanough. You forget how soon it was that I was your prisoner and how, in your triumph, you took me throughout your land and into every village so that your people could see your power and greatness. While I was thus being seen by your people, I was myself seeing your people. I saw their wide fields full of every kind of fruit, and your hunters who daily brought back great quantities of meat from the forest. Powhatan well knows what victuals I require, and it is he who continues to starve my people in spite of my many offers of friendship. Does he think that I am a simpleton?

"I well know that his son and his nephew would not have attacked my people without his consent. Why does he continue to make war upon us when all we desire is to live in peace and happiness forever? Take my words and your victuals back to him and tell him that he may have his kinsmen when he is ready to talk fairly and trade honestly with me."

Captain Smith and Opechancanough stared at each other for a long time, like two bulls claiming the same plot of ground. Then Captain Smith spoke, with a contrived note of friendliness in his voice.

"Opechancanough, as a sign of my trust, I will give your son to you and ask nothing in return save that you speak truly of what I have said to Powhatan. Tell him I would prefer it if he could come himself to settle the differences between us."

"I will do as you ask," Opechancanough said, taking a step back and making a motion with his hands for the women to pick up the baskets.

They did so, and the young fighters surrounded them. Opechancanough waited, looking straight ahead with his arms folded. Captain Smith had already ordered Lieutenant Webster to release Opechancanough's son. There was another movement in the crowd, and a path was cleared as the Lieutenant led the young man, bound by the hands, to his father. The Lieutenant stopped in front of Opechancanough, cut the young Indian's bonds, and stepped back next to Captain Smith. Opechancanough, without the slightest change of expression or hardly so much as a glance at the young warrior, led his people out of the fort.

When the gates were closed, Captain Smith turned and spoke quietly to the Lieutenant who, after the captain had finished, ordered the crowd to disperse and the soldiers and men to resume their arms and their work. At the Captain's bidding, the Lieutenant followed him into the President's House.

The Lieutenant later told me that he had asked the captain if letting Opechancanough take back his corn and one of the hostages was particularly wise, and that Captain Smith had said perhaps it did not seem so. The Captain knew Powhatan and that the old man would soon meet his price, but he did not expect to see him come to the fort himself.

The Lieutenant also told me that two expeditions were to be readied for the plantation of men at the falls of the river and across the river at Nansemond. I asked the Lieutenant if he could recommend me for the settlement at the falls, and he said that he would but that he doubted the Captain would consent to it, my skills as a carpenter being needed more at the fort.

Richard was extremely pleased that Tatahcoope was to remain in the fort. His lexicon was half finished, he said. At least he had used up half of his paper, and that the remaining half would have to serve. He felt sorry for Tatahcoope also and not a little angry with himself for wishing the Indian to remain until his work was completed.

I explained that it was better for the Indian to endure this small suffering so that all who could read might learn the Indian tongue, and thereby come to be friends much more readily. Wilcox and Ben Holt laughed greatly at this. Although I pretended to be offended, I knew that they could see into my liar's heart.

Richard, however, was content with my explanation. It was not in him to see evil in men, and the possibility of one of his dearest friends being untruthful with him was as alien to him as this land of Virginia was to me.

That night, while returning from our visit with Tatahcoope, Richard confessed to me that he desired to marry Anne Breton and that he was going to present his proposal to her this very night. I asked about her service obligation to Mrs. Fitzsimmons, and Richard said that he knew that Mrs. Fitzsimmons was pressing her husband to return to England.

"It might be possible," he said, "for Anne to leave her service and remain here so long as she has a husband."

"And does she want to stay here and deal with the mosquitoes?" I said jokingly, not believing that it was possible for any woman of delicate sensibilities to want to struggle in this wilderness.

"I believe so," said Richard. "She seems to feel the same about the place as I do, and she is a good girl, Matthew; kind and strong and as pure of mind and heart as the Virgin herself.

"Isn't it strange," he continued in a dreamlike way. "Back in England I thought of marriage as the most distant, hardly possible thing I could do, but here, I don't have to tell you, everything has changed. It's as though the future expects it, even demands it. I could almost believe, and perhaps I do, a divine hand is intervening. I tell you, Matthew, I am free of fear for the first time in my life."

"And what if she refuses you?" I asked.

Richard smiled tolerantly at my lack of understanding.

"She may well do that, but I don't think she will."

Wilcox and Holt were in the house when we arrived, eating their day's rations. Holt eyed me strangely at first, then pretended to ignore me. Richard packed away his lexicon and took a book of poetry from his chest.

After he departed to visit Anne, I started preparing my rations.

"Have you heard," Wilcox said, looking up from his half-cooked piece of meat, "that the Captain is getting up two expeditions?"

"No, I haven't," I said, without looking at him.

"Then you must be the only one, for everyone else knows it, except your scholarly friend, of course."

"Idle rumor," I said.

"Not this time," Wilcox said, tearing off a piece of meat with his hands and dropping it into his mouth. "I know it for a truth. That the noble Captain is to send one expedition across the river and trade with the friendly Indians there, and the other to go up river to search for minerals. Jamestown is too small for us, you see, and the company wants its profit. Ben and me will be going up river. Will you be joining us?"

"I don't know. If I had a choice, I would prefer to go up river," I said.

"I thought as much," said Wilcox. "You haven't been study-ing that book your friend's been writing on the Indians for nothing. Me and Ben have been noticing that you're beginning to change your ways. That maybe you're starting to see the real reason for coming to this place. After all, what is wealth and power among the savages? A few beads, a hatchet, a little gunpowder."

I ignored him and finished preparing my supper. He was right, though, and he knew it. It is an easy thing for one scoundrel to see into the heart of another. There is nothing complicated there, no confusion, no unanswerable questions.

CHAPTER 6

Proposal of Marriage

Shortly after I had finished my supper, Captain Smith sent for me. He was sitting at the table with Lieutenant Webster, drinking watered-down ale and appearing very angry when I arrived. He thanked me for coming.

"The Lieutenant has conveyed to me your request to go upriver. I hope you haven't got it in your head to get rich."

I denied that any such notion had entered my thoughts.

"Good," he said, "because I've decided that you should go. That blockhead West will need someone of your skills and good sense, and you should know that you are going with him at my insistence. He thinks he is going to show me by dragging that assembly of gentlemanly rogues and common street ruffians upriver. He thinks I don't know what he's up to."

The captain let out a short laugh, which sounded more like an angry shout, and then held up a list of names.

"You see this?" he said, waving the piece of paper in front of me. "It's a list of the men he wants to take with him—everyone fit only for prison or cuckolding the clerks of London, and everyone opposed to me. I'm putting you in charge of the buildings. I'm sending Lieutenant Webster along also, to help you accomplish that work. He is my man, and I want you to be his. God willing, maybe we can prevent those fools from destroying the work we've already accomplished here."

I thanked the Captain and said that I would do all that he expected of me, and afterward took my leave of him.

I despised myself as much as if I had lied to my own father. I felt as low as any worm crawling through the slime. Yet, in spite of my wretched state, I resolved to follow through with my new ambition. From what I knew about the Indians, they had no need of tailors or cobblers or bankers or any of the things we needed in England, so they would certainly have no need of gold or other precious metals. Was I so wrong? We were all exploiting this land in one way or another. Like Wilcox, with his cruel, indifferent avarice.

Even Captain Smith had his reasons for being here, reasons that would eventually drive the Indians out of their land. And Richard. Perhaps he was the worst of all, for his reasons seemed the most right, a divine mission which would seep into the Indian soul and begin the process of destroying them. Richard would learn their language so that he, or others like him, could teach the Indians about Christianity and English customs. Soon the Indians themselves would need tailors and cobblers and all the other miseries of that cold and hard island across the sea.

Thinking this way, I felt much refreshed by the time I reached the house. A shaft of white moonlight shone through the opened window and fell directly on Wilcox, covering him in a deathlike pall. He lay on his back, sour wine fumes swimming up from his opened mouth, and an empty bottle of Canary wine lay by his side.

Holt lay hidden in darkness near Wilcox and made his presence known by an occasional snort. Richard wasn't in his bed, which was unusual for him. I imagined that he had had to persuade Mrs. Fitzsimmons of his honest intentions which, I was sure, her natural suspicions caused her to doubt.

I slipped off my shoes and crawled over to my bed and lay

awake for a long time, acutely aware of a strange feeling of separation from all that is good. I could hear the night birds cooing their mournful notes.

Cooling embers snapped in the fireplace. All of the night sounds of nature dominated our little town, like a nocturnal army of occupation.

Something warm and comforting seemed to have gone out of me and left in its place was a cold knot of antagonism. I was afraid, I was angry, I was impatient, and I hated myself for feeling this way. Everything, every person became a potential enemy, even Richard.

The next morning, Richard was in his bed and, it being the Sabbath, the church bell was sounding the call to services. Wilcox rolled onto his knees and held his forehead in his dirty hands.

"God split me down the middle if I ever touch that poisonous Canary brew again."

Holt sat up, gripped his stomach, and stumbled over Wilcox, trying to get out of the house to make it to the latrine.

I got up, grateful to see warm daylight shimmering outside our door.

Richard rose to his feet and covered a yawn with his hand.

"Did the lady accept your offer of marriage?" I asked, loosening my belt and stuffing my shirt into my britches.

His eyes took on an amused look.

"Not precisely, but she did not refuse me either."

"Trouble with Mrs. Fitzsimmons?"

"No. That lady gave Anne complete freedom to do whatever she wishes."

"Will Mrs. Fitzsimmons be returning to England then?"

"On the first ship leaving Jamestown," he said, brushing the dust from his clothes.

"Aren't you going to tell me, Richard?"

"Of course. I'm sorry for being neglectful. Anne says she is not sure that she wants to stay in Jamestown, that she is frightened by the wilderness, the Indians, and the distance from home. But she will get over these fears."

"How do you know that, Richard?"

He looked at me with a tolerant smile. "I just know she will."

"Are you saying that it's ordained?"

"Yes, I suppose I am. I don't mean it to sound boastful, Matthew. Please forgive me if I do. I simply mean that I believe that our being here is a part of an immutable divine plan, and that Anne is to share in it in a particular way."

"By being the mother of a new race?"

"Yes. I believe that is what her presence here means."

Wilcox moaned pitifully. He was still on his knees, holding his head.

"Lads," he said, "would you help me to Vespers? If they catch me absent again, it'll be a flogging for sure."

Richard helped him to his feet and held on to him until he regained his strength.

"What of your friend?" I asked Wilcox.

"If he don't make it, then that's his misfortune. That'll teach him to steal the meat from a ship what made the crossing too long."

Wilcox tried to laugh, but the added sickness in his stomach and head caused him to immediately abandon the attempt. Richard placed his arm around Wilcox's waist to further support him.

"Just let me walk between you, lads. I can't let them see you hauling me to God's house this way."

"Yes, we would not want you accused of drunkenness."

Wilcox cast his shiny, red veined eyes at me and, for a

moment, they were as sharp as swords' points before they faded into something more like shallow pools of water. I walked over to where Richard was supporting him and motioned for Richard to step aside.

"Don't soil yourself with this son of Satan," I said to Richard, who appeared shocked at my words. "Make him pay. That's what he knows best. Isn't that the truth, Wilcox?"

Wilcox raised his head for a moment to look at me, not with hatred or even in reproach, but more like an accomplice.

"I will see that you get to Vespers, Wilcox," I said, putting my arm around his waist. "But you will owe me for it."

He uttered an oath, and I let my grip on him go. He swayed several times, then caught hold of my arm. I pulled it away. He started to fall and grabbed my shirt for support.

"Well?" I said, and he looked up at me, almost smiling, and nodded his consent. I knew he had no intention of recognizing the debt, yet it was gratifying for me to hold this small measure of power over him.

We walked together to the church, me dragging Wilcox along as though he were a wounded man, and Richard walking a short distance behind. We were the objects of no little amusement, especially from the sailors whom Wilcox was most acquainted with.

The Reverend Albright stopped us at the door of the church and said that he would not allow a drunken man to enter God's house. I explained that Master Wilcox was not drunk, only sick from drink and that certainly God had punished him for the sin of drunkenness by making him so.

"Surely," I said, "the words of God would be the right liquor to cure him in body and spirit."

The Reverend still refused us entrance and said that Master Wilcox could find the same cure by listening outside of the church. I sat Wilcox under one of the opened windows where he immediately rolled to one side and retched up a yellow fluid.

One of the sailors came over to him and, squatting down beside him said, with much laughter, "I've got an old bottle of aqua vitae that you can have for a good price."

Wilcox looked up at him and, half smiling, said, "God damn you for a son of a whore; what is your price?"

"An hour of love," the sailor said in a lowered voice.

Wilcox made a weak lunge for him. The sailor jumped back, laughing, and after kicking dirt at Wilcox, walked away.

"If the Reverend asks, tell him you've repented and will never touch another drop of that infamous liquid," I said.

Wilcox agreed that he would follow my directions, yet he seemed, still, more like a beast quietly enduring his captivity and waiting for the first chance to bolt.

I could hear the Reverend's sermon faintly above the general noise of the men outside the church who were near us. He spoke of kindness toward our brother Indians, of the necessity for gentleness and patience with those who were ignorant of the truths and joys of Christianity. Lastly, he reminded everyone of our duty to those who were financing our work in Virginia and of obedience to those in authority over us. The service concluded with a prayer and hymn which, surprisingly, Wilcox knew the words to. He even sang them as loudly as those in the church.

After the service, Lieutenant Webster announced that all of the men in the fort were to assemble in the yard outside the church, except for those soldiers presently on guard. We drifted with the flow of men to the center of the yard. The Reverend, carrying his prayer book tucked under his arm and still wearing his robe, walked past us, totally ignoring Wilcox and me. He stopped, looked at Richard, and motioned for him to follow.

Richard was puzzled. For a long moment, fear shadowed his face.

"What do you think this is all about?" he whispered to me.

"I suppose you'll have to go and find out," I said, trying to sound encouraging.

The Reverend put his arm around Richard's shoulder and led him away, out of the crowd. After a long wait, during which the men began to grumble, Captain Smith appeared. He stood up on the top of a barrel and made the official announcement that two expeditions would be leaving Jamestown on the next day with the morning tide. He held up two pieces of paper.

"The names of those men who have been selected are from both volunteers and others. They have been written here and will be posted. I don't need to tell you, men," he continued, "that you are to treat the Indians with courtesy, yet don't trust them. There will be men with you who know the language of Powhatan, both in words and signs. Those men are also good soldiers. They will be your guides, both in your intercourse with the savages and in matters of defense. Obey your leaders and your instincts and, for God's sake, practice good sense."

"Those men whose names appear on this list will have the day to make such preparations as are necessary for themselves. The rest of you will go about your work as before."

Having said this, the Captain leaped down from the barrel, walked over to the post, and nailed the lists to it. The men moved with him and closed around, each trying to look over the head of the man in front of him.

My name was on the list of men going to the falls, as the Captain said it would be, along with my occupation written next to it. Wilcox's name was also there with his occupation listed as laborer. Wilcox was starting to behave with more vigor and less like a dying man. I told him that I was going to fetch my rations and eat before making my preparations and invited him to join me. He declined, however, saying he had more urgent business to attend to.

I picked up my rations but decided not to prepare them since I already had prepared food left over from the day before, and I thought it would be better if I took these unprepared rations with me upriver.

The house was empty. I was the first to return, and I think it was the first time that I became aware of the foul smell of the place. The stink of men's bodies, unwashed in months, the sickening odor of rotting pieces of discarded meat, the musty, damp stench of our straw bedding was overpowering. Yet, in spite of this, I took out the uneaten portions of yesterday's rations from my pouch and began eating them.

The meat had started to become rancid and the cornbread stale, but I forced it down since it was a punishable crime in the colony to waste rations. I fought back the sickness that swam to my head. The house began to appear to me as little more than a waste pit. Vermin seemed to be everywhere, crawling over our beds, on the floor, on the walls. The very air seemed laden with fever and disease.

As soon as I knew that I wasn't going to lose my breakfast, I left the house and walked toward the river. I had few preparations to make before the coming journey, save washing the filth from my body and my clothes, a task I began to earnestly look forward to doing.

Outside the fort, the world was dazzled with the summer light of these latitudes. The birds chirped freely. A warm, gentle wind blew from the south. The fort had become a kind of prison that we had grown accustomed to in the month or so that we had been in this place, and seeing the land outside the fort, when I had leisure to see it, reminded me of what a promising, beautiful place it was. I could forget for a while the threat of the Indians or starvation. Perhaps, by washing in this Virginia water, I could also wash away the stain of sin and corruption that had lately afflicted me.

I walked along the shore, past the ships and pinnaces that would take us farther into this land. I walked past the firing field where Lieutenant Webster was training more men in the use of weapons, and past a group of men and women washing their clothes. Had I two suits to wear, I would have gladly joined them, but since I had only what I wore, I continued on my way to a less populated part of the peninsula.

Once clearly out of sight, I waded into the cool water of the river and stripped my clothes off. I soaked them through, twisted them, pounded them with my fist, churned them around and around in the water until I was convinced that I had either removed the filth from them or had torn them apart.

I took them back to the river's shore and laid them on a large log to dry in the sun. Then I happily returned to the river and, scooping up handfuls of the bottom's clean sand, I began to scour my body with it until I had rubbed it red and sore to the touch. I swam for a while out into the river but, feeling quickly exhausted, I swam back to shore.

My clothes were drying well. The sun was approaching its zenith and beat down with increasing heat and intensity. I stretched out on the sand near my clothes and let the sun dry my body. I had a brief thought of the Indians which I knew were somewhere nearby, and I hoped that they would not be offended at my nakedness.

I thought briefly of what lay in store for me in this journey to come. Perhaps I would find something there more worthwhile than gold, but I quickly dismissed that notion since the only other wealth that would be greater than gold, for me, was the love of a beautiful woman. Yet I had resolved not to do as Richard had done and take a wife here. I thought it would be the utmost cruelty to subject a wife to the rigors of the wilderness and children. I did not want my children to grow up running like beasts in the forest. When I marry, I thought to myself, I want it to be in England amid fine comforts and wealth. I wanted my children to be educated in the arts and sciences and move and speak with grace among the best sort of people.

I lay there for a long while, absorbing the heat of the sun and entertaining wild fancies, until I heard a noise. Thinking that it might have been caused by an Indian, I quickly jumped to my feet and threw on my clothes. I moved cautiously to the edge of the woods, but seeing and hearing nothing more, I decided it must have been an animal.

The incident did, however, put me in mind of my own carelessness. In spite of what pleasure there was to be had in these simple delights of nature, I was reminded that there was always death lurking somewhere out of sight. I started walking back along the sandy river shore and, as I was rounding a shallow curve of the land, I saw a figure walking toward me. Drawing closer, I could see that it was a woman. Moving still closer, I recognized the person as Anne Breton. She seemed not to see me and when I called to her, she appeared frightened at first, then waved as she recognized me. She started to walk away, so I picked up my pace to catch up with her.

"Wait, please," I finally managed to say between short breaths. Coming up beside her, I said, "Please let me escort you back to the fort. It's not safe to be out here alone."

"And what about yourself?" she asked in a teasing way.

"It's true also for me. Only a little while ago, I heard a sound in the woods that could have been an Indian."

"And what were you doing so far away from the fort, alone?"

"Washing my clothes before the vermin eat them off my back."

"I see," she said, with a slight smile.

"What are you doing here alone?" I asked.

"The same," she said, "washing for myself and my lady. It seemed like such a lovely day. I finished early and thought of walking along the shore, for it looked so inviting. Living as we do, there is no place to go to be alone."

She hesitated for a moment and, looking out over the river at the sparkling dark greenery of the opposite shore, said, "Do you think there are Indians on our peninsula now, at this moment?"

"Probably," I said. "The forest is their home."

"Just as Ragland is ours."

"I suppose you can look at it that way."

"Then if they were to paddle their canoes across the ocean and settle on the banks of the Thames, they would be in about the same situation as we are?"

"I don't think so. For one thing, their canoes cannot reach England."

"What's that got to do with it?" she interrupted sharply.

"Well, it means a great deal being able to do something, doesn't it? It sort of gives you the right to try it, I think. And for another thing, England is a civilized country. No one roams in the forest unless he has a license."

She laughed lightheartedly. "Do you suppose they're watching us now?"

"Yes, I imagine they are."

"Then why don't they try to hurt us as they often do some of our men?"

"I don't know. Indians, from what I have learned, are very strange and temperamental and unpredictable."

"I don't blame them for hating us."

"Oh? Why do you say that?"

"They may be savages as everyone says, without Christianity, but they are people much like us. Did you ever hear your parents speak about the Spanish fleet and what it was like when they believed the Dons would invade England?"

"Yes."

"Then isn't that the same as us landing here?"

"Perhaps. But we do not wish to subject the Indians to servitude. We only want to live in peace with them. Captain Smith has said so himself, and you have heard Reverend Albright speak with nothing but kindness toward them, reminding us always that we are brothers."

"Do you believe that, Matthew?"

"Yes, I believe it."

She glanced away. She seemed to know that I had my doubts about the reasons and justifications for Jamestown.

"Will you be going back to England?" I asked, thinking to remove the unpleasant subject of our settlement.

"I don't know. You know that Richard has asked for my hand?"

"Yes, he mentioned it. Please forgive me for being bold, but will you accept him?"

She stopped, and for a long time looked at me with questioning, dancing eyes. There was wonder in those clear blue eyes and pleading and fear and something so obscure that I felt mesmerized for an interminable period and stricken to the core of my being.

She turned quickly away. "I'm not sure," she said in a strained voice.

I was afraid that I had offended her, but before I could speak, she glanced back over her shoulder at me and started running along the shore, toward the fort. I shouted after her that I was sorry if I had stepped out of place, but I don't think she heard me.

Lieutenant Webster stopped me upon entering the fort and asked me to go with him. I followed behind the lieutenant, walking at a brisk pace to keep up with him. I noticed that he walked with his hand on his sword hilt, and I remembered that he had always done so. The metal parts of his armor clanked with authority at each of his steps.

We went directly to the storehouse where the soldier's equipment and other tools were stored. I followed the Lieutenant inside and stopped beside a large, roughly-made box containing an assortment of carpenter's tools.

"The Captain says that you will need these, but until such time as more tools arrive, these must be considered the property of the colony."

I asked the Lieutenant if I would be held responsible for them. Would I have to replace them at my own expense?

He said that unfortunately I would, but if more should come while I was in the settlement upriver, I would be informed, and that I would be given these, without obligation, to practice my trade independently. I thanked the Lieutenant but greatly wished that the tools had not been placed in my charge since I well knew how tools may be lost even in the best of conditions. We stepped back out into the glaring sunlight and noonday cooking smoke of the fort. I thanked the Lieutenant again and tried to make it sound sincere.

"We will make this a success, Matthew," he said with a

boyish smile. "Our settlement at the falls will be second only to Jamestown and, God be praised, we'll make a nation out of these villains yet."

I didn't want to question the Lieutenant's vision or his confidence. It was far too late for that. Like the rest of us, he preferred his own view of our journey. He saw justice and God on his side. Why shouldn't he feel fearless?

"Good," he said, almost as a shout, and slapped me on the shoulder. "I'll see you in the morning before the fifth hour." He smiled again. "And don't worry about missing the time. I'm having a man go around to all the houses and wake those men who are to embark in both parties."

I thanked the Lieutenant for his planning and thoughtfulness, and staggered back to my house, dragging the box of carpenter's tools behind me.

Wilcox and his friend Holt were there, lying on their beds and drinking a thick wine from a green bottle. When Wilcox saw me dragging in the tools, he burst into laughter.

"God's blood! What will you be doing with those?" he asked, spitting wine on his britches and the dirt floor.

"Building a city," I said, as Wilcox's laughter became a seizure.

Richard returned soon and appeared very pleased with himself. I, of course, asked the reason, and he said that the Reverend had heard about his lexicon and wanted to see it.

"I showed it to him, and he seemed quite interested and said that this may well be the instrument he needs to spread the word of God to the heathens. He told me of what the printing of the first English Bibles had done to help reform the old church by bringing the Light to everyone who could read. He also wants me to become his assistant."

"Will you do it?" I asked.

His brow knitted, and he shook his head slowly, more in unresolved thought than in rejection.

"I don't know. I did not come here to work in holy orders, although I certainly know its importance."

"But I thought . . . "

"Then why, pray tell, did you come here?" Wilcox interrupted.

Richard looked straight at him, honest as a saint. Although his lips moved, he did not speak. Whether it was that he thought Wilcox unworthy or that he chose not to fuel the man's mockery, or he had begun to doubt his own reason, I do not know.

Soon afterward he turned to me and said he was sorry that he had not been chosen to go upriver, but that in view of his coming marriage it was probably for the best. Then he offered, truly insisting, that I take a suit of his best garments for my own.

"Not for social wear," he said with a happy smile, "but made of very strong material, and by the best tailor in Plymouth."

Of course, I accepted his kind offer since my own clothes were becoming torn and threadbare. I purposely decided not to tell him that I had seen Anne or had spoken with her. He seemed so sure of the future and of his destiny. Then too, she did not tell me that she would not marry him or that she did not care for him the way lovers should. The truth was that, at that time, I was more concerned about what lay in store for me upriver than I was about what should happen to those in the fort.

I spent an anxious night sleeping fitfully, often waking with a start, wondering what time of the night it was. Finally, Captain Smith's soldiers appeared in the doorway and announced that it was time for my departure.

I was out of bed in an instant, followed by Richard, who

insisted on helping carry my load down to the ship. Wilcox and Holt arose with their usual curses. They stomped around their section of the house, threw their few belongings into an old shirt and tied it into a crude bag.

The men flowed like ants out of the fort to their small ships, each carrying his personal belongings and each ominously silent. A fresh, warm breeze blew from the east and carried with it a faint odor of the sea. The waves in the river slapped at the sharply cut shoreline and gave a gentle roll to our pinnaces.

We stopped and assembled around the Reverend, who said a few quiet prayers and gave us his blessing. We said our goodbyes to those friends and relatives who were present. I looked around quickly for Anne but did not see her. I thought she might have come to join Richard and, although I did not admit it to myself at the time, I had hoped to have a last sight of her before departing.

After Captain Smith had spoken to our leaders and admonished us to be courageous and to do our duty, we began boarding the shallow draft vessels: one hundred and fifty men, all eager for conquest, gain, and adventure.

CHAPTER 7

The Falls

As soon as we were on board our ship with our tools and supplies, the Master gave the order to cast off and make sail. If the wind held and providence kept us from accident, it would be less than a day's journey to the falls.

We soon separated from the other party as their destination took them across the river. We glided upstream, swept along by a flooding tidal current and a reassuring wind on our starboard quarter.

It was one of the most pleasant journeys of my life. The water, though dark and turgid, fairly danced and sparkled with the morning light. Fish of all kinds seem to leap everywhere in a kind of unspoken joy. The shore glowed with greens and blues. Nature was to me that day almost like a lover unbound with soft sweet kisses and whispered promises of a happy life on earth.

The canvas sail of the pinnace stretched and drummed with its load of wind. Lines creaked with strain but held fast. Few of the men talked. Those who did spoke, as always, of the minerals they expected to find and of the hidden wealth of the Indians.

We sailed quietly past the village of Paspahegh and attracted some attention from the Indians, who came down to the shore and made gestures that the Lieutenant said meant friendship. Our course took us near another group of Indians in several canoes who gave us a wide berth by making for the shore as hard as they could paddle. We passed other Indian towns on our voyage upriver, but for the most part they appeared deserted.

Twenty or so miles beyond Paspahegh, the river narrowed with many bends, requiring careful navigation. The wind, although still blowing well, was disturbed and often impeded by the river's high banks and trees. The force of the tide also slackened until it began to flow against us. Nevertheless, we came upon our destination several hours before nightfall.

A party of men was selected to go ashore under Lieutenant Webster's command to reconnoiter the place. We were not far from the town of Powhatan where the great Mamanatowick, Powhatan, made his home at various times of the year.

Our party returned after about an hour to say that there were no sightings of Indians and no hostile action. The Lieutenant and Captain West discussed at length the best location for the sight of the new fort. Lieutenant Webster strongly disapproved of Captain West's choice as being too low, too exposed to the elements, and too vulnerable to attack. Captain West was insistent, however, and his subordinates agreed with him against the Lieutenant.

Rations were prepared and a watch was posted for the night. We were to spend the first night aboard ship, which offered the best protection from the Indians, and in the morning begin the establishment of our town.

That night it rained, and rained hard. I would have gladly traded an Indian's hut for what we had that night. As many men as possible crowded into the hold of the pinnace and formed themselves into round snails in order to fit into the small spaces. Yet it wasn't much better than we had on deck. I managed to find a piece of torn canvas and, although it did not keep me fully dry, it did keep off most of the pelting rain.

A few hours before dawn, we were swept with several

thunderstorms. The lightning crashed to the ground, making the whole earth tremble. On those occasions, when I peeked out from my covering and saw the blue-white flash of the lightning, the rain seemed to be suspended for that instant like a shower of glittering diamonds, frozen in a sphere around the cross of the mast and yard.

The thunderstorms passed, and a strange calm settled on the river. Water dropping from the yard sounded like heavy stones striking the surface. The morning was cool and sunlit; the ship and the land around us bejeweled with twinkling drops of rainwater. Our spirits rose as the men wormed out of the hold and crawled on deck to stretch themselves into full human form again.

We soon had the pinnace warped in close to the shore so that, by laying out long boarding planks, we could disembark without having to walk in water above our knees. I was one of the first to go ashore with my tools. The Lieutenant had already begun marking off the perimeters of our fort even before the men had finished landing. We assembled in the center of this area, and Captain West divided us into groups.

Twenty men were sent to gather straw and reeds along the river for thatching. Ten men were to gather green poles so that we could construct temporary housing in the manner of the Indians. Ten were left as guards for the camp and to help with the vessels. The remainder, Captain West would take with him and contact the Indians to arrange for future trade.

We, the men in my group, decided to gather enough materials to construct three large mat houses. Half of our men were to begin work on these structures immediately, the other half were to go with me and begin the task of cutting trees for our permanent houses. Tents had been supplied to us, but these were not enough to house all of us. We discovered later that most of the tents had been sent with Captain Ratcliffe to Nansemond.

Lieutenant Webster and Captain West had heated words over the construction of the fort, the Lieutenant saying in a loud voice that erecting a palisade was more important than housing, and Captain West disdainfully arguing the opposite. After a while, the Lieutenant wheeled around and marched off toward the ships. Captain West, gazing after him with fury in his eyes, turned with his party and headed into the woods.

By afternoon we had the three huts framed out and ready for their coverings. The Lieutenant had taken charge of the guards and of sorting the supplies of rations and hardware. About the same time, Captain West returned with about twenty Indians, each bearing a basket of corn, fish, or fowl. They seemed well disposed toward the Captain and spoke with much laughter and gesticulations. They showed our men how to weave their kind of mats quickly. They wandered through our camp and looked freely over our stores. Most wanted guns and swords, but Captain West kindly refused them, offering instead large amounts of copper. The Indians accepted this, although they did not seem as pleased, and many gazed at the weapons with a covetous eye.

Since I knew a portion of the Indian language, the Captain asked me to serve as his interpreter. He began straight away by asking them the location of the mines he had heard of.

"Not copper mines," he assured them, since the Indians valued copper highly, "but the gold and silver mines which do much to restore our Englishmen to health."

The Indians protested that they had no such mines. They added that those mines they knew about which gave the metals that we sought lay to the west, in the land of the Monacans. They themselves had not seen the mines, since the Monacans were their bitter enemies and came almost yearly to make war upon them.

The Captain asked where the boundaries of the Monacans extended.

"To the mountains and to the Manahoac," they answered confidently.

"Will one of you guide us into the land of the Monacans?" the Captain asked in a most friendly manner. "I will pay much in copper and even provide he who is chosen with much wealth in blue beads. And he need not fear the Monacans, for we will protect him with our weapons."

I conveyed this message as best I could. The Indians discussed it quietly among themselves for a while. Then the one who was their spokesman said that the Captain's offer was most generous, but if one of them was seen in the land of the Monacan, it would mean a general war between the two nations.

The Captain then wanted to know if the Monacan spoke the language of Powhatan. The Indians replied that they could not understand a word of the Monacan language. The Captain then thanked them most courteously for their corn and their information and won assurances from them that they would return the next day with more victuals.

When the Indians had gone, Captain West immediately sent for Lieutenant Webster and waited impatiently for him to arrive. When the Lieutenant came before him, the Captain ordered him to keep silent and listen. The Lieutenant looked as though he had been slapped across the face, but he remained silent.

"Take a number of men," the Captain said. "Twenty will do. And follow the river into the land held by the Monacans."

He then took out a small map from his shirt and opened it before the Lieutenant.

"Newport got as far as here on his last trip."

He pointed to a place next to the river on the map.

"The Indians say that the sources of the metals are here. You see these two villages here? Try to procure a guide from one of them. Do what you have to, but find those mines. Don't come back empty-handed, and while you're about it, make a survey of the river. Go all the way to its head if you have to. Live off the land and from trade with the Indians, but do not return without something. The Company cannot continue to operate this venture at a yearly loss. If we don't show a profit soon, everything will have to be withdrawn, and all of our work here will have been for nothing."

The Lieutenant said that he would do as the Captain ordered, but that he felt obligated to remind him of Captain Smith's instruction regarding the establishment of fortifications.

"Goddamn Smith!" Captain West shouted, squeezing his hand white on his sword hilt. "I am in command here. You will do as I say, and if I ever hear you mention that son of a whore's name to me again, I'll have you arrested and sent back to England in chains."

Lieutenant Webster bowed like a polite courier.

"Good," Captain West said, hissing out his last ounce of rage. "Take Matthew here." He motioned toward me with his hand. "He has some knowledge of the Indian language. There is a good chance the Monacans will have a translator. At least I have heard that the various Indian nations have some people skilled in all of the Indian languages for trading purposes.

"Make preparations straight away," he continued, "I wish you to be on your way before nightfall."

Without another word, the Captain walked away toward the ships and supplies, calling several of his subordinates to accompany him.

The Lieutenant motioned for me to step closer. His lips were drawn into tight, thin lines. His eyes smoldered with anger, but he did not speak against Captain West. He asked me to choose the men who could best handle a musket and hatchet and report to him with those men by two of the clock. He had decided to leave his few soldiers to guard the settlement.

Wilcox somehow caught the scent of what I was doing, and soon he descended upon me, demanding to be included in the party.

"You well know that I am good with a musket, even better with a knife, and I can outlast any man here."

I knew it was true that he was good with a musket. And I knew from firsthand experience that he could handle a knife with competence. But I had never seen him use a hatchet and told him so, whereupon he walked over to the wood supply, picked up a hatchet and split in half the first log he came to.

I said that he could go, but he would have to obey the Lieutenant as his superior in all matters. He said that he would and requested at the last moment that Holt be taken in. I consented, thinking that Holt could, and might, restrain Wilcox if he took it upon himself to endanger the company in any way.

We were gathered at the specified time and, after a short speech from the Lieutenant, we were given our muskets and knives. Seven hatchets were allotted for the whole company, along with three day's rations, fifty rounds of shot, and about two pounds of powder apiece. More powder and shot, plus the hatchets and other tools, were to be drawn in a small, hurriedly constructed handcart. The Lieutenant carried his weapons plus a hand compass and a few navigation instruments for mapmaking.

The Lieutenant was the kind of man you put your faith in. He never seemed in doubt, always knew ahead what he was going to do, and he seemed to always know what the Powhatans were about. Nevertheless, I could not get it out of my mind that the Powhatans and the Monachans knew the forest like the deer they hunted. After all, it was their home that they had lived in since the creation. I couldn't stop the uneasy feeling that crept up my spine as we made preparations to start out.

By four of the clock, we had started on our way, following at first Captain Newport's old route up the north side of the river. We passed many of the Indians' stone fish weirs and saw no evidence of Captain Newport's former expedition.

We trudged along the riverbank for almost three hours until the Lieutenant signaled for a halt and said that we should make camp. He directed us to the highest ground and ordered that we surround the camp with armed guards.

He took out his map, studied it for a while and said, "We are near the village of Mewhemcho. Not many people live there, but I will send out a few scouts to reconnoiter the place. Choose several good men who can be trusted to keep their heads and bring them to me."

I did as the Lieutenant bid and picked two men who seemed to fulfill the requirements.

"Scout upriver," the Lieutenant told them. "Try to go as far as this village."

He pointed out the marking on the map to the two men.

"If you find you cannot reach this point and return back here before dark, then do not waste time trying to locate the village. Learn the condition of the river and the land along your route. Above all, do not be seen. If you do make it to the village, learn what you can of their numbers, how many young men, and if they are a fortified town."

The two scouts nodded, and the Lieutenant watched

confidently as they started out, moving swiftly along the riverbank and into the trees, like Indians themselves. Lieutenant Webster then informed the guards that, upon sighting an Indian, they were to leave their post immediately and let it be known to him. If they were attacked, they were to use their muskets with restraint.

We began by clearing away much of the underbrush and making fires with which to prepare our rations. I asked the Lieutenant if it was wise to make these fires since they would give our position away to the Indians. He said that he was sure the Indians knew of our coming the moment we left the falls, and would probably not attack because of our number.

"What of the two scouts?" I asked.

"If they are careful, they will not be seen. The Indians expect us to all remain in camp. They know that it is our best protection."

After having our supper, which the Lieutenant spiced with several herbs he had gathered from around the camp, I tried my first draught of tobacco. Wilcox had obtained an Indian clay pipe from someone in Jamestown and some tobacco from his acquaintances among the sailors. He was insistent that I try the weed, and at first I found it exceedingly nauseating and bitter, but later it had an agreeable effect upon me, and I came to see why it is highly valued among our people.

Darkness came, and the scouts had not returned. The Lieutenant became most agitated and spent much time pacing back and forth along the river bank. The firelight reflected on him in orange and yellow flashes. We became so concerned with the scout's return that every small noise in the forest would cause us to jump.

I was preparing to sleep when I heard something crashing its way through the trees and bushes. One of the scouts fell into our camp, face first, and lay for a while next to the fire like a dead man.

The Lieutenant examined him and called for water. He turned the scout over and held his head up with much gentleness. The scout opened his eyes. The water came, and the Lieutenant held it to his mouth. The scout drank thirstily from the pitcher, making moaning sounds as he did. He was badly bruised, and his face, arms, and legs were covered with scratches. His hair on the left side of his head was matted with blood.

"We came upon the village, sir," he said to Lieutenant Webster.

As he said this, I noticed for the first time that he was a youth, a youth of about my age. I looked at the Lieutenant and saw that he, too, was scarcely older than the scout. Most of the faces glowing around us in the firelight were young faces. It seemed strange that I had not noticed this before. In the cities of England, where most of us came from, we would have behaved like young men, ready for love and frolic in an instant. But here youth began to mean the necessary strength to survive, and the will and determination to prevail.

"And they fell upon us from behind," the scout was saying.

"How many were there?" the Lieutenant asked.

"I don't know, sir, maybe twenty . . . maybe fifty. They were all around, howling like wolves and shaking their clubs at us."

"How did you escape?"

"They put us into their canoes and started to cross the river." The scout paused and gasped, trying to catch his breath. "I pretended to faint." He continued. "And they released their hold on me long enough for me to leap out of the canoe. I managed to turn the canoe over when I jumped to prevent them from coming after me, and I stayed under water as long as I could, going with the current. I thought I might drown, sir.

The first time I came up, I saw the Indians swimming for the shore, and the other canoe which held Benjamin had landed, and his captors were dragging him toward the village. He was kicking and screaming, I remember. I remained in the river for as long as I could, until darkness came. Then I made it to shore, where I struggled through the woods until I saw the campfires. Thanks be to God."

The scout sighed, and the Lieutenant slowly lowered the man's head back to the ground.

"Let him sleep," said the Lieutenant. "When he wakes, give him something to eat and see to his wounds."

He turned to look at me, his eyes glaring like two mirrors.

"Who was on guard at the place where this man entered our camp?"

I said that I did not know his name, but that I would know his face. I looked around at the men standing by the fire and did not see the guard. The Lieutenant requested that I go with him, so I followed him into the woods where the scout had come through, and found the guard asleep on the ground, nestled with his musket as though it were his wife.

The Lieutenant looked down at the man's dark figure.

"I'm tempted to discharge my pistol next to his ear. That will teach him not to sleep while on guard, but he is a lucky man. The penalty for this offense in any army in Europe is death, with very little chance of mercy."

The Lieutenant crouched beside the man who, like most of us, was but a boy, and gently nudged his shoulder. He woke slowly and, in his state of half sleep, called someone's name.

"Wake up!" the Lieutenant demanded. "If I had been one of the savages, you would not be waking until Judgement Day."

The guard sat up quickly and, using his musket for a crutch, got to his feet. The Lieutenant was not as harsh with him as I had expected, but explained to him, in a fatherly way, the importance of keeping vigilant. The boy listened and did not offer complaints or excuses, but promised to stand his post faithfully in the future. We left him in a renewed state of readiness, confident that he would remain awake at least for the next hour.

The Lieutenant asked if I would take charge of posting the watch and seeing to it that the men were properly rotated. I said that I would. He thanked me and bid me a good night.

Before trying to sleep, I made a list of the men's names and posted the time of their watch for that night. I passed it around for all to see. Several could not read their own names, so I made sure that they were made aware of their duties, and I asked the man posted to watch the camp to wake me at midnight.

He did, and promptly. I struggled out of sleep and went around to rouse those men who were to relieve the perimeter guards. I went with them to each post and inquired how the watch went. All said they had had no trouble, not even a sound that was out of the ordinary. I returned to the camp and told the relief camp guard that I was to be awakened at four of the clock.

I did not find sleep so easily this time and lay awake for a long while, listening to the crackling of the fire and watching the dark tops of the trees sway gently in the wind, dusting the winking stars. The occasional hoot of an owl or the short, sharp cry of a wild animal would, for an instant, disturb the quiet.

While I was in school, I had heard that this land was unlike England or Old Europe, but I had never truly thought or believed it to be so. Indeed, there were many things here very similar to those in England. Yet nothing was quite the same. Everything, no matter what, was different in some way. The birds flew the same way but were of different markings and songs. The plants looked the same, yet they, too, were different in the smallest ways. And the Indians. They were like us as men, though it seemed that they surely inhabited another planet. I had the uneasy feeling that Captain Smith's implications were true and between our Atlantic and Captain Drake's western ocean lay a vast and wild land that could easily swallow us up without a trace.

CHAPTER 8

Monocans

At the appointed time I changed the watch and returned to my place near the fire. I had no trouble sleeping after this, until we were aroused by the Lieutenant at daybreak. We had our usual breakfast of boiled pork and cornbread and began the day's march. The scout who had returned the night before was much improved in health, and we all looked forward to recovering Benjamin, the captured one. The Lieutenant suggested that he was probably being held for ransom, and laughingly said that we had enough beads to buy him back.

After several hours of climbing over small hills and treading our way through the woods so as not to be seen easily, the Lieutenant ordered a halt. He spoke quietly with the scout for a few minutes, then signaled for me to follow. We followed the scout through the woods in single file, keeping the river in sight to our left. He stopped after a while, looked around, and studied the ground.

"It was near here," he said. "But we have to get closer to the river."

We waited, but the scout seemed reluctant to move. He glanced around continuously and appeared to even sniff the air like a hunting dog.

"Wood smoke," he said finally.

"Then come on," the Lieutenant said impatiently.

We crept slowly to the riverbank and, lying on the ground, crawled up to the shallow embankment at the edge of the river. There, perhaps several hundred yards away, was the village of Mewhemcho. A thin curl of smoke drifted lazily up from its center, forming a flat, translucent cloud over the village. We watched for a long time, in strict silence, without moving.

A noise in the woods caused us to jump, and the Lieutenant snapped his head around to look behind us. There was nothing to be seen, so we continued our vigil.

The village appeared deserted, not even a playing child or a canoe on the shore. We saw no Indians along either bank in the woods, not even the sound of a wild animal. The river wasn't very wide at the place from where we watched, and the Lieutenant suggested that he and I and the scout swim across to the opposite side and see for ourselves what news the village held.

We crept down to the river and waded in. The bottom was covered with slick rocks where we entered, but the current wasn't fast. The crossing was made quickly, touching our toes on the rocks of the opposite shore after a short swim. We entered the woods and, crouching low, carefully made our way to the village. Once at the village clearing, we stopped and waited. Still we saw no one. Lieutenant Webster drew his sword and looked nervously around at us.

"Let us make sure, lads," he said.

He stood up and, with us following, he walked slowly into the center of the village. We stood looking around in silence for a long time before the Lieutenant spoke. He instructed us to look into all of the houses and if we found anything of use to take it.

The first hut I went into was empty, as I had expected. A few deer skins lay on the beds. There was a lingering smell of wood smoke and cooked meat and the faintest odor of recent human inhabitance, but there was nothing of value; no food, no weapons, nothing; not even the straw mats used for sitting on the ground. I looked into several more huts and found about the same conditions.

We met again in the center of the village. Lieutenant Webster shook his head in puzzlement.

"Where and why have they gone?" he asked.

I suggested that they knew we were nearby and had probably learned of our intentions from the scout they had captured. They knew that we would be coming this way and would not take the capture of our man as a friendly act.

The Lieutenant agreed and asked our scout to return to the rest of the men and have them cross the river and meet us in the village. The scout immediately did as he was asked, and we watched as he swam back across the river and darted into the woods like a young deer.

Mewhemcho was a small village with not more than fifty or sixty inhabitants. Lieutenant Webster told me that, according to what he had learned from Captain Newport, it did not have a werowance or even a priest, which made it a village of lesser importance among the Monacans.

There was certainly no werowance's house in the village or a temple where the priest lived. The Lieutenant believed that the people had probably fled to Massmacack where there was a larger population and a strong werowance.

"We should approach that settlement with caution," he added.

It was not long before we saw our men swimming across the river, wisely carrying their muskets, with their powder bags tied to them, over their heads. Those who could not swim cut logs for themselves and, using these as buoys, were pulled across by the others. Fallen branches were also gathered and tied into a primitive raft. The powder barrel and other supplies were floated across in this manner.

The men were joyous at seeing the village empty of people. They began to say that the Indians feared their wrath over having captured one of our men. The Lieutenant, however, advised caution and told the men that he did not know what the Monacans meant by leaving their village, but that we should not assume that they greatly feared us. He again admonished us to always be vigilant and to obey his orders.

We started up the south side of the river, keeping to the woods whenever possible, and crossed several deep, muddy streams along the way. Around midday we came upon a path which, the Lieutenant supposed, was an Indian road leading to other settlements, possibly leading to Massmacack. He proposed that we should take it.

Several of the men disagreed, saying that this path would lead us surely to certain destruction. The Lieutenant reasoned that by taking the path, we would demonstrate to the Monacan that we had no fear of them and that we meant peace. I felt that we should have remained in the protection of the woods, but I sensed that the Lieutenant knew what he was about, having been in the colony since its founding and also, like a wise leader, he was not saying all that was in his mind.

Lieutenant Webster took the lead, and we followed the path in a single file for many hours. Several times we heard movement in the woods, and my heart would bound inside my breast. My hand would tighten around my musket without my being aware of it. Nothing daunted the Lieutenant. He marched without a falter knowing as we all did that the Monacans were at all points around us.

As we turned a curve in the path, three Indians appeared ahead of us. They looked very similar to the Powhatans, with stern expressions, and carrying their bows ready with arrows.

The Lieutenant signaled for a halt and summoned me forth. He asked me to make signs of peace to them. I placed my musket on the ground beside me and, holding one hand over my heart, pointed to the sun with the other. One of them stepped forward and made the same sign.

"Tell them we have come in peace," the Lieutenant said.

I repeated the words as best as I knew them in the language of Powhatans. "Lchick chammay peya quagh."

The Indian laughed and said something to me, of which I understood the words "Friends. Come." Then he made a sign for us to follow. The Lieutenant turned to us and told us to stay together, but not to fire unless we were attacked or unless he gave the order.

The Monacans moved very swiftly along the path. We had to run to keep up with them. In a short while, we ran into a clearing several hundred acres broad, and in the center was the village of Massmacack, walled in by strong palisades sharpened to points at the top.

We entered the village amid a throng of people, all pressing to get a closer look at us, and went directly to the werowance, who greeted us outside his house in a haughty manner. One of the Indians who had brought us spoke to the werowance in his own language. The werowance listened without so much as a muscle twitching in his face. Then he spoke angrily and with much vehemence. The interpreter turned to me and said that his werowance wanted to know why we had come into his country from the land of his enemies.

The Lieutenant stepped forward and said that we came

from a great island kingdom far across the great water to the east, beyond the lands of Powhatan, and that we were not his enemies.

"We have come in peace and friendship and wish only to trade with your people as brothers."

On hearing this from his translator, the werowances' expression softened, and he commanded that meat and tobacco be brought. Mats were placed on the ground, and he made signs that we should be seated. After we had eaten our fill, clay pipes were passed among us, and we followed the werowance's example in lighting the tobacco and drawing the smoke into our mouths. The werowance seemed much satisfied and asked what we had to trade.

The Lieutenant brought out his bag and poured out a few blue glass beads, which immediately delighted the werowance and all those around us. The Lieutenant, seeing the people much pleased, ordered one of our men who was carrying a hatchet in his belt to step forward. The Lieutenant took the hatchet from the man and presented it to the werowance, whose eyes fairly danced with excitement. The Lieutenant made it known that he could obtain many more for them if they wished. All that he would require would be a guide to take us to the headwaters of the river, and corn and meat for a journey of seven days.

Lieutenant Webster also asked the werowance where our man, who had been taken by force by his men, was being held. The werowance said that he knew nothing of this act, and added that perhaps the men the Lieutenant spoke of were a raiding party of the Manahoac from the north, and that his men were in no way responsible.

The werowance offered his translator for our guide, and ordered his wives to bring our rations. The Lieutenant handed him enough beads to make a long necklace, and said that he would bring more hatchets with his return. The werowance stood and spoke at length with our guide. He made a sign of friendship to us and returned into his house.

Our rations were quickly distributed, and the remainder loaded into a sack and bound to the cart with leather straps. While this was being done, the scout came up to the Lieutenant and demanded to know why we were not searching the village. The Lieutenant pulled him closer.

"Don't look now, you fool, but every house in this village has four or five of their warriors hiding behind it. Their bows are fixed so that if we make one move to do as you suggest, our bodies would be full of arrows before we could go a single step. We will come back for the man when the time is proper. Other than that, he must surrender himself to his fate like the rest of us."

The scout saw that the Lieutenant was right. There were few young men in sight within the village. We went about preparing to leave with a surface calm so as not to arouse suspicion.

After a few hours, the Lieutenant called a halt and, taking out his map and compass, said to me that this was the extent to which Captain Newport explored.

"From here I will have to chart the course of the river and make careful notes of the geography and other natural oc-currences that would be of information to our people."

Our pace slowed down considerably now that the Lieutenant was engaged in his calculations and note-taking, and we had not gone far from Massmacack when we made camp for the night. Guards were posted for the night. After eating liberally of the new rations that the Monacans had given us, I went early to my bed.

Later that night, before the watch change, I was awakened by Wilcox, who whispered to me that he had a bad feeling about our guide and warned that I should not trust him. I assured him that I did not trust our guide, but what could one Indian, who is unarmed and unskilled in the use of our weapons, do to harm us?

"Nevertheless," said Wilcox, "he's got the look of the devil in his eyes. I've seen it enough to know."

"Wilcox, you trust no man. They all have the devil in them by your reckoning."

"That's true enough, but him being a savage and a heathen makes it all the worse."

"Return to your bed, Wilcox, and do not disturb me further with your suspicions."

The next day we were on our way by first light. The Lieutenant stopped many times to sight with his compass and make notations on his map. Once a man shouted, "Gold!" Every man in the company dropped his musket and whatever else he was carrying and ran to the man who had shouted. The gold turned out to be a kind of mica that sparkled like fine grains of glass when held up to the sun's light. The Lieutenant noticed other minerals; pieces of earth containing iron ore, rocks with traces of copper and, he believed, tin deposits lying nearby.

About noon we reached a stream flowing from the south, which was unusually wide and deep where it emptied into the river. Our guide said that he knew of a place upstream where it could be easily forded. The Lieutenant hesitated, but it was clear to all of us that the stream would not be crossed at the place where we stood without considerable risk to our supplies and men.

The Lieutenant agreed, reluctantly, that we should try the crossing at the place our guide suggested and come back to this point on the river on the opposite side of the stream. The woods and underbrush were too thick to make fast headway along the bank of the stream, so our Indian guide led us to higher ground where the trees were still large and closely spaced, but the entangling vines and thorns were not so heavy.

We walked single file for a mile or more, hacking down bushes and vines with the butts of our muskets. The Lieutenant remarked that we sounded more like an army of ten thousand Turks beating their muskets together.

Our guide suddenly signaled for a turn toward the stream, which we did, and he led us down between two long ridges, almost completely obscured by trees. The Lieutenant sent five men forward to clear away the dense undergrowth. They were not long engaged in this task when one of the men called out in alarm.

Moments later, the air was rent by the scream of a man to our rear. We all turned toward the sound of the scream and saw Wilcox pressing the Indian guide against a tree. His powerful left hand was squeezed around the Indian's throat while his right gripped the handle of his knife, which was buried up to the hilt in the Indian's midsection.

The Lieutenant instantly drew his pistol and pointed it at Wilcox.

"Good God, man," he yelled. "What do you mean by this contemptible action?"

Wilcox withdrew his knife with a jerk and held the quivering Indian against the tree.

"1 knew this heathen was up to no good, sir. The moment he heard our man call out, he made as if to escape from us. I tried to reason with him, sir," Wilcox said, wiping the blood from his knife on his britches' leg. "But as you can see, he would not listen."

"Wilcox," the Lieutenant yelled. "You'll hang for . . . "

But before he could finish, a wave of arrows fell among us, thudding into the trees, the ground, and wounding several men.

A great howl of animal-like voices rose from both ridges. Every tree and bush seemed to turn into an Indian, making ready to shoot an arrow. The Lieutenant ordered a run for the stream.

"We will make a stand on the higher ground across the stream," he yelled.

The men ahead of us had only cut a short distance into the thick woods. When we arrived at their position, we saw the cause of their outcry. The body of our scout, Holt, lay bound hand and foot, among the bushes where he had been thrown. He had been scalped and the skin had been stripped from his face and the front part of his body. His forehead had been split open from the blow of a spiked club, and there were numerous broken arrow shafts sticking out of his body. He looked, strangely, like a newborn infant, with the skinless part of his body covered in a shiny, clear film. His torturers had taken care to make sure that the look on his face was one of horror.

The Lieutenant turned away in disgust at the sight. Another wave of arrows swept into us. The man next to me dropped, with a groan, at my feet, an arrow halfway through his neck. The Lieutenant ordered five of us, myself and Wilcox included, to form a line facing the Indians. The rest he told to cross the stream and form a defensive position where they could offer us protective fire when we followed. The five of us facing the Indians, he ordered to shoot at will.

I fired blindly at first, catching a glimpse of an Indian, then pulled the trigger. The Indians moved toward us gradually, by jumping from tree to tree after shooting their arrows.

"The trick," Wilcox said to me in considerable haste, "is to pick out one, wait till he jumps behind a tree, then when he steps out to shoot his arrow, let him have it. Timing and steadiness are the most important things."

I took his advice since my other shots had only wasted ammunition. I picked my man, a tall, agile Indian, brightly painted with red and black designs and with several feathers decorating his hair. He was very quick. He would jump behind a tree, wait several seconds while placing an arrow in his bow, step around with the bow already drawn, and let an arrow fly. All of his shots came very close to our heads.

He did this several times, each time getting closer. The fourth time I was ready, calculating that he would move out to the left of the tree. He did, and I fired. His head jerked back, and his arrow shot toward the sky. He fell where he had stood. I reloaded quickly and, using the same method, wounded my next man.

I became aware of the general firing all around me. Most of our men had reached the other side of the stream, scaled the high bank, and had begun firing over our heads. There was an unexpected shout from the Indians, and they started retreating back up the ridges, always jumping from behind one tree to another. In a few minutes they disappeared over the tops of the ridges, but the firing continued for a while in sporadic shots from the men behind us. Then suddenly, as though all our men obeyed a voiceless command, it was silent, not the faintest twittering of a bird, nor the buzzing of an insect.

The Indians had dragged their wounded with them. Those dead that lay upon the ground seemed melted into twisted, grotesque patterns. Nothing moved, nothing stirred, not even the steaming air.

"There's no time. The positioning's wrong for pursuit." The Lieutenant said to himself, unaware that he had been heard.

Wilcox jumped up and started running for where our guide lay.

"There's no time!" the Lieutenant shouted after him. "Come back, you fool."

But Wilcox wasn't in pursuit of the fleeing Indians. He stopped and knelt down beside the dead Indian guide. I saw his knife flash. He held the Indian's head up by the hair and with his other hand holding the knife, he quickly circled the Indian's head. In another moment he was running back, still gripping his knife in his right hand and swinging the Indian's scalp in the other. He slid to the ground back at our position, and the Lieutenant met him with a drawn sword pointed at his chest.

"I should run you through, you dog. If you ever leave your position again without my order, that is what I will do. Now let us cross the stream in all haste."

Wilcox smiled at me and tied the bloody, dripping scalp to his belt by its hair and started off behind the Lieutenant. We crashed our way through the bushes until we reached the stream bank only a hundred feet away. Our guide had known what he was about. The stream was particularly wide at this point, and deep. Fortunately, several large trees had fallen from the high banks and lay almost spanning the stream.

Our other men had been able to cross singly and were waiting anxiously for us on the other side. The Lieutenant stood guard while we made the crossing, at times waist-deep in muddy water. Then the Lieutenant crossed while we protected him from a position at the top of the high bank. One of the men asked if we should not set a powder charge to the trees to hinder the

Indians from crossing. The Lieutenant doubted that the Indians would cross.

"There are too many natural obstacles, and besides," he said, "They know this forest as well as any rabbit. The only device that would hinder them would be the proper use of our guns."

He emphasized once again, as he had often done, that we should take loving care of our muskets and powder.

We had lost three of our men to mortal wounds, and two others had been badly wounded, one in the hand and the other in the chest where an arrow had grazed his ribs. None of the wounds would prevent them from moving with us.

One of the men spoke up and, in an angry voice said, "We are Christian men and should not leave our dead without proper burial!"

Lieutenant Webster, matching his anger with reason, said, "I agree. It is not a good thing to let our men lie in the woods for the crows and wolves to eat. But we are not fighting against Christians, and to venture back across the stream would be to invite the deaths of us all.

"If we are to survive," he continued, "we must put as much distance as we can between us and the Monacans."

The man was silent after this speech, but morose. Lieutenant Webster added that if he felt so strongly about it, he was given leave to cross the stream and do his Christian duty, and that he could catch up with the rest of us later.

The man looked across the stream at the rough, entangling brush and at the dark heart of the trees from which we had so recently escaped. His temper changed almost at once. He quickly became more jovial and ready for the march ahead.

We made our way along the stream bank back to the river. Each man moved with caution from one tree to the next, listening as keenly as any hunting dog. Once at the river, we wasted no time in starting our journey upriver. We walked for several more hours, stopping at various turns in the river so the Lieutenant could check its course with his compass, and to make calculations of the miles we had traveled.

We found a good camp site at the top of a high hill. The trees and bushes were thinner on this hill, making it a good place to defend. I posted guards immediately. Lieutenant Webster forbade the making of fires since he reckoned that we were still in the country of the Monacans. Fearing that they might now be tracking us, he did not want to lead them to us by the smell of our cooking. I posted the guards near the base of the hill, with instructions to fire a warning shot if they should see any signs of the Monacans.

After this was done, we settled down quickly. The men were near complete exhaustion. We mixed raw cornmeal to a thick paste with water and chewed endlessly on our dried beef. The Lieutenant busied himself with writing in his notebook, noting his observations of the changing land: its flora and fauna, its fertility, its minerals. By nightfall we fell asleep like men who had suddenly and quietly died. Indeed, I remember nothing until awakened about two o'clock. It was my turn to stand guard.

I crawled to my feet with the greatest reluctance and walked to my post, in a groggy stupor, with the other men. I stumbled halfway down the hill, and so did not need to identify myself to the man I was to relieve. In fact, he seemed most perturbed at the noise I was making.

After standing guard for not even a half hour, I understood his impatience with me. Silence and the night seemed one and inseparable. I began to see strange, unnatural shapes in the darkness. Disembodied sounds seemed to surround them. All noises were sudden and magnified tenfold. The movement of a small nocturnal animal was like the tramping of a great beast, nearby but unseen. The hooting of an owl was to me like the crying of a lost soul. If a twig snapped, I would whirl and aim my musket in the direction of the sound, all the while seeing nothing but dark, unearthly shapes.

Until then I had never considered what it must be like to be blind and forced to live in absolute darkness without even these unearthly shapes to ponder. I promised myself that if I ever returned to England, I would not pass a blind man on the street without first emptying my pockets to him.

The night slowly yielded, as it always does, to happy daylight. Never was I so happy to see it come. The dark, strange shapes slowly became bushes or the trunks of trees covered with vines, or they disappeared altogether—mere night shadows. All manner of birds awoke and greeted the day with their particular songs. The sun warmed and dried the ground, which yielded a sweet, wild scent.

The Lieutenant himself came to fetch us from our post, saying to me that we were less than a day's march from the land of the Saponi, and there we might expect to bargain for fresh victuals and peaceful relations. So, after breakfasting on more dried beef, we continued our march along King James River, going further into the interior of this strange land.

The men had begun to grumble about the value of our undertaking and openly doubting that any of us would return alive. Lieutenant Webster did his best to appease them but, as the day wore on, their complaints grew stronger. The Lieutenant ordered a halt. He reckoned that we were well out of the land of the Monacans, and ordered camp to be made on a height next to the river. There were many hours of daylight left, and he ordered our best marksmen, of which I was not one to go into the woods and kill the fattest deer they could find.

The Lieutenant himself went in search for whatever fruits the land would provide. He soon returned with his hat and shirt full of berries which looked similar to English strawberries but with a sweeter, juicer taste. We heard a musket report not too far off and, in less than half an hour, the marksmen returned, bearing a large male deer strung on a carrying pole.

Every man in the camp, including myself, was most happy over the prospect of fresh meat. We set about dressing the deer and constructing several roasting pits. In a short while, we had the best cuts of the venison sizzling over glowing wood coals. The unusable parts of the animal we buried away from our campsite. To clean ourselves of the blood and animal fat, we bathed and frolicked, like schoolboys, in the running cool waters of the river.

When the meat was done, we sat around the fire, naked as Indians except for a loincloth which the Lieutenant demanded that we wear. We feasted on well-cooked meat until we could not force another mouthful down. We then lay by the fires, gorged as the most gluttonous of Romans, and instantly fell asleep. I hardly gave a thought to whatever Indians might be lurking about.

Lieutenant Webster stood guard while we slept, and at dusk he woke me with a gentle nudging.

"It's time to post the guard," he said.

I dressed in my clean clothes, which now smelled strongly of river mud, and roused the men who were to go on the first watch. They protested most bitterly, but they dressed and went to their duties.

The night passed as peacefully and uneventfully as if we

had been back in our beds in England. The next morning we ate, with less desire, what was left of the venison. One of the men on watch had discovered a spring of fresh water nearby, and from that we replenished our water for drinking.

The land had become very rocky with sheer cliffs and sharp hills. We had entered the territory of the Saponi. By midday, we came upon a height from where we were confronted with the sight of a high mountain range, extending north by east and south by west, as far as we could see. The mountains were blue-green, almost the color of the sea, but with a hazy quality that shimmered at places where the sunlight touched them. They stood before us as a great wall, jagged at the top like the teeth of a giant beast, some even touching the clouds that sailed over them.

From our heights we could also see the glimmering band of the King James River, winding from the west and sharply turning to run south along the base of the mountains.

"What's it to be, Lieutenant?" Wilcox asked, leaning on his musket and gazing at the mountains with a slight grin.

"We have come in search of the western ocean," the Lieutenant said, "and with God's help, we will climb to the top of those mountains from where, I pray, we will see our objective."

CHAPTER 9

Fool's Gold

We made camp at a large stream at the base of the first line of ridges. The Lieutenant asked me to accompany him and two other trusty men. A third he left in charge of those who would wait for our return. We took four days' rations, powder, shot, match, and started off, following the stream for about seven miles through a gap in the first ridge, until we reached the base of a cluster of three peaks, each higher than the other. The highest was exceedingly lofty and bald at the top. The Lieutenant stared up at the mountains, smiled and said that we would be able to see all that we needed to see from the top.

"We will approach it from the north," the Lieutenant said, "since that side is not so steep."

Not a man among us had ever climbed such a great height before. We started off, following the Lieutenant's every step. The climb was hardly noticeable at first. We had been climbing over hills since shortly after leaving the falls. But soon the slope became rockier, steeper, the trees thinner. My musket and other equipment began to grow heavier and heavier. We breathed like mules pulling a plow through a muddy field.

We came to a rocky ledge where we could see from west to east over the tops of the trees below us. As far as we could see, there were swells of motionless blue-green mountains, all varying in sizes like waves in the sea. For a moment it seemed to me that we were in the midst of an ancient ocean that had been suddenly turned to stone.

The Lieutenant did not have time for such fancy. At this height there was not the first sign of a western ocean. There was a column of smoke not far to the north, meaning Indians of perhaps an unknown nation. We could also see a goodly portion of the rocky summit that was our destination; closer, but still too far to be reached in daylight.

We rested, legs dangling off a stone ledge like children finding themselves accidentally at the top of the world, and breathing hard, yet not seeming to satisfy our lungs. The Lieutenant said that we should push on and find a camp site as close to the summit as we could get. No one objected. No one cared. We had gone halfway up the cluster of mountains already, and there seemed no point to not go to the top.

As for myself, I had become a little curious about this western ocean, and at least wanted to give the discovery my best effort. Our other two men, William Gardner and Francis Lynn, wanted to go on because reaching the summit would be a clear end to this expedition and a return to the falls.

The climb became exceedingly difficult after we left the ledge. The rocks were sharper and often loose, so that every hand or foothold threatened to fall away beneath us. Many of the rocks on this side of the mountain were also covered in slippery moss and slime, adding to our difficulty.

Our progress to the top became slower as the rocks and sheer ledges became more numerous. The Lieutenant took longer contemplating his next move up, once taking near half an hour to decide on a path that brought us only a few feet closer to the summit.

At dusk we reached a clear ledge without much slope, but with enough open floor for us to lie on. However, there was not enough room to move about unless we crawled over each other. Every move we made had to be planned in advance and executed with the most extreme caution. There was not room for a fire, so we ate our dried beef cold.

We lay in one position all night. Rolling over would have sent one of us plunging many hundreds of feet to the next level of the mountain. I slept little, not only because of our cramped position, but also because there began a cold rain. A strong wind whipped at the trees and our bodies with unrelenting fury. The wind boomed and tore through the mountains like a beast gone mad.

I began to fear that this would be the time when the sun would not rise, that the end of the world would come in darkness and find me here on a cold, wet mountainside in the midst of this hard and unhappy land. Day did come, however, and as soon as it was light enough, we resumed our climb.

The rocky cap of the mountain was wet from the night's rain and worn smooth as glass in many parts from the continual wind. Our last few hundred yards of progress were very treacherous. With much slow going, we reached the top long before noon and sat down to enjoy our cold breakfast. There were pockets of rainwater collected in lower portions of the impervious rock, and we drank from those, not quite like dogs, but lifting the trembling clear liquid carefully to our mouths in cupped hands.

The Lieutenant stood up, despite the thundering wind at the top, and gazed around the horizon. He saw a glowing sliver of the King James River to the east and reckoned the position of our camp near to it. To the north and south ran more spines of mountains and to the west, no ocean was present; not the smallest sign of any water; no lakes or rivers or even streams. Nothing but higher mountains and broad blue-green valleys.

The Lieutenant stared out at the western horizon for a long while before he turned and shouted to us above the wind.

"I cannot see it. I cannot hear it. I cannot smell it. But, most importantly, I cannot feel its presence. There is no ocean near. I suspect that this land is like that of the Russias—endless dry land with no water avenue to the spices of the Orient."

He knelt beside us, drank a handful of water, and said that we should be starting back.

"Traveling down the mountain will be faster than the climbing up. We should be at the stream well before dark. And we will follow it, even in darkness, until we reach the camp."

After a short rest we started down, and at midday we were well into the trees again, feeling our way down the slopes, endeavoring not to surrender to the temptation of haste which would have meant a careless step or a faulty handhold.

The Lieutenant had marked the path that we took up the mountain, but we overlooked one of the marks going down and lost the trail, which forced us to find another way at a slower pace. We reached a ledge and paused for a rest. One of our men, Francis Lynn, was the last to come down and had not quite reached the ledge when he shouted for the Lieutenant and the rest of us to come.

We climbed, with labor, back up the slope to his position. He was digging at the ground with much excitement, clearing away rotted leaves, moss, and loose rocks.

"Look!" he shouted, even though we were close beside him. He held bits of rock and dirt in his hands. "Gold!"

The Lieutenant looked at the dirt in his hand, stirred it with his own finger, and said nothing. Lynn took this silence as an affirmation of his find and got to his feet.

"It must have come from up there," he said, nodding his head toward a rocky, sheer cliff.

Before the Lieutenant could restrain him, Lynn had started scrambling up toward the cliff. He looked like a man fleeing for his life. The Lieutenant called to him, ordered him to stop, threatened him with arrest, even took out his pistol and warned that he would shoot, but nothing stopped the man. There was only one course to take.

We started after him but, not having Lynn's blind obsession, we were forced to pick our way with more care and less speed. We saw him climb onto the ridge. The Lieutenant once again shouted for him to stop, this time promising him understanding and leniency.

Lynn began to scale the ridge. He looked like a small insect trying to climb the sides of a wash tub. The Lieutenant shouted again, promising complete forgiveness and all the victuals he could eat. Lynn ignored him, seeming not to hear or even to be aware of our present efforts to stop him.

By the time we reached the base of the ridge, Lynn was far ahead of us. He stopped climbing and started digging with his knife. We watched from below as chips of rock and dirt tumbled into our faces. Then, in an instant, he appeared to let go of everything and, just as though the mountain had pushed him away, he fell backwards, arms and legs spread out, falling without a sound.

He fell past us and into the tops of the trees a few hundred feet below. Lieutenant Webster stared, open mouthed, toward the place where Lynn had fallen, but we could not truly see him from our position.

"There might be a chance he's still alive—the trees serving as a cushion, perhaps?" Mr. Gardner suggested.

The Lieutenant agreed, through reluctantly, and said that he would go down to the place and see. If any of us wanted to remain and wait for him, we were welcome to do so. Of course, we said that we would go. If Lynn was alive, the Lieutenant would certainly need our assistance, since it was doubtful that Gardner would have escaped injury.

Finding him wasn't as easy as we had supposed. After a considerable time searching, Mr. Gardner shouted for us to come to him. He stood there, beneath an oak tree, among several freshly broken branches, looking up. Lynn lay about a third of the way up the tree, his body twisted as though it had been made of straw. His head hung down from the mass of branches that were threaded around his body. It was certain that he was dead. His eyes were gaped open and empty as a dead fish's. Blood had filled his nostrils and had run down to his forehead, but it did not flow as blood from a living person. It had stopped running and now only dripped slower each time, covering a rock at the base of the tree. His hands were still wet and covered with dirt from his digging.

"There is no point in tarrying longer," the Lieutenant said. "We must get to the stream before dark and back to our camp. We have been away from the falls too long already."

"Aren't you going to say anything, sir?" Gardner asked. "Not even a prayer? He was often a foolish man, sir, and often a knave, but not always. There were times when he was wise, and times when he was honorable. He was a man like the rest of us and when a man leaves this life forever, he deserves a good word from us, some comfort for his soul."

The Lieutenant stared silently at Gardner for a while, the secret conflict that raged in his heart showing only in his eyes. He turned toward the body of Lynn and, bowing his head, led us in the familiar Anglican prayers of a Sunday service.

Hearing those prayers had a strange effect on me, although I had heard them daily at Jamestown and had not been moved by them. They brought to my mind days of my careless childhood when I attended Sunday services with my mother and afterward spent the day at children's play. These Virginia woods would have held all forms of enchantment for me. The terror and horror and privations that they offered to me now would not have entered my child's world. After the delightful Sunday play, there was always my return home to my mother's supper, which she had spent the entire afternoon preparing. I thought of my own mother's death just as I was growing into manhood. An icy feeling swept over me that I was truly an orphan. And now, even England was lost to me forever. For a few brief moments I wept uncontrollably, but I soon had it stopped. The Lieutenant and Gardner ignored my outburst, and we started once again for the stream and our camp on the King James River.

We approached our camp near the James about midnight and were exceedingly weary and hungry, having eaten all of our provisions. We could see the fire flickering a long way off and, as we drew near, a shot split the night air and a ball crashed through the trees above our heads. We dropped to the ground, seeking protection behind whatever was close at hand.

"We are English," the Lieutenant called out.

A voice answered from the darkness, "Come forward, near the fire."

We moved very cautiously into the clearing where we had made our camp, and stood motionless by the fire.

"Thanks be to God, it is you, Lieutenant," came the voice from out of the circle of darkness around us.

A man appeared out of that dark circle, one of the men we

had left to guard the camp, whose name was Nicolas Greene.

"I didn't know but that you might be savages, sir, come to relieve me of thinning hair. They can do so many things. Curse me if there isn't one who can speak our language as good as you or me. Would not surprise me if one couldn't imitate the voice of Christ Almighty, if he was to hear it, I mean."

"Where are the other men?" the Lieutenant asked.

"Gone, sir, I'm afraid."

"What do you mean, gone?"

"I don't rightly know, sir. You see, the morning after you left, come a savage into the camp. A big, strong fellow he was, not in dress and manner like those other nations we have seen. This savage come boldly into our midst and pulled out from his pouch a chunk of metal like unto purest gold.

He passed it freely among our men and, after our men had all examined this piece of metal, he said that he was acquainted with men of our race and would gladly show us where this gold was mined if we would give him in exchange our knives and hatchets.

"Our men seemed to go mad all at once and, God save me, I among them. We dropped everything we was doing and struck out behind this savage, every man urging him to hasten. Then something like good sense got the better of me and, without the Indian seeing me, I returned here. Toward dawn, the next day, methinks I hear shooting off in the distance. But I can't be sure, it was so faint. I knew, sir that you would be coming back. My faith told me that. So, I hid in places all around the camp, never spending more than a few hours in one place for fear they might smell me out with a hunting dog, if they have such things. And then, God Almighty be praised in his Heaven, you have arrived, thanks be to God!"

The Lieutenant looked at us, and then he walked over to a

nearby log and sat staring into the fire.

"You think they might be dead, Mr. Greene?" he said after a long silence.

Greene looked at me as though he expected me to answer for him.

"Aye, sir, that is what I think."

Lieutenant Webster nodded. Then, looking around the clearing, saw our equipment piled in one stack.

"They took nothing with them?" he asked.

"Not even their rations, sir," Greene answered. "They were like men who had all gone mad, sir. There was no reasoning with them."

"You did well, Mister Greene, having the good sense to return and wait for us."

"Shall we go after them?" Will Gardner asked.

The Lieutenant shook his head sadly.

"No. They knew my order, and they disobeyed it in their greed and lust for gold. You saw what it did for Mister Lynn. If I cannot take time to bury the dead, I certainly cannot take the time to go in search of them. No, we will stay the night here, doing as Mister Greene did, sleeping in a protected place and leaving the fire to serve as a beacon for any of those who might be on their way back. But if they are not here by the morning, we will wait no longer. We must make haste back to the falls."

We found a good place in the forest close enough to the fire to see it clearly, yet far enough away so that its light would not expose us. The Lieutenant took the first watch and I would take the second, until dawn. In spite of the rocky, wet ground, I slept well, and it seemed only an instant before the Lieutenant woke me for my watch.

"Come with me," he whispered.

I followed him to a place far enough away so that we would not disturb the other men.

"I've been thinking," the Lieutenant said, his voice tense, his words emphatic. "We will go back to the falls over land. The Indians usually make their cities close to the river. If we follow the course I have laid out, we can avoid the Monacan settlements, passing to the south of them, and reduce our time by as much as a day."

He anticipated my question.

"I know that it is unexplored territory and we will have to survive by our wits, but the map of the river is accurate enough, and we can reasonably suppose that the land will be much the same as we have thus far experienced. We will take only what we can carry, destroying the rest. We will have to move as swiftly as an Indian, stopping for nothing."

He looked at me intently. Orange and yellow firelight danced on his face, giving his eyes a cat-like glow.

"Not even for the wounded?" I asked.

He said nothing for a few moments.

"We can't leave our men to fall into the hands of the savages," he said. "You have seen what they do. If any are wounded and cannot travel, we will have to dispatch them ourselves. It would be the only merciful thing to do. I have thought over this plan many times and what I propose seems like the best course of action to take. Our mission here is completed. Now we must return with all possible speed. God, I would give all of my paltry wealth if we could put on hawk's wings and fly back. But we cannot, so we must use our legs to carry us, like the plodding beasts we are."

He touched my shoulder gently.

"I will tell the others in the morning. Meanwhile, have a good watch and wake me at dawn."

I said goodnight to the Lieutenant and listened as his foot sounds faded into silence. I leaned against a high, tooth-shaped rock and stared at the fire which had begun to die. I thought of those foolish men, most of whom had never seen a forest wilder than a town park. I knew that none would survive and, for a long while, I felt a deep sadness. I couldn't, in my heart, cast blame on them. Had I been left in camp with them, I might have succumbed to that shining temptation offered by the strange Indian. I would have run with them, no doubt leading the way, and would have been among the first to have my head smashed.

I told myself that if a man were to survive in this land, he must turn his attention to the land itself; to clearing the forest. I was beginning to believe that the sweet-smelling ground was the true wealth that this new country had to offer and that gold, especially the lust for it, was the way to certain destruction. Had it not been proven to me many times? All those good men casting away their own safety, their own lives, for Satan's fondest temptation.

I decided that, although I was as guilty as the rest, I had been spared for a reason known only to God, a great and noble task lay ahead of me. I had only to wait and do my duty to goodness and honesty, and it would come. I was thinking about this and the events of the past few days and trying to recall all that I had seen, when I heard a movement in the woods behind my left shoulder. I held my breath and listened. A twig snapped, leaves crunched. It sounded like an animal slowly making its way toward the fire. I thought of a wolf or a bear. We had seen their tracks throughout this journey. Perhaps it had caught the scent of our victuals and intended to raid them. I leaned closer to my rook and readied the match in my musket.

In a few minutes I could see the hazy figure of a man's silhouette moving through the trees. He stopped at the edge of the woods, near the fire. I couldn't tell if it was an Indian or one of our men. I pulled back the cock of my musket, blew gently on the smoldering match to increase its fire and aimed. He heard the metallic click of the weapon and turned toward me.

"Vtteke neer pokatamer," I said in the language of Powhatan, meaning "Get you closer to the fire."

The man stood motionless. I repeated my order in English.

"Matthew, is that you?"

I recognized the voice. "Wilcox?"

"Yes, yes," he said with undisguised joy. "I thought, I prayed . . . "

"Let's move closer to the fire so that I can be sure."

"Believe me, Matthew, I am Wilcox."

He walked closer to the fire and I followed, still holding my musket ready for use.

It was Wilcox standing before me, but he was almost un-recognizable. His clothes were torn to ribbons, his face and arms covered with blood and dirt, his hair and beard matted and as stiff as leather. I lowered my musket.

"Matthew, I must have something to eat."

His voice was dry and hoarse.

I walked over to our supplies and took out a large piece of dried beef, a water bottle, and several wild onions. He was sitting on the ground next to the fire when I returned. He ate, biting into the onions as he would have bitten into a sweet apple, and he tore the meat with his teeth, chewing until his jaws were as distended as full wineskins. He swilled the water until it overflowed his mouth and ran down his chin and neck.

When he had finished, he pushed away the water bottle and lay back on his right elbow and, for a moment, stared into the bright glow of the fire.

"Oh, God, what I would give for some fresh red meat and good Spanish wine," he said wistfully.

"Be thankful you're alive," I said.

"I am, Matthew, I am. And I'm also thankful that you returned safely. What about the Lieutenant?"

"Sleeping. With the others. We lost a man, Francis Lynn."

"Too bad, he was a good man."

"What happened here?" I asked.

Wilcox, still staring into the coals, bit his lower lip. His face wrinkled.

"This strange Indian came into camp. It might have been one of them that the Lieutenant mentioned or, as I now believe, he might have been the devil come out of Hell to take us. Anyway, this creature shows us a handful of gold nuggets. That is, he said it was gold, and it looked like gold. And he said that he would take us to it if we would give our knives and swords in exchange. I was against it from the start. It was too easy, too suspicious. I tried to warn them but after they got a look at that yellow substance, there was no holding them.

"What was I to do? Abandon them? Let them rush headlong into disaster without one voice of reason to aid them? No. It was my duty to go with them and try to bring them to their senses. The Lieutenant wasn't here. You were not here. There was no one in authority, and you know how mischievous men are, left to their own devices, without proper leadership.

"I went with them, much to my shame, and for nearly six hours followed that devil to the place where he said he mined his gold. It was a large cleft in a rock wall, looking like the very gateway to Hell itself. The men were so wrought up in their madness that they threw aside everything, including their weapons, and commenced digging like dogs in the earth, every man trying to outdo the other.

"Then, all at once, a screaming rose up from among them and, looking around, I saw four or five of our men falling dead, with arrows sticking in all parts of their bodies. I, myself, was grievously wounded in the leg. The Indians had taken our weapons, without our knowledge, and we were like hogs to be slaughtered. And they, having nothing to fear from us, rushed at us from all sides. There was nothing to do but seek what protection we could in the cave.

"It was a trap. I knew there was no way out the moment I entered it. The Indians lit torches and came in after us. Our men were wild with panic and did nothing to defend themselves. They cowered behind rocks where the Indians easily found them and killed them with their hatchets, some even using our own swords.

"One of them found me, and I pretended to cower down. I found a large stone about the size of an English brick and hid it behind my back. The savage wanted to have his fun first, so he shook his hatchet in front of my face and, smiling like a fiendish demon, drew back his weapon to strike off my head. He was a horrid sight with that torchlight flickering on his painted face. His eyes seemed to smolder with Hellfire itself.

"Just before he had drawn his weapon completely back, I flung the rock at him with all of my strength. It bounced off his head and ricocheted against the wall of the cave. I did not want to take a chance that he might still live, so I wrenched the hatchet from his hand and stove in his head with it. God! What a sound it made, like popping open a ripe melon! Then I dragged his body behind a rock and waited. The slaughter went on for a while longer, and the howls that came from that cavernous darkness were such that I hope never to hear again in my life.

"The savages were soon finished with their orgy of murder

and left the cave to commence a vile and disgusting dance not far away from the entrance. I waited until they were possessed with this barbaric rite, then I slipped out of the cave and, without being seen, made my way to the river where I floated with the current for well over an hour, after which time I climbed ashore because I could no longer stand the cold water. I made my way along the riverbank until daybreak. I covered myself with dead leaves and branches to wait for darkness again. That is how I came here, thanks be to God, who is my only keeper."

"Lies!" a voice shouted behind us.

I turned to see Greene, the Lieutenant, and Will Gardner standing just inside the clearing.

"Lies! All lies!" Greene shouted again, walking quickly toward us. "Wilcox, you are the lowest dog made in a mother's womb. He is the one, Lieutenant, who is responsible for what happened. He is the one who got our men worked up into a frothing madness for gold. He marched side by side with that roguish Indian out of the camp, and I'll wager he saved his own life at the cost of the rest of our men. Or perhaps he bought his way out by promising to turn us over to the savages."

Without warning, Wilcox jerked the musket out of my hand, leveled it at Greene, and pulled the trigger, but the weapon misfired, and before he could reprime it, the Lieutenant pinned him to the ground with the point of his sword pressing over his heart.

"Too many of our men have died already. Whatever the cause, it doesn't matter now. If you'll swear before God that your story is true, we will believe you, and that will be the end of it."

"1 swear," Wilcox said, "I swear before God, his angels, and all of his saints."

Wilcox was so sincere that only a hardened man would not

have believed him. And, even though I doubted much of his story, he had managed to escape from the killing wrath of the Indians, and that was what was most important to us now. Truth or lies seemed of little importance to me at that moment. My mind was most concerned with reaching Jamestown in safety.

CHAPTER 10

Friendly Fire

I t was beginning to grow light in the east. The Lieutenant ordered us to divide the rations up evenly among ourselves. We were to take only what we could carry, which included powder and shot. The rest we would sink in the river.

I stuffed every pocket lining and belt with cornmeal and dried beef, as did the others. The Lieutenant had an extra burden with his map making instruments. We covered the fire with dirt and pulled our cart, bearing the excess baggage, to the river, weighted it with stones, and shoved it in.

We recrossed the river on a series of exposed rocks. The level of the river had dropped in spite of the rain the night before, and the Lieutenant informed me that it appeared to him that Virginia was subject to drought, especially in late summer, and that the soil would drink up the rain water without much runoff. The Lieutenant had studied such things when he was a student at Cambridge, along with other math and sciences, and had served as an engineer with an English army in Holland before finding employment in Virginia.

We traveled through the forest as fast as we could, often breaking into a run when the way was clear enough. Lieutenant Webster stayed ahead of us, leading the way with his compass. It was exceedingly hard going and, after a few hours, we were required to rest. We were worn and weary from hunger and sleeplessness but, once on the move, the pace was always fast until one of us dropped from exhaustion.

We had not seen a sign of an Indian all day—no hunting trails, not even the smell of smoke in the air. So that night we slept with considerable peace of mind. Lieutenant Webster reckoned that we were in the land of the Monacans, but that we were well south of them and that we should keep this distance for the next two days, then turn north and pick up the river again. Only one guard was posted that night and the next day, after a quick breakfast, we resumed our flight through the forest.

We had been moving for many hours with only one brief rest. The sun was well past the noon when we heard a great commotion in the distance. Supposing that the noise was being made by the Monacans, we proceeded with extreme caution. Coming to the top of a high ridge, we saw below us, at a good distance, a large party of Indians, well-armed with bows and arrows. Fires had been built in a large circle and the Indians stood between these fires, all yelling and some dancing and shaking rattles, made from gourds, over their heads. The Lieutenant noted that the wind was behind us and blew the smoke to the southeast. Near the center of the circle stood a small herd of deer, eight or ten in number, all huddled together in a revolving group.

We lay on the top of the ridge, not caring about the wet, musty leaves under our bellies, and watched as the upwind fires burned closer and closer to the center. The closely packed group of deer began to revolve faster inside the decreasing circle of fire until they suddenly uncoiled and, led by a large buck with tall antlers, made a galloping charge at a point of the circle. The Indians at that section rushed at the deer, flinging their arms up and down and leaping and shouting at the tops of their voices.

The buck then wheeled around with a toss of his head, and led the frightened deer on a wild race just inside the perimeter of fire. We could hear their hooves clattering on rocks or thudding in softer ground, not as heavy as the sound of running horses. Once in motion, they seemed unable to stop or to slow their pace, but raced at top speed around the circle. The Indians cheered and shouted as they passed. After many circuits the deer began to tire. The fight had gone out of them. The inevitable must happen.

The Indians all raised their bows, drew back their bows and, as the running deer passed by them, they let go their arrows. The deer made one more circuit, then began to drop to the ground. The youngest first, the smallest, then the others; females and males together until only the large buck remained.

The buck slowed his pace. Tossing his head from side to side and snorting, he trotted to the center where, after revolving once, he stopped to face his tormenters. He was pierced all over with arrows and as he stood looking with his wild, bright, dark eyes, he wavered for a moment.

The Indians stood their ground, saying nothing, waiting for the fall of the buck. The animal wavered again. Its head dropped. The Indians moved closer into the circle. Then the buck jerked his head up and, in a final act of defiance, charged at the Indians who were closest to him. The Indians flung themselves aside, some rolling on the ground to escape the kicking hooves as the buck darted past them. With a great effort, he leaped over the fire. His legs retracted against his body like a giant bird's.

The effort proved too much for him, and the buck crashed against the ground and rolled over on his side. He tried to rise again, but it was hopeless. One young Monacan rushed upon the deer and, with a chilling yell, buried his hatchet in the deer skull.

We slipped down from the ridge so as to be out of sight.

"There will be much dancing and feasting now," the Lieutenant said, "and they will stay here until the carcasses are dressed and the meat divided. We will have to go farther south to avoid them, though I believe this to be the only hunting party in this area."

I did not ask him why he believed that to be the case. His judgement had been good so far, and he knew the Indians better than any of us with him.

"I wish to God I could get ahold of some of that venison," Wilcox said. The other men muttered their agreement.

"That would be a very foolish thing, Mr. Wilcox," the Lieutenant said, looking hard at him. "There will be fresh meat at the falls, and the sooner we get on the move, the sooner we will enjoy it."

For two days we traveled south and east, stopping only for rest and sleep. On the second day the Lieutenant reckoned that we were out of the land of the Monacans, and we turned northeast and marched without stopping until we came to the river. In all that time we had not seen an Indian nor heard another human voice except our own. When we did speak, it was never more than the most basic communication.

It was dusk when we reached the river, a few miles south of the falls. We made our way north along the shore until we came upon two Indians fishing from their canoe. Lieutenant Webster called for them to approach us, and they promptly paddled their boat over to us. The Lieutenant asked them if they would take us to the falls.

The Indians said that they would, but first they wanted beads and our knives. The Lieutenant drew out his pistol and, grabbing one of the Indians by the locks of his hair, put the muzzle of the pistol against the Indian's throat and said that he would take his head off if he did not take us to the falls. I held my musket on the other Indian who stood trembling in ankle deep water.

It was dark when we reached the settlement by the falls. We stepped quietly ashore. The Lieutenant shoved the canoe back out into the water and told the Indians to be gone at once. We could see only a few burning torches in the settlement and, not thinking that we were in any danger, we started walking toward it, talking loudly of our deliverance.

A shot rang out. We heard the ball sing close by us, then another, then a volley. Will Gardner groaned and fell next to me. I felt a ball tear through my thigh, and I dropped to the ground. The Lieutenant yelled for the men of the settlement not to shoot, calling out our names and declaring that we were Englishmen.

The firing stopped abruptly, and I looked up to see many men, with torches, running toward us. I reached back and felt my thigh. Warm, thick blood covered it. At that point there was no pain, only a numbed tightness in my flesh. I looked up again. Someone was holding a torch near my face. A bearded white man was looking at me intently. I didn't recognize him.

"This one's alive," he shouted to someone in the darkness behind the torch.

"Good God! What did you fools think you were doing? Couldn't you have sent a messenger or waited until daylight? How were we supposed to know that you were not savages?"

I recognized the voice of Captain West.

"The usual procedure is to challenge an intruder before you shoot him, sir," the Lieutenant retorted angrily.

"Not here it isn't. Not with these savages."

"How would you know, sir? You've only just arrived." Lieutenant Webster said.

I heard the metallic sound of swords being unsheathed.

"By God's wounds, I'll run you through before I'll have any more of your insolence."

Another voice boomed above the rest. "Put away your swords, you fools, and tend to these men."

It was Captain Smith's, and I was never more relieved to hear it. I knew then that I would not die. Such was his power over men, whom he stirred to either great love or great hate for him.

"West, you are a simpleton: Get these men to shelter and see that their wounds are cared for. I will speak with you afterward."

I was able to walk with the help of the Lieutenant, though my thigh felt like a block of wood over which I had little control. We, the wounded, were carried to a large tent and placed on straw mats. I was placed facedown on one. Mr. Greene was put beside me. A ball had shattered his hand and had continued on to pierce his upper arm. He was beginning to moan with the pain. Will Gardner was placed on the other side of the tent. He was dead.

The Lieutenant encouraged us to be of good cheer and not to worry over our hurts. He then excused himself, saying that he had to report the findings and events of our expedition and, as soon as that business was concluded, he would return to us and personally see to our comforts.

Shortly after the Lieutenant left, I began to feel cold and sweaty, then hollow inside and weak as though my flesh were falling from my bones. My bowels loosened, and I feared that I might disgrace myself. The numbness in my thigh was fading away and quickly being replaced by a burning, throbbing pain.

Mr. Greene was now whimpering and rolling from side to side, holding his wounded arm.

A man entered our tent, looking more like a traveling jester than anything else and, indeed, I think that was what he truly was. He had a bucket of water and a few dirty cloths with him. He said immediately that he was not a physician, but that if we wished to believe him one, then it was all right with him, and that such a belief would probably heal our wounds as well as the strongest medicine.

The man took one look at Gardner and said, "He will not be needing my imagined services."

The man laughed and giggled much while he was cleaning Greene's hand. All the while Greene was moaning in agony. Finally, he came to me and commenced to clean my wound with the same cloth and, at the same time, fondled and stroked my left thigh, saying as he did so that it was an abomination to wound buttocks as handsome and lovely as mine. I asked if he would be pleased to leave us alone since his physic was more painful than the wound itself. He laughed heartily at this, thinking it a clever jest and, in a few minutes, he left our tent with a wish for our speedy recovery.

The pain now spread to my leg and pounded like the blows from a blacksmith's hammer with each beat of my heart. I made an effort to turn my head and see the wound for myself, but I could not manage it, since to move any part of my lower body was unbearable. I reached back to feel it, but touching the skin felt like a touch with a hot fire poker.

The Lieutenant returned an hour or so later and brought with him Captain Smith. The Captain knelt down beside us and sat on his heels.

He smiled his usual merry smile and said, "I am terribly sorry over what has happened here tonight. Isn't that the way of fickle fortune, to have gone all that distance in the wilderness and then to be shot by our own men at your return? And that poor man!" He looked over at Gardner's body. "What a wasteful thing to have happen, and all because of that incompetent viper. He should be the one lying there and not your unfortunate comrade. But have no fear, I will not leave you here. Both of you will return with me to the fort as soon as it is day."

We thanked him with feeble effort.

"I am powerless against these men," the Lieutenant said. "They have put themselves against me on every issue. They have denied and refused my authority. But worse, they have rejected my advice and experience. So I will have to leave them to their own devices and pray that they do not suffer much."

He pulled out a bottle from his shirt and showed it to us.

"This is good English brandy. That scoundrel West has been keeping it for himself, but I persuaded him to part with it for medicinal purposes. I learned another use for it while I was a soldier in the army of Prince Sigismund, the Hungarian."

He reached over Green and poured the brandy liberally over my wound. The pain was blinding at first, and I could not hold back a sudden scream. He then poured the rest of it over Greene's arm, and Greene screamed equal to that of a woman giving birth.

"I know it stings now," the Captain said softly, "but it will prevent the wound from becoming putrid."

He stood up, and he and the Lieutenant exchanged glances.

"Try to sleep, my men," he said to us. "I shall return for you in the morning, and we will quit this place where men have lost their reason."

Sleep, of course, was impossible. I was conscious that night of only a few things, the greatest of which was the spreading pain in my body which never eased for a moment. The other was the near constant moaning and whimpering of Greene. And another, which alarmed me most in spite of the pains of the living, was the growing smell of death from Gardner's body.

In the morning, Captain Smith returned with the Lieutenant and a few men carrying litters and one carrying my toolbox. Two of them went immediately to Gardner's body and rolled it, with the toe of their boots, onto the canvas litter. Next, we were moved onto those rude carrying devises, with not-so-gentle hands, and taken down to the waiting pinnace.

All of our surviving company was there. Wilcox and Captain Smith were the last to board. There were some heated words exchanged as we pushed away from the shore, and Captain Smith shouted that they should not come a-weeping to him the next time the savages attack. A few men on shore shouted an insult, but we were too far distant from them to understand it.

"I have wasted many days among those jackasses. I never in all my days knew men who could be so pig-headed. Good God, if they are the best England's got, then the King may as well turn the country over to the Spanish, because they will have it soon enough."

A few of the men laughed and so did the Captain. Then he sat down in the bow section of the pinnace and, taking out the map that the Lieutenant had made, began marking on it.

We drifted down the river with the tide, the wind being slack. Our sail hung in folds from the yardarm and occasionally slatted lazily against the mast. It was going to be a hot day. Already I could hear the flies and mosquitoes buzzing around our ears. I still could not sit, so I had to pull myself up to the gunnel to see over, and lay on my stomach in the seats with my back arched nearly to the breaking point. I was determined not to spend this voyage staring into the sloshing black water of the bilges.

I seemed to never grow tired of looking at the green and muddy shore float past me. I knew this part of the river from the falls to the bay was well populated with Indians, but I saw only a few of their canoes pulled up on shore, resembling large logs skinned of their bark. Perhaps English ships had become too common a sight for them. What was more likely was that the Indians already knew of Captain Smith's departure from West's fort and were deliberately staying out of sight.

Captain Smith

C aptain Smith was considered by Powhatan's people to be a very powerful man, not easily deceived, quick to revenge a wrong. More importantly, however, he was believed by many of them to have certain spiritual powers that enabled him to see into other men's hearts. It was believed that his power could ward off arrows and other blows. He had been attacked many times by large parties of Indians, all shooting their arrows at him, and yet not one struck him; though, at times, they were as thick as hail. Did he not defeat the giant werowance of Pospaheagh, single handedly, without receiving the smallest wound?

"In two days' time," the Captain was saying, "there will hardly be one man alive at the falls and, though it pains me to say it, they will deserve their fate. They have been cruel and faithless with those good and simple people of Powhatan. They are not even as clever as Satan himself who, by cunning and persuasive words, did tempt the mother of all mankind to eat the forbidden fruit. Those fools with West, having all of the sins of our first parents in their hearts and none of their gentleness, would rob and murder the original inhabitants of this place and pursue their selfish hunt for gain like a pack of braying dogs. God knows, the Spanish could not have been a greater trial to me than those cloven-footed imps. And God knows what new mischief that trinity of evil has prepared for us at Jamestown."

Several canoes, manned by two men in each boat, appeared from the shore, rowing for us. The Captain ordered our muskets to be made ready, but to be kept down out of sight until he ordered their use. The Indians came closer, hailing Captain Smith in their own tongue. The Captain, recognizing one of them, returned his salute, "Netoppew, Netoppew, Matowas."

The canoes came swiftly up alongside our pinnace. One of the Indians who knew Captain Smith was smiling broadly, much like a child's happiness at seeing a long-absent parent.

"My captain," he said in his own tongue. "I have only now returned from Powhatan and was grieved that I might have missed you. Here, see." He pointed into his canoe. "I have brought you corn and good meat so that you may know that we are still friends."

The Captain bowed slightly and said, "Matowas, you have greatly honored me with your gifts and your proven friendship." He pulled out a bag from under the boat's seat, and from it took a handful of blue glass beads. "Please accept these in exchange. They are all that we have and poor proof of my undying friendship."

Matowas bowed, imitating the Captain, and accepted the beads.

"Accept also my promise that I will do all in my power to rid you of the plague that has descended upon you at the falls."

Matowas grinned happily. "Thank you, my captain, for you are a great man with much power from Heaven, and I know your promises are good."

They talked a while longer as we drifted down the river in company. When they had finished, Matowas pushed away from the pinnace and, with a farewell wave, paddled toward the shore. The Captain watched until they were mere specks in the distance. Then he ordered our matches to be put out.

"A friend?" one of the men asked in a mocking tone.

"Yes," the Captain answered, "like the rest of his people, he cannot feel indifferently toward others. He is either a devoted friend or an equally devoted enemy. Yet Matowas is also devoted to his people. If Powhatan ordered him to bash my head in, he would immediately take his tomahawk and come after me."

"That's very sad, sir," said the same man, but this time without ridicule. The Captain took a deep breath and turned away, putting his attention on the man who had spoken.

"No sadder than passing a poor beggar on the streets of London and hardly giving him a glance, much less a single coin. Matowas, if he were taken to England, would be as much appalled at our world as we are at his."

A little breeze had picked up from the southwest and was filling our slack sail. I felt the pinnace move under me and gather speed. The breeze was cooling and carried with it the smell of water and earth. I don't know why it happened or how, but I had the intense feeling—it would have to be called a feeling since there was no reasoning for it—that I was going to recover from my wound. I knew, by some mysterious means, that I was going to be well, that I would not die of this bullet. At that moment the pain seemed to diminish. I seemed to be able to feel the flesh knitting together and healing. My fears for my recovery vanished, and I was anxious to be up and about and helping with the task of managing the ship.

I asked Greene how he felt, but he only looked at me with wide, hollow eyes and did not answer. His hand was blue and twisted and had swollen to twice its size. The Captain examined it.

"Don't worry, lad," he said. "The savages have excellent cures for battle wounds. I have myself seen them apply their medicines to wounds much worse than yours and overnight the humors were drawn from the injury so that the very place of the wound looked as pink and subtle as baby's flesh."

Greene smiled at this and seemed to rally his spirits.

That night we anchored in the river and, for a long time, we were entertained by the Captain's stories of his services with the Earl of Mildritch. He told us of his defeat of three Turkish champions at the battle of Regall. For that service he received a coat of arms of which he was very proud. He then went on to enthrall us with the tale of how he was wounded and left for dead after the battle of Rebrynk. In the morning the scavengers, searching the dead bodies for loot, found him alive, restored him to health, and sold him as a slave in the city of Axopolis to a Turk named Bogall.

Bogall was a man of considerable wealth and power in his country, and he had a young wife who preferred to live in comfort in Constantinople. Bogall, wishing to glorify himself in his wife's eyes, sent Captain Smith to her as her personal servant, along with a letter saying that Captain Smith was a Bohemian Lord whom he had captured in single combat and whose ransom would adorn her in glory.

The Captain laughed as he told this story.

"The young wife was very pleased to have a Bohemian Lord as her servant but, knowing her husband to be advanced in age, and being more of a man of business than of arms, questioned me about how I came to be captured. I told her the truth and the young lady was much displeased that I wasn't a true Bohemian noble. As a result, she sent me to her brother-in-law, Tymor Bashaw, in Nalbrits who was a very cruel master, indeed, and hated Englishmen exceedingly.

"After many months of extreme hardship such as a dog would not endure, I managed to club Tymor to death while he was in his fields, and escape to the town of Aecopolis on the river Don. From there I made my way back to England, after receiving a handsome reward for my former services from the noble Prince Sigismund."

The Captain was a natural storyteller. We all listened as intently as if we ourselves were the participants and had actually seen the places and had known, firsthand, the difficulties that the Captain related. I had even forgotten about my own discomforting wound while listening to the Captain and was much disappointed when, owing to the lateness of the hour, the Captain cut short his tales and advised us to rest. One of the men who could play the horn pipe took out his instrument and played us a merry tune, one that I had heard often in the streets of Exeter.

One man was left on watch. Shortly before daybreak, we were all awakened by a muffled explosion and a shrill cry of pain. There was much confusion in the semi-darkness. My first thought was that we were being attacked by Indians. Others in our company had the same thought for, in a moment, several shots were fired out into the darkness. There was much shouting and men stumbled about in the boat, groping for invisible hand holds. Someone shouted that the Captain had been injured and thrown overboard.

Finally, a lantern was lit and there, struggling in the murky water like a stricken fish, was Captain Smith, his long hair and beard hanging in sodden strings, clinging to his face and neck.

The Lieutenant thrust a boat hook toward him. He grabbed it with one hand and held on weakly. Several men leaned over to get a grip on his shirt, but could not reach the distance. They then tied lines around their waists and leaped into the water beside the Captain. Using the lines to pull themselves up to the boat, they hoisted Captain Smith up by his armpits to where others, with grasping hands, could gain a good hold on him.

They pulled him back into the boat as they would have pulled in a large, clumsy seal. The Captain cried out in agony. The wound in his thigh was instantly visible, a red and black hole about the span of a man's hand, spread out. The clothes around the wound were burned and torn into strips and the stringy remainder of the Captain's powder pouch hung on his belt just above the mound. The injury was exceedingly ugly, and blood oozed from it as it would from a piece of burned beef.

"Hold the lantern up!" the Lieutenant shouted.

He drew out his pistol and leveled it at the man who had been on watch.

I had never seen the Lieutenant so angry. He was totally possessed by his rage. He pulled back the cock and fully intended to shoot the man, had not the Captain forbade him to do so.

The man cowered in the stern of the boat, holding his body and shivering as if it were freezing instead of a warm, late summer night.

"I was asleep, sir," the watchman said in a shaking voice. "I'm sorry, sir. I've had no sleep in two days. I couldn't help meself, it being a warm night and no Indians about. I didn't even know that I was going to sleep, it happened so fast."

"Don't shoot him for that, Webster. Shoot him for stealing food or giving arms to the Indians or for taking another man's wife by force, but don't kill him for falling asleep," the Captain pleaded.

"What about for this?" the Lieutenant said, motioning toward the Captain's wound.

"He didn't do it. That man could not murder another man in his sleep. It's all he can do to shoot at the Indians, and I don't think that he's ever hit one, have you?"

"No, sir. That I haven't," the watchman answered quickly.

The Lieutenant lowered his pistol. "Someone here is responsible, and I will throw you all in jail if I must until the guilty man steps forward."

"Never mind that now, Lieutenant," the Captain groaned. "Get me back to the fort. We still have a long way to go. Perhaps Matowas will have medicine good for this."

It was still dark. The Lieutenant ordered the anchor to be raised and the boat to get underway with oars, as there was little breeze. We put out our lanterns so our movement would not be seen from the shore and, being as quiet as we could, we rowed down the river. The Lieutenant served as coxswain and steered the craft as carefully as he would have handled a hen's egg. Even so, we grounded several times, and each time managed to free ourselves by pushing against the bottom with oars and boat hooks.

———————

After an hour of floating around blindly, the blackened void of the sky at last began to grow lighter. Soon we could make out the dark lines of both shores, and later it was light enough to see the bends and snags in the river itself. The stillness continued, however, causing the surface of the water to appear like a smooth, brown syrup. Except for hidden movements beneath us that sent random swirls of water to the top, the surface was disturbed only by our wake, which spread out from our boat interminably and as unalterable as the flight of an arrow. The mist over the river glowed white as the first fingers of sunlight touched it. The smell of rotting wood and brackish water rose from the river and clung to our bodies as did the damp, stagnant air we glided in.

We rowed, as mindless as machines; not thinking, not feeling, only doing our mechanical work without falter or hesitation. Only the occasional groan from the Captain reminded us that we were earth men and not lost souls journeying over the river Styx. I even took a turn at the oars and found that I could rest my weight with reasonable comfort on my undamaged thigh and keep pace with the rest of them. I watched the Lieutenant at the boat's helm and saw him as a frightened man. His face and body seemed turned to stone. Only his eyes moved, and they were alive with dread. He looked at only two things—the Captain and the horizon ahead.

I had never before thought of the possibility of the Captain getting hurt or killed like the rest of us. Perhaps, like the Indians, I believed, without knowing it, that there was something supernatural about the Captain. He was to me the very essence of our people's desire to succeed and to survive in Virginia. He was the best among us, and the thought of the colony going on without him seemed impossible.

I was angry with him at that moment, I must admit, for being like us—mortal and subject to death. I was angry with him for not being a god, for not having the supreme, invincible powers of a god. I felt that, in an obscure way, he had abandoned us to the greedy, indifferent clutches of most of the leading men now in the colony.

I was soon ashamed of myself for thinking and feeling unkindly toward the Captain. It was clear that his wound was serious and possibly even mortal. He was suffering greatly, and there was nothing any of us could do except to get to the fort as quickly as we could.

We rowed past Paspahegh and saw many Indians on the shore, making signs for us to land. We ignored them and kept to our endless rowing. After rounding the point at Paspahegh, with the Chickahominy River on our left, we had the fort in sight. It looked surprisingly small and vulnerable, perched as it was like a small animal cage on the edge of the island. It had seemed much larger in our imaginations, much stronger, much less likely to slip off into the river.

A mile or so from the fort the Lieutenant fired off his pistol, the standard signal for danger or distress. The doors of the fort swung open and a group of soldiers, along with other people of the settlement, came running down to our landing place.

"Captain Smith is grievous wounded," the Lieutenant shouted to the soldiers on shore.

The soldiers looked taken aback for a moment. Then they all rushed to our boat, splashing out into the water and leaping at the gunwales, all anxious to help the Captain. They saw that Greene and I were able to walk, so they took my litter and, with great gentleness, placed the Captain on it. Captain Smith groaned and gritted his teeth so hard that the veins in his rough neck stood out like heavy cords.

The Lieutenant and Wilcox helped Greene and me out of the boat and, leaning on the Lieutenant, I managed to hobble toward the fort's entrance. By this time there was a large crowd gathered, and we made our way, with some difficulty, through them to the door. People were pushing and shoving to get a look at us and inevitably someone would bump into my hip, sending a shower of pain through my body.

The familiar smells of woodsmoke and sour clothes still filled the air inside the fort. I heard a voice calling me from the crowd, and I recognized it as being that of Richard's. I informed the Lieutenant of who he was and that he could take over the burden of my weight and allow the Lieutenant to pursue more important matters. Lieutenant Webster stopped and called for a path to be made way for Richard. In a few minutes this was accomplished, and Richard emerged from the heart of the crowd looking as healthy and sincere as I had left him.

"Take them to your quarters. Greene can take Holt's bed since he will not be returning," the Lieutenant said. He looked sympathetically at Greene and me. "I will come around with the physician as soon as we have seen to the Captain. It will not be long, so be of good cheer and rest as much as you can."

The Lieutenant turned to the crowd.

"Disperse, you good people, and go about your work. A report of these happenings will be made known to you in due time."

"Go with them to their quarters and see that they are not molested," the Lieutenant said to a soldier near us.

We waited as the crowd slowly dispersed. Then, led by the soldier, we made our way to the quarters. Greene held his lifeless arm and I, propped up against Richard, limped along on one good leg. I was never happier to see the rude door and framing of our wattle house. It seemed better than the finest palace to me and as sacred as a church.

The soldier stopped at the door and, saluting us, departed in the direction of the President's House. Wilcox was already in the house when I limped in with Richard and Greene.

"You'll not sleep here," Wilcox said, motioning to his straw bed. "This has always been my place. You take Benjamin's, over there." He pointed to the darker corner where straw and pieces of clothes lay in a disheveled heap.

Greene shrugged and said that he did not care where he slept so long as his arm healed. Richard helped me ease down to my bed, and he sat down beside me.

"How bad is the Captain's wound?" he asked.

"I don't know," I said, "but I think that it is not good."

"Not good!" Wilcox blurted out. "If the man doesn't die

of that wound, it'll be a miracle. Why, half his arse is gone. Putrefaction will set in, especially in this unhealthy climate, in no time. It'll surprise me if he's still alive by next week this time."

"You sound as though you almost wish it," Richard said, with an unaccustomed strain in his voice.

Wilcox smiled. "I wish no man such unpleasantness, my lad, but the truth is one thing and a miracle is another. I put my faith in the truth of experience, lad, and that tells me that the Captain will be a dead man in a fortnight."

"Miracles do happen, Mr. Wilcox," Richard said. "Witness your own safe return."

"Aye, I have returned safe this time, but I doubt that it was owing to some miracle or other."

"Then to what do you attribute it, sir?"

"To the toss of the coin, to the fates, to the four winds, to luck. I don't know, but if God wishes to preserve me when he takes others more deserving of his mercy, then he is a poor judge of men."

"God has his reasons, Mr. Wilcox. Perhaps he has a plan for you."

Wilcox laughed and slapped his knee. "Lord preserve us."

When his laughter had subsided, he said, "I must be about some business down at the ships. Matthew, can I bring you back anything?"

"Not if it costs money," I said.

"Fear not, I'll bring you back a present. We can celebrate our miraculous return." He laughed again and left the house.

Richard looked disturbed and then said, "He's going to get drunk, I suppose."

"Let him get drunk if he wishes. He deserves it," I said.

Richard looked at me with full sympathy in his eyes.

"Was it very bad for you, Matthew?"

I told him that it was, and I proceeded to tell him all that had happened until our return to Jamestown. He listened intently to every word, and when I had finished, he took my hand and patted it gently, the way a mother does a sick child's. He told me that he was convinced now, more than ever, that a divine hand had intervened in our behalf and that we were not to mourn the dead since their deaths had been pre-ordained by God and were, therefore, not an evil thing.

"And," he continued, leaning back in his chair. "I have some most happy news for you." He hesitated, studying my face. "Anne Breton has consented to become my wife."

I said that it was good news indeed and congratulated him, although I thought to myself that taking a wife at that time and place was a most foolish thing. He beamed with such pride and happiness that I could not bring myself to tell him of my true feelings.

"When is the ceremony to take place?" I asked.

"Next Sunday," he said, grinning. "In the church. We will live outside of the fort. Everyone has given some of their time to help us build a small house, and it is almost completed. When you are well enough, I will show it to you. The house and land will belong to the community, of course, and is not to be sold by me. But I am free to live in it and garden the land as I see fit, for as long as I wish to." He clapped his hands together, excited. "I've also applied for a large track of land near four miles north of Jamestown, to be paid for from a percentage of the land's annual yield. Close to three hundred acres of good soil. Can you believe such a thing happening? Many of the great squires in England hardly own as much, and here in Virginia there is no limit to good land. I dare say in a few year's time I could own a thousand acres, Matthew. It is true. All that I have prayed for has come true and, my friend, I want to share what I have with you. If my bid for the farmland is granted, then I wish you to have a hundred acres of it, any hundred acres you wish."

He clasped my free hand in his and shook it.

I expressed my sincere gratitude to him for his generous offer and said that if he should be granted the land I would not deprive him of it, since I had no skill at farming, but that I intended to pursue my trade as a carpenter as soon as conditions allowed it.

"There is much to be built and a boundless forest from which to build it. I should not lack for work or satisfaction in the future."

The Lieutenant entered with the doctor while I was speaking to Richard, and we ended our conversation. Richard clasped my hand again, wished for my speedy recovery, and left for his work in the fields.

The doctor, who had been in the colony since the second year, began by examining Greene's wound. He roused Greene from his stupor and looked at his hand and arm. He spoke in a low voice so that I could barely hear it.

"The bone is shattered in your hand, and there is no way I can treat it here that will save it."

Greene started to speak, but the doctor held his hand up for silence. "If you wish to live, the hand will have to be removed."

"No!" Greene shouted. "I will not let you do it. Die if I must, but with both my hands, for I would die as quickly here with one."

The doctor stood up.

"Have it your way, sir, but I have given you warning. Do not come to me when it is too late, for there will be no way I can help you."

He then came to examine my thigh. He was a very gentle

man, and touched the areas of my wound as though his own fingers were sensitive to the pain. He then softly applied an ointment which burned at first, then left the place with a numb feeling.

"The wound is still clean," he said. "No sign of putrefaction. The ointment will aid in the healing, but you must be careful to keep the wound clean. Take pieces of boiled cloth and use it as a dressing until a scab has formed. It will continue to pain you for a while, but there are no bones broken, and the soft flesh should knit together in a few weeks."

I thanked the doctor for his kindness, which he seemed hardly to acknowledge, and watched him as he left the house carrying his box of medicines and instruments. The Lieutenant waited behind to tell me about the Captain.

"If he lives, it will surprise us all. You know, Matthew, that I am not a strongly religious man, but I have prayed since that morning. Every moment I have prayed for his recovery. I cannot see the colony going on without him. He is a strong man with a will of iron and, although he is delirious and often cries out for people in his past, he still clings passionately to life. He is as close to being a dying man as I have ever seen and still not die. God knows what will happen now that he is surrounded by his enemies and cannot defend himself. Unless he regains his senses, they will usurp his authority and undo all that he has done since the beginning of the settlement."

"What does the doctor say?" I asked.

The Lieutenant looked very much troubled.

"He says there is nothing he can do. That the Captain's wound is greater than he has medicine or skill to assuage. The doctor says that if the Captain is to live, he must have better surgery in England, but he doubts that the Captain could survive the voyage. The ship will be leaving in a few weeks and I will try to persuade him to leave with it."

"Do you know anything of how his powder pouch came to be fired?" I asked. The Lieutenant shook his head.

"No. But someone in the boat had to do it, and I suspect it was one of those men at West's fort, no doubt paid by the Captain's enemies there to kill him. And I am going to have all of those men watched. The scoundrel will no doubt try it again, knowing his first attempt to be questionable. I will be gone now, Matthew. I have much to do. We are in a den of inequities here. Get you well quickly. I will have need of you."

He stood up, his sword and armor clanking and creaking against his leather undercoat, his eyes full of cause and determination. How I envied his strength and unflinching concern with the problems of the settlement.

He stopped by Greene's bed and spoke a few words to him in a low voice. Then, turning, he gave me a reassuring smile and departed.

"What did he say to you, Greene?" I asked.

There was a long silence from Greene, who gazed at the wall opposite his bed.

"He wants me to have my hand cut off."

"Are you going to do it?"

There was another long silence.

"No," he said, and he remained still, gazing at the empty wall with the most despairing look I had ever seen in a man.

I thought it best to leave him to his silence. I lay back on my straw bed and listened to the muted sounds of busy people outside, the distant sounds of wood sawing and the ringing of metal tools at work. Soft footsteps could be heard, and clouds of yellow dust floated in through the open door and window. I was tired but unable to sleep. My thoughts jumped from one fearful thing to another without coordination or cohesion.

CHAPTER 12

Convalescence

I do not know how much time had passed before a shadow passed into the one-room house. I looked up and saw Anne standing over me, holding a basket of fruits, nuts, and other fine things to eat. She knelt beside me and placed the basket down next to my arm.

"Richard said that you had returned and that you were seriously wounded." Her eyes darted at my wounded thigh. "I brought these for you. My father always said nothing restores health but good fresh fruit. I picked them outside the fort where they are clearing the land. Richard showed me what to pick, and he even knows the Indian names for them. Oh, don't worry. They are not poisonous. I tasted each one and found them quite sweet and delicious. The nuts have a hard shell, so you will have to break them with something. Perhaps one of your hammers."

She reached for my toolbox.

"No, don't bother. I'll manage soon enough, please."

She stopped. She looked frightened.

"I'm grateful for yours and Richard's kindness, truly I am," I told her. "But the wound is not serious. I will be recovered in a few days."

She seemed hesitant, distant. I wondered why she had not mentioned her forthcoming marriage.

"Richard has told me of your plans."

She nodded.

"Are you not looking forward to it?"

"It means never seeing home again. It means dying in this wilderness," she said, casting her eyes down at the floor.

"Hasn't Richard expressed to you what being in this land means to him?" I said.

"Yes. They are noble thoughts, full of goodness, but . . . " She stood up abruptly. "I hope that you will be well recovered soon. Richard had wanted Captain Smith to give me away, but now, of course, he will not be able to. Will you do it?"

"If Richard wishes it, yes."

"He wishes it. It was the last thing he said to me today."

"Do you wish it?"

"Yes, I do. I will return tomorrow with more fresh fruits and whatever I can find to aid your recovery."

I thanked her, and she left with a swish and rustle of her clothes. I tasted one of the berries and found it as she had said, sweet and delicious.

I dug a file out from my toolbox and cracked the shell of the nut and found its fruit exceedingly tasty, almost as satisfying as if it had been the finest meat.

I offered Greene a portion of these fruits, but he would not answer me. He continued lying on his side, gazing at the wall. He had lost touch with where he was; the house, me, even the pain in his hand and arm did not seem to trouble him. I looked at his hand. It was swollen to almost twice its normal size, and it had begun to turn a darker blue.

The air in the house had become heavy and oppressive. The sweat under my clothes felt like hot water next to my skin, and the stink in the house was like that of a dead rat that had crawled away to die in a secret place. My hip continued to feel like a chunk of wood, and I could not stand without the aid of a crutch, which I did not have. I made up my mind to endure the heat and the smell, at least until I could procure a suitable crutch.

That did not happen for many days afterward, until the doctor had given his permission. During that time, he came to visit every day and applied his salve and spoke to Greene, who remained silent, even refusing to eat the poor rations provided in the fort and brought to him every day by Richard.

Anne came also, bringing new baskets of berries and such edible things as she could find. She even erected a curtain over our door to keep out the dust. The Lieutenant had not returned to visit me for a few days, and I had begun to worry that he might have found some displeasure with me until, on the third day, he came late in the afternoon and brought the Indian Matowas with him. He explained that Matowas had come to treat the Captain's wounds and, at the request of the Captain, he would treat ours also.

I felt very strange letting an Indian look at my wound, being as he was of a people of whom I had little real knowledge. But I trusted the Captain and the Lieutenant. They had knowledge of his healing power, and that was enough recommendation for me.

I bared my hip, and Matowas examined it for a moment and called for a cloth to clean away the doctor's salve. He was very diligent and gentle with the injury, though the pain was inescapable. I gritted my teeth and tried to suppress a groan. He then poured a small quantity of ground leaves from a pouch, decorated with small seashells, into his hand. He looked up, closed his eyes, and said a prayer in his own language over the medicine. He applied the ground leaves directly to the wound. Each one felt like a small knife cutting into my tender skin. He then tied a cloth around my hip to hold the medicine in place.

"In six days," he said, "remove the cloth and look to the

wound. If it be red and crusted over with dead flesh, then you will live. But if it be white and running with a foul liquid, then you will die."

The directness of his approach stunned me into speechlessness. The Lieutenant smiled apologetically.

"You should not be in doubt now, Matthew."

"Not until after six days more," I said.

"Will you look to Mr. Greene?" the Lieutenant said to Matowas.

The tall, strongly built Indian shook his head.

"No," he said, and would not even turn his face toward Greene. He said to me, "I will return on the seventh day."

He stepped back a few times then left, brushing aside the door curtain.

"If the situation with my wound is as he says it is, why is he returning?"

"He wants to see to it that the Captain has the proper burial rites and, no doubt, he will be looking to see if his services are needed with you."

"What is he?"

"He is a conjurer, believed to have strong curative powers and the gift of prophecy."

"And Captain Smith believes in him?"

"This is a strange land, Matthew. Some of our people say that it is a land that Christ forsook, choosing instead to shed his light in our Europe and leaving this place to the savages and their devil worship."

"Do you believe that, Lieutenant?"

He waited for a long while before answering. His brow twisted in thought.

"No," he said, but not with absolute finality. "I don't subscribe to that view. Yet this is a very strange country with strange people. The powers of speech and reason are themselves mysteries beyond our comprehension. These Indians were, until now, unknown to us and we to them. What powers of the mind they may have developed over the centuries may not be fully understood by us.

"I have heard of men dying after one of their Quiyoughqui-socks had cast a spell upon him, or some men driven mad by lesser spells. I saw with my own eyes a Quiyoughquisock touch a man, who had treated us rudely, upon the arm with his hand, and such welts were raised on that man's body that it looked as though he had been given a hundred lashes at the pillar. And shortly did that man plead for the mercy of death. You would do well to trust Matowas in matters of healing. But his honor, his allegiance lies with his nation."

"Isn't that the way it should be, Lieutenant?"

The Lieutenant looked at me strangely for a moment.

"Yes," he said, "that is the true obligation of every man."

"His healing knowledge will be enough for me," I said jokingly. "He can have his honor and his nation."

The Lieutenant smiled at me in a way that I had seen Richard smile at an ignoramus. He asked me if I needed anything that he could get for me. Many things to eat came to my mind, things that I had not eaten since leaving England. I appreciated the spirit of his offer but did not want to tax his kindness further. So I told him that all my wants were satisfied and that if I should have a real need, I would tell him of it.

He stopped at the door on the way out and looked at Greene.

"Mr. Greene," he shouted, "Greene!"

But Greene ignored him, preferring, as always, to stare at his wall. I believe that Greene heard him, for I saw his eyes blink each time the Lieutenant shouted his name.

"The doctor will be in tomorrow to see you," the Lieutenant

continued speaking to him. "He is under orders to do whatever he thinks best to save your life. Surely that means something to you."

Greene did not move. He did not answer. He had totally shut us out of his mind, and he continued to lie motionless, holding his blackened and swollen arm as though it were some offering in a pagan sacrificial rite.

The Lieutenant shoved the door curtain aside and departed, his armor and military hardware ringing as he walked. I watched Greene for a while. He remained indifferent to my presence. He was beyond my power of communication, and I thought it best to get some sleep and pray that the healing power of Matowas would work for me.

I drifted off to sleep and when I awoke, the heat of the day was beginning to be felt in our little mud-covered house. Greene was there, unmoved since the last time I saw him. The odor of human waste was strong and filled the whole house. I stood up and hobbled over to the door and tied the curtain back to let in some air. I was immediately met with a blast of hot air, smelling equally as nauseous, of animals and unclean men. The light was so bright and piercing that I had to cover my eyes.

The atmosphere outside was as still as that inside. The only movement to be seen was what the men of the fort made, dragging themselves under the burden of the oppressive heat. I hobbled back to my bed and stopped to lean against the wall for a few agonizing seconds before dropping. I was suddenly very angry with Greene.

"The rest of us have to live with you, you fool!" I shouted. "By what right can you lie there and cut yourself off from us? This isn't just your world or your house. We are all dependent on one another here. None of us can afford the luxury of your kind of self-pity. The least you can do is clean yourself, man!"

My words had no effect on him. He remained as frozen in his place as before.

I flopped onto my bed and, feeling a sudden lightness in my head, lay still while my heart pounded like a runner's feet. Richard came in shortly and if he noticed the odor, he did not show it. He spoke to me gently and saw that I was not well. Then he started preparing our rations. They turned out to be a true delight; fresh meat, onions, a soup of many vegetables, and two apples apiece.

He offered a goodly portion to Greene, who did not so much as turn his eyes. Richard and I ate heartily, and the delicious food made the unwholesome air considerably more tolerable. After finishing, Richard sat in the chair next to my bed, and lit a pipe of tobacco. I asked him where he had acquired a taste for tobacco, and he said that Tatahcoope had taught him the proper use of it as a medicine.

"Tatahcoope vows that drinking in the smoke has kept him in the best of health, that tobacco is also much prized by their gods. Tatahcoope says that every morning his father, along with many important members of his tribe, goes down to the river and offers a libation to that god in the hope that he will not take away their fish and oysters. No priest of their nation is without his tobacco pouch, and it is believed by many to have the power of summoning spirits from the heavens."

"Good Lord!"

"Is something wrong?"

Richard was startled by my outburst.

"Look at this and tell me if it is tobacco."

I pulled away the bindings that Matowas had placed over my hip. Richard bent down and looked closely at the dressing.

"Well?" I asked.

He sat up straight again.

"I'm quite sure that it is not, but I can't tell you what it is. It is not a plant that I am acquainted with."

He asked me how I came by this dressing, and I told him of Matowas's visit and of the Captain's and Lieutenant's faith in his skill. Richard nodded and said that he agreed with them.

"We have much to learn of Powhatan's people, and even if the preparations are tobacco, I doubt that it will injure you further. Perhaps tobacco does have curative power. The Indians certainly would not continue to use an herb that had proven to be useless."

I agreed with him that his logic seemed sound. In any case, the wound was healing before Matowas applied his medicine and, by having no effect, it would certainly not inhibit further healing.

We drifted into a conversation about England, including Exeter and Plymouth. We talked about the differences in the two countries, especially the climates. Useless talk, really; the sort of things we had discussed before. Yet the harmless, pointless conversation with my friend was very soothing to my spirit and, for the first time since my return from the falls, I felt safe. Speaking of familiar things with someone who had shared my young manhood gave me a sense of comfort and peacefulness. As for any thought of gold and wealth, I had lost such notions somewhere in the stony, inhospitable mountains to the west and did not care to regain them.

We talked until well after dark and until Wilcox returned, drunk and staggering about, holding a half-empty bottle of wine in one hand and a flickering candle dripping hot wax in the other. He stopped a few paces inside the door and, holding up the bottle, drank from it until the wine overflowed his mouth and ran like thin blood down his neck. He then sat the candle and the bottle on a ledge he had made above his bed.

"Those goddamn sailors," he said, spitting his words out. "They'll stick you in the arse and steal your last shilling. A savage is a better Christian," he said, flinging off his hat and then pulling out a pistol from his shirt. He aimed it out of the door in the direction of the ships.

Richard leaped up and, with kind words, took the pistol away from him and helped him to his bed, where he instantly fell into a snoring sleep. Richard looked at the pistol for a moment, then placed it on the shelf beside the wine bottle, then blew out the candle.

I had lost the appetite for further conversation, and Richard, sensing I was weary, excused himself, saying that he must visit Tatahcoope while he had the time allotted.

I soon fell asleep and did not stir until I was roused early in the morning, about two o'clock, with a shout, then a pistol report. Ordinarily I would have thought nothing of it, shouts and gunfire being a common thing in our fort at night. But I had a particularly uneasy feeling. I quietly got out of bed, slipped into my britches, and felt my way to the door.

Several men with torches were bent down over the crumpled form of a man lying near the center of the fort. Other men were running, with torches held high, toward the scene. I hobbled over to them and pushed my way through to the center. There, twisted into a small snail-like shape, lay Mr. Greene, his eyes staring now with the gaze of death. His bloody face, turned up, looked like the horrible face of a demon rising from Hell. His hand still gripped the pistol that he had used. It was Wilcox's pistol, the one that Richard had laid over his bed.

One of the soldiers who had been on guard recognized me and, knowing that Greene had come with me from the falls, sought to explain.

"I thought he was a drunken sailor, but I wasn't sure. He could have been a savage, disguised as one of our men. How was I to know? I ordered him to identify himself, and when he didn't, I commanded him to stop. He did, and then he shot himself. There was only the weak light from the church and the storehouse. I couldn't see him clearly."

I said that he should not blame himself.

"Greene was a sick man in mind and body," I said, and promised to explain his action to the Captain myself.

"Poor devil," someone said. A hush settled on the men gathered as they looked down at what remained of Greene and his last act on earth.

Finally, the soldier who had spoken to me said above the windy noise of the torches, "We must bury him before daybreak. You know the policy. Anis," he said to the soldier beside him. "Go fetch the Reverend. There is unhappy work for him tonight."

The man left immediately and walked hurriedly toward the Reverend's house.

"Some of you men help. You," he said to another man, "go and find a burial shroud and a proper litter. Several of you draw your shovels and dig the man a deep grave. We don't want the savages getting to him."

I tried to help with the preparations, but the soldier advised me to stay my efforts because of my wound. They told me I could be more useful if I went to inform the Captain, and that he, Sergeant Johnson, would oversee the disposal of the body.

I found it difficult to think of Greene as just a body, a carcass, something to be disposed of quickly when, only a few minutes before, he had been a living man, in pain. His decision to take his own life must have been a lonely, desolate journey.

My hip was beginning to feel better; that is to say, I was regaining much of the feeling back into it. I could put more weight on it and so walked less like a peg-leg sailor. As I approached the President's House, I heard the Lieutenant call to me. I stopped and answered.

"Do you wish to see the Captain?" he asked.

"Greene has killed himself," I said.

"Damn, that is too bad. But perhaps it is best. The physician said that he doubted that Greene would recover . . . but the Captain need not know of it just now. He is sleeping for the first time in many days and should not be disturbed. Who is seeing to the burial?"

"Sergeant Johnson," I said.

"Good. He's a good man and will take the proper course."

"How is the Captain?"

"The wound looks and smells bad. The physician does not think he will live, and truly it does not seem that he will. He confided to me today that he is giving the Presidency to Sir George Percy, and it will be a sad day when that happens. Captain Smith sees no way to fight them now without creating what could be a bloody civil war right here in our own fort. By putting one of their own men in the presidency, especially a weak man like Percy, we might still control most of the colony's future through seats on the council. Also, most of the soldiers are loyal to Captain Smith, though I'm loath to think of it that way.

"The presidency was never intended to be the office of power that Captain Smith had made it into, mainly because no man here is capable of wielding the influence or power over the Indians that he is. We have much to fear from the likes of Percy and his conspirators."

"What will the Captain do after he resigns his office?"

"I must hold you to your word that you will tell no one."

"I swear, I swear."

"I am almost certain that the Captain intends to return to England, if he lives. He believes he can find better physic there. He refuses to accept the real possibility that he might die. God—if I could corner the dog who did this thing to him, his life would be as worthless as a twig's."

"Do you truly believe someone in the pinnace was responsible for the Captain's injury?"

"Yes, I do. But the Captain is unsure, what with the burning match for the watch. He believes it could have well been an accident. No accident could have been more timely: in the early hours of the morning, shortly after leaving the camp of 120 enemies. It would have taken an utter fool to have caused such an accident. And if it was, why hasn't the knave owned up to his mistake? The Captain is a forgiving man."

"But are you, Lieutenant?"

The Lieutenant was silent for a long time. In the weak torchlight of the storehouse of the President's House, I could see that he was stunned by my remark.

"Tomorrow, then, I will offer a full pardon to the man responsible. That will show my good intent."

"And if no man steps forward?"

"Then I must assume that there is an assassin among us who will try his evil act again."

"When the Captain awakens, Lieutenant, would you inform him of Greene's death? I would like to attend the burial. Will you accompany me?"

"No, what is the use? Nothing on earth can bring a man back to life again and, perhaps in Green's case, nothing should. I have had my fill of funerals and church services and empty words. There is nothing important to me now but the present and how one can shape it by direct action. Being in charge is what's important to the man who wants to prosper."

I started to take my leave, but the Lieutenant stayed me for a moment. "If you know anything about the Captain's accident, I can trust you to tell me, can't I?"

"Of course, but I truly know nothing. I was asleep in the bow section of the boat, as you know. Give my deepest respects to the Captain."

"I see your injury is better."

"Yes, owing, I'm sure, to the skill of Matowas."

I returned to where Greene now lay wrapped in canvas. It had begun to rain. Several men were lowering him on to a litter. Most of the curious had left and only six of us remained to attend the services. We carried Greene out of the back side of the fort and up the small hill to the ridge not far away. The gravediggers, working by torchlight, were up to their waists shoveling wet dirt from the oblong cavity where we were to place Greene. We waited in silence, listening to the crunch of the spades piercing the earth and the low thuds as their loads of dirt were dropped beside the grave.

This seemed to me like a foolish attempt to hide our deaths from the Indians. They were out there watching, day and night. They knew of our losses. They knew we were mortal and subject to wounds and sickness. And the torchlight was bound to draw their attention, as surely as any church bell.

Perhaps there were Indians watching this night. Something disturbed the murmuring sounds of the night and set off a chorus of frogs from the swamp. They reached such a pitch that the Reverend was forced to shout in order that his service be heard above them. He was reading from the Book of Common Prayer and shouting about the resurrection on the last day, when the frogs suddenly ceased their off-key music, leaving the Reverend shouting like a man raving. It was a long while before he realized that his competitors in the swamp were silent, and then only because the Sergeant nudged him.

When the Reverend finished, we lowered Greene's pathetic body into the grave, and I shuddered when I heard it splash into water at the bottom. The Reverend concluded his service with a blessing and left for the fort while we all lent a hand shoveling and kicking the dirt back into the grave. The task was completed quickly, and we scattered the remainder of the dirt around the hill and covered the grave with branches and such things that would hide its location. Richard and I walked back to the fort with the Sergeant.

"It wasn't Greene's pistol," I said to Richard, who nodded, knowing exactly what I meant.

"Then whose was it?" the Sergeant asked.

"It belongs to our housemate. Like us, he had no idea of what was in Greene's mind."

"Yes. I know the man. Here. Return it to him."

The Sergeant withdrew Wilcox's pistol from his belt and handed it to me. The weapon felt heavy and cumbersome. I tucked it into my breeches, and it lay like a hard knot at my stomach.

"He can't be blamed for what Greene did," the Sergeant said. "You men forget about what happened here. It's over and done with. God knows what tomorrow will bring to us. Get your rest, and keep up your strength. I bid you all goodnight."

We said our goodnight to the Sergeant and returned to our house. Wilcox was sound asleep, snoring like a handsaw and stinking, as usual, of sour wine and filth. I replaced his pistol on the ledge above his bed and went to my own bed, feeling frightened and alone.

CHAPTER 13

Thank God For An Honeſt Man

R ichard was up early and had prepared the morning rations before leaving for services. Wilcox struggled to sit up. He wiped his dry, cracked lips with his tongue, reached for the wine bottle and drained it, holding the bottle straight up to catch the last drop.

"Ooh, wine is a bloody curse. May the miserable wretch who first discovered it roast on the spit of Hell."

He threw the empty bottle into a corner and got shakily to his feet.

"Ooh."

He held his head in both hands.

"The wages of sin, the wages of sin. But good Lord, a man must drink himself into oblivion or else spend his time thinking on women. That will surely drive a man to madness as quick as drink and with none of the advantages."

He picked up a flask of water next to our breakfast and drank a long time from it, gulping the water down like a man who had been parched from days in the sun. He tore the cornbread with his teeth and ate it and the fresh fruits without interest.

"That's what this colony needs, more women to curb our passion. There would be far less fighting among ourselves. More women like that little one who's going to wed your friend. Mark my words."

He stuffed his mouth with the rest of the cornbread and spit some of it out as he continued to speak.

"I'd know how to treat a woman like that. No, sir. I wouldn't waste a woman like that on praying and hymn singing and talking on books and such like. I'd have her in bed most days and every night, doing what God created her to do."

"Hold your tongue, Wilcox," I said with something more than simple anger.

"You need not tell me that you haven't thought about taking her to bed. I seen you look at her when she brings her little baskets of figs."

"They are not figs."

"Aye, but you get my meaning. I seen you look at her when she walks away, that round little bottom of hers, and knowing that scholar is going to have it all. I know what you're thinking, lad. I know what you're feeling."

"Wilcox, you don't know anything but your own filthy, sinful, greedy mind—if it can be said that you have a mind. I swear, if your pistol had a ball in it, I would use it to end your miserable life."

"My pistol, no ball?"

"Aye. Greene used it during the night to blow his brains out."

"Did he? Used my pistol without so much as asking me? The thieving swine."

Wilcox looked to the ledge. "That pious friend of yours returned it, I suppose."

"No. I returned it, knowing how much you would miss it."

"Thank God for an honest man."

Wilcox walked over to the ledge, picked up his pistol, and bounced it a few times in his hand as though to feel its weight.

"Damn me if it weren't my last ball. Could you spare me one from your pouch?"

I reached into my bullet pouch and took out the right sized ball.

"And some powder? If you don't mind, that is."

I handed him my powder pouch also and watched him reload the pistol, overcharging it with powder and wiping the residue on his breeches.

"And what, may I ask, became of poor Mr. Greene?"

"We buried him on the ridge with the others."

"You should have called me from my sleep. I would have been pleased to be of assistance."

Wilcox turned to look at Greene's bed. "He didn't leave nothing, I suppose."

"Only the clothes on his wretched back. That was all."

"And you didn't take them?"

"Steal clothes from a dead man? What kind of horrid act is that?"

"It be not stealing, lad. What use are clothes to a dead man? Good Lord, the thought of that beautiful leather jerkin and those fine boots of his rotting in the grave with him drives me near to weeping."

"If you want them that badly, then go dig him up and strip them from him."

Wilcox looked horror stricken.

"What, and violate a grave? Not this son of a whore. That'll be one sin that I shall always be innocent of. My father, God bless his damned soul, always said that to rob a grave would mark a man with the face of the dead, and that he would bear the burden of the sins of the dead all his life. Violate a grave? Lord, no. Once a man is in the ground, all that he takes with him remains there as far as concerns me . . . but I did so admire that jerkin and those boots. Still, a body wastes time fretting over broken eggs."

Wilcox finished the water.

"I must be off to services or take my punishment . . . though at times I don't know which would be worse."

I was still angry with Wilcox for his remarks about Anne, when the doctor came to visit me. He was hurried and agitated and complained of the heat. When he saw the dressing that Matowas had bound to my wound, he was furious and demanded that I remove the dressing or that he would have nothing more to do with me. His outburst frightened me at first. I could not imagine that a man of learning could be so unwilling to accept methods outside his knowledge. He did not even look at my wound but kept repeating his demand that I remove the Indian dressing and cast it into the fire.

I did not want to make an enemy of the doctor, but my wound felt much improved and I would rather he made a judgement of its condition than to behave like a jealous apprentice. I asked him if he would first examine the wound before discarding the Indian dressing. He said that he would not and stood as defiantly as a soldier on the battlements.

"I don't wish to remove the dressing until the time has passed," I said, thinking the next move on the doctor's part would be to strike me with his sword.

"Very well then, you traitorous scum. Go the way of Greene, for all that I care. You are all Turks in this place, with more need of a gravedigger than a healer. And I'll spend not one minute here longer than I have to."

I was very sorry that I had angered the doctor and felt, in spite of how I tried to reason with myself, that I was guilty of some grievous wrong.

I lay in bed for a long time worrying over it when Anne entered with her full basket of fruits. She was smiling beautifully. Her face seemed to radiate light and happiness. Lord, the mystery that draws a man to a woman is beyond comprehension. One can describe the elements of beauty to the smallest detail and yet never fully explain it. I realized that I had yearned for her visits. Being in her presence justified every act that I had done thus far. Her visits and her concern over my health had in themselves given me strength. Why this was so, I did not have the courage to admit to myself at the time, much less to speak it to another soul.

She had picked a handful of wildflowers and arranged them in an earthenware cup on the window ledge. Sunlight streamed in from the window, lacing her hair with strands of silken gold. She seemed at once too delicate, too frail, to be among such rude and masculine surroundings. But such were her angelic powers that the perennial stench which filled the air of our house vanished, and the filth and disorder left by men living together in the wilderness seemed covered by a soft, opaque veil.

She came and sat next to me in the only chair we had. It might have been a throne from the way she sat in it, with such grace and poise. She could easily have been a princess, and she was more beautiful than the proudest queen.

She talked for a long while, in her musical voice, about her former life in London where her father was a tailor, not poor but not well-off either. Her mother had been in service to a cousin of the Lady Fitzsimmons and got for her a position in the Fitzsimmons family. She told me of how the Lady Fitzsimmons had left London with no intention of settling in Virginia, but merely to appease her wandering husband, until she could steer him back to London.

She asked me why I had come, and I told her the truth, that a return to England for me would mean arrest and probably imprisonment. I had no choice but to stay, like many others who had come over with us, and dig out a place to live.

"Richard," I said, "is the only one of us who has come for the right reasons."

"Yes," she agreed, "but not for unselfish ones."

I asked what she meant, and she said that it was selfish, and possibly even blasphemous, for anyone to believe that he has been selected by God to start a new race of people, and that no matter how much she talked with him, nothing she said could disillusion him into seeing that Virginia was not a new Garden of Eden or that the Indians were not childlike innocents, waiting for Christianity.

"He refuses to see it," she said, "and I fear that there will be much trouble ahead. You are his only friend. He trusts and respects you. Could you not persuade him to take a different view?"

"One like Master Wilcox's?" I suggested.

"That horrid man!" she said, curling her top lip. "Certainly not. But surely he can be made to see that Virginia is not a poet's dream world, surely—"

"Richard has his own mind, and I'm not so sure that he isn't right. He knows what he must do to survive. He knows that he must learn to farm and to shoot. Richard's enemies are not nature or the Indians, but his own countrymen who would rob him blind at the first opportunity. If I could convince him of anything, I would caution him not to trust these men here. They are like dogs broken from their leashes. Nothing but the iron will of Captain Smith restrained them and now that they have nearly murdered him, there is virtually no law here at Jamestown."

She looked away briefly to hide her disappointment.

"Will you go ahead with the marriage?"

She nodded, and I saw tears welling up in her eyes.

She stood up, walked to the door, then turned quickly to me and said,

"Would that some other had my heart."

She darted out of the house. I stared at the space she had stood in and at the swinging door curtain and wanted to shout for her to wait, to come back, but my voice left me. I could not make it speak. I thought of getting up and going after her, but my strength failed me and I fell back on the bed, not from a weakness of the body but more a weakness of the will. For a moment I wished that the roof would fall in, or that a stray Indian arrow would find me and relieve me of this heavy burden of friendship and denial.

I had pushed all thoughts of Anne from my mind the moment Richard told me of his plans to marry her. His future in Virginia was assured, I felt, whereas I drifted without conviction or destiny, like the rest of those men who came across the ocean with us. A woman, a girl, like Anne should not bind herself to someone like me. I believed in little, not even God most of the time, regardless of how often I pleaded His name. Richard, however, believed in everything, even me.

I had tried not to think of her. Most of the time I was successful, but there were moments on the march to the mountains—when every sound, every smell, every second could have been my last—when I thought of her as a lover. I saw myself coming to her and taking her in my arms and knowing the deliciousness of her body. At such times I wanted to restrain myself. I did not want to think of her in a lustful way. She was to be my best friend's wife and thinking this way, I had been told, was the same as committing adultery. I owed some measure of loyalty to Richard for protecting me in Plymouth, and for bringing me here for a new start. My visions of Anne and I, coupled in a lover's embrace, would inevitably fade away, and the terrible dangers of the night would return.

Now, practically on the eve of her marriage, she had revealed herself to me. Now, when it was too late for both of us. I still thought of going after her, but that would serve no real end. If she had wanted the situation other than what it was, she would not have consented to marry Richard. She would have, at least, made him wait a little longer.

The wound in my thigh was beginning to throb with pain. I did not care. I wanted it to hurt. I wanted it to hurt so much that it would totally possess my mind. I wanted only to think about the pain.

CHAPTER 14

Dissension

The next day Matowas returned with the Lieutenant. The Indian was stone-faced and spoke little. He removed the dressing and examined the wound, his fingers poking the still-tender places. He grunted a few times. Then he stood up beside the Lieutenant.

"Some white men have the flesh of the devil. We will leave it to heal in the air. There is no sign of the white death, no blood, no odor of death. He will live."

He spoke these words to the Lieutenant and, after having said them, he departed without a single glance in my direction.

"What is the matter with him?" I asked the Lieutenant. "Why did he say a thing like that?"

"It was, strangely, a compliment. You see, these Powhatans worship the devil as their most powerful god. From their point of view, it makes sense to try to please the god who can hurt you the most. They don't waste much time praying to a good and benevolent god as we Christians do. They believe that their benevolent god will always do good by them, regardless, so why bother? It's the bad ones they most fear and respect."

"That is why they respect Captain Smith?"

The Lieutenant nodded. "They see him command men and guns that can do much damage. Therefore, they think he has great influence with our devil god. They know him to be a powerful werowance and when they captured him in the

Chickahominy River not one arrow caused him harm, though there were as many as seven hundred Indians in that hunting party. After that, they believed him to have supernatural powers, and his life was spared until he was taken before Powhatan. That great werowance is a very clever man who holds onto his kingdom by force and superstition. He saw a rival in the Captain and was determined to have him murdered. It would prove his power over the white man's god."

"Why did he fail?"

"Powhatan's daughter, Matoaka, whom the Indians tell us is named Pocahontas, offered her life for his and she, too, is believed by the Indians, a notion strongly encouraged by Powhatan, to have the gift of spiritual vision. They refrained from killing the Captain, believing now that Matoaka saw his partial divinity and, by placing her own head on the Captain's, did save the entire kingdom of Powhatan from destruction by their Okee."

"If the Captain then dies or leaves for England, the Indians will think that we are unprotected."

"I believe so, unless we can convince them that one of our new leaders has supernatural powers. And, judging by the candidates, there is many a devil worshiper to choose from."

"Why was Matowas angry?" I asked.

The Lieutenant laughed softly.

"He and the doctor got into a quarrel at the Captain's residence. The Captain ordered them to cease, whereupon the doctor said that if he was going to take the advice of a savage as equal with his, then his services were no longer needed and he would return to England on the first ship. The Captain told him to get out if he could not show more respect for Matowas. The doctor wheeled around and, with a look of the lowest contempt at Matowas, left the Captain's residence. I imagine the doctor is, at this very moment, gathering up his saws, hammers, and potions in preparation for an immediate departure from here."

"That's unfortunate," I said. "We have need of a doctor more than any place in England. Is there no persuading him to remain?"

The Lieutenant shook his head.

"I don't believe so. I think he has decided that there is far more profit to be gained by treating the colic and gout of the overfed rich than there is in speculating for land in the wilderness of Virginia. Still, I will try to dissuade him from going."

A strong desire came over me to get out of my bed and to do what I could to rejoin the world of living men again. My wound no longer hurt as much as it had. My back and side were sore and stiff from lying on crushed hay. I rose to a sitting position. Then, after a few deep breaths, I stood up. My undamaged hip could easily bear my weight. I walked around our little mud house. Most of the stiffness had gone from my wound, so that I walked now with only a slight limp.

"Lieutenant," I said, "I want to return to my work here, today."

"Perhaps you had better wait another day or so."

"No, I feel strong. I know I can do my share."

The Lieutenant bit his lower lip.

"I don't deny that we can use your skills. There are new houses to be built outside of the fort, more land—endless land—to be cleared. I must stay here with the Captain and carry out the instructions he has given me for maintenance of the fort, but I can take you to the works now being done outside. I think it's the true beginning of our permanent Jamestown."

I walked with the Lieutenant across the dusty, hard-packed earth of the fort, exceedingly happy at hearing the metallic clanking from the blacksmith's shop and feeling the invisible stream of heat from his forge. There was the ever-present smell of men and burning wood outside the riverfront gate. We walked across the firing range to where the new dwellings were being built. They were much more substantial buildings than those already in the fort. They had heavier timbers for framing and clapboard for siding instead of our crumbly mud plaster.

The Lieutenant suggested that we might consider the construction of wood shingles from the abundance of cypress trees now being taken from the swamp.

"When peace has been achieved with the Indians, I might consider going into the mountains again and open a mine for roofing slate. There is going to be a great outcry for construction materials in the years to come, and it would be wise to obtain a proper grant for those lands in the west likely to bear slate and timber. It would be a long-term prospect, and none of the men here are interested in long-term profits. They consider the land worthless unless gold can be found on it. If I ask for a grant of that mountain land, surely the men will think that we lied about the absence of gold, if they don't believe that already. You could do it, Matthew, without angering anyone. Have the grant exclude all rights to gold or silver."

I must have looked doubtful, for the Lieutenant said quickly, "Think on it then. It may be a chance for future prosperity when the colony is firmly established."

The Lieutenant's suggestion for my future prosperity sounded grand indeed, but I wondered why he had not pursued this himself.

"I am first a soldier," he said, after I had asked him. "To settle down here would put an end to my occupation. Soldiers such as the Captain and I can never remain in one place for long. We take our employment because someone is in need of our skills, and when that job is done we move happily on to where we are needed. I have seen enough of these merchants to know their ways. My own father was a grain merchant in London, and I decided early that it was not the life for me.

"One day Virginia will become as settled and tame as England itself. Then the lawyers and merchants will take over. Men like the Captain and I will become useless and feared. Those of us who have not found new employment in some wild and distant land will be fettered and chained by those people we helped to prosper. You see, we soldiers do not make the world what it is. We are only the instrument of those who do, and when our utility is over, we are put away like all other tools. Yet, I do not loathe those fat, soft, devious swine who employ us to do their unclean work, and then, when they are safe, parade about in fine clothes and think of themselves as just and honorable men."

The Lieutenant showed me the partially cleared site of a new dwelling. I, along with two helpers, was to clear the lot and estimate and issue a request to the store master for the materials that would be needed. It seemed like a simple task. The house was to be built like the one next to it, with rooms and allowances for future additions. The occupants would dig their own well and lay out their stock pens the way they wished. The Lieutenant explained there were to be streets, and a common grazing pasture behind the lot.

My two helpers were young men about my own age who had come from the weaver's trade in London. Their gnarled and scarred hands showed their new labor. Their bodies were as frail as street waifs. One, John, had a continual cough and his eyes were streaked with blood vessels. The other man, Frazer, was a redheaded, wiry Scot, with no discernible trade except a gift for talking. Both said that they had seen me working in timber when we first arrived but had heard that I had died by my own hand. I said that, as they could see, I was very much alive and that it was a man who had returned with me from the mountains who had died in such a manner.

They asked if I had ever built a house before and I said that, as an apprentice carpenter, I had built many such constructions, some of which were near to being palaces. In truth, most of my work for Mr. Dorn had been simple repairs, and I had never stayed long enough on one job to see the finished construction. But these men seemed disposed to challenge my position and neither one of them looked fit enough to swing a hammer, much less to strike the nail. I thought that my small expansion of the truth would be a harmless way of preventing future conflicts.

Most of the large trees had been taken away, leaving the stumps and smaller trees and brush. We started clearing the smaller trees first and found it an easy enough job. The brush we also easily chopped down. The larger tree stumps gave us the greatest difficulty. It would be winter before all of them could be cleared sufficiently to build a house.

I knew that horses had been shipped with us out of England. I did not know the number, although I had heard that as many as twenty had completed the voyage. I had seen six of them myself but, as to the others, I had no knowledge. Just two of those horses would be sufficient to pull all the stumps from our lot in less than a week's time. I, therefore, resolved that we would have them and, straight away, took myself to the Lieutenant who, upon hearing my request, took me straight to Sir Percy, then acting in the President's name.

"No!" Sir Percy thundered. "Those horses are not common work animals. They belong to various gentlemen here, who must use them for hunting game to supply our people and for the hunting down of Indians near the fort."

"The meat," Lieutenant Webster reminded Sir Percy, "is

supplied through barter with the Indians. If the gentlemen who claimed the horses killed any game, they kept it for themselves. We at the fort have seen none of it. And our object here, as written in the charter, is to make peace with the Indians, not to hunt them down for sport."

Sir Percy was red-faced. He jumped up out of his seat, his beard trembling down to the tip end.

"More talk such as that, and I'll have you shot for mutiny."

The Lieutenant wheeled around on his heels and stomped out of Sir Percy's residence. I followed, feeling that my intention of using the horses had little chance of success.

Outside, the Lieutenant headed straight for the store house where the arms were kept, and ordered the guard there to summon ten of his men, including Sergeant Johnson, and bring them to the store house with all haste. The Lieutenant then handed me a loaded pistol from the arms store, and put on his armor and burgonet. He took out his sword, examined the shiny blade, and slid it back into its sheath.

"Confound it. It's time something was done about these unruly dogs masquerading as gentlemen. It's time for a good thrashing, and that is what is now required."

I could see some of the soldiers jumping from the ramparts of the fort and running, holding their muskets in front of them, toward the arms store house. They assembled in front of the Lieutenant without undue clamor or questions, in ranks of five. The Lieutenant ordered them to face left and to follow him.

We marched in good order, the Lieutenant at the head of his troops, and me beside him, to where a temporary stable had been constructed to house the animals outside of the fort. The Lieutenant positioned his men on either side of the stable and told me to pick the two horses I thought would be best for the task.

I went into the stable with noticeable hesitancy and selected two of the strongest stallions. I untied them and led them out into the open. A number of gentlemen had noticed our action in the fort and had followed us at a distance to see what we were about. When they saw us stop at their crude stable and saw me go in, they rushed headlong to where we were. When I came out, leading the horses by their bridles, five or six of these gentlemen had assembled in front of the Lieutenant's men and angrily demanded to know what we were doing.

The Lieutenant quickly addressed them. "As military commander here, I am requisitioning these horses for work in the field. It is within my authority to do so. You gentlemen have enjoyed the use of these animals long enough, and to the disadvantage of the colony. They are now to be used for the general good of all the people. You gentlemen will have to take your pleasure elsewhere."

"Goddamn if we will," one of the gentlemen shouted while drawing his sword.

He was close enough to the Lieutenant to make a quick lunge before the Lieutenant could adequately defend himself. The gentleman's sword struck the Lieutenant's breastplate and glanced off. The Lieutenant then knocked the gentleman away with the back of his arm and drew his sword.

I heard ten musket cocks snap into firing position. The other gentlemen had made a move for their swords, but the soldiers checked their intention and held them frozen at the end of their musket barrels.

The gentleman and the Lieutenant circled one another like two fighting cocks, the red feather in the gentleman's cap fluttering in the breeze, the sun glowing dully from the lieutenant's armor. They circled and circled, kicking up a thin layer of dust. Then the gentleman feinted to the lower part of the

Lieutenant's body and lunged for the upper. The Lieutenant parried and returned the attack, but his thrust was parried, and he narrowly escaped the gentleman's counterattack by leaping to the side.

They parried and thrust at each other for a few minutes, each trying to probe for the other's weakness. I saw what the Lieutenant was trying for. The gentleman was slow parrying attacks to his upper right torso. The Lieutenant concentrated his attacks on the low quarters, forcing the gentleman to parry furiously to protect himself. It was a sickening sound to hear the swords cut the air, singing like whips, then clang angrily together. I wondered how even the best steel could stand such punishment—*whip, clang, whip, clang,* on and on.

I gradually realized that no one else was making a sound, no cheers from the men standing around, no shouts of encouragement. Men were lined up along the palisades, watching the fight through gaps at the pointed ends. Their faces showed that they were not enjoying this spectacle. They were concerned, and some were even frightened, that this fight would determine who ruled in the colony. This was a fight between one class and another, between old England and new Virginia.

The gentleman was a good swordsman, better than the Lieutenant. He fought with a style learned in the best fencing schools in Europe, whereas the Lieutenant was army trained. What he lacked in style he oversupplied with untiring ferocity and an anger that seemed to come from deep within him. The gentleman had finesse and confidence, but not the Lieutenant's stamina or his depth of feeling. Soon the Lieutenant had him backed against the fort's palisades.

The gentleman was breathing hard and, for the first time since the fight started, he looked frightened. The Lieutenant lured the gentleman into his trap by lunging low and feinting to attack a high quarter. His feint to the upper quarter was deliberately high. The gentleman parried slow and mild, carrying his sword blade too high. Then the Lieutenant quickly, almost imperceptibly, brought his blade around in a double feint and lunged home, piercing completely through the gentleman's body and into the wood palisade.

The gentleman looked astonished for a moment, as though he could not truly believe what had happened. Then a look of pain came on his face, such as I have only seen Indians bring to their victims.

The Lieutenant withdrew his sword with a jerk and stepped back, still holding the sword but lowering the bloody point to the ground. The gentleman's eyes rolled back, and with a long exhaling of his breath, he slid down to the ground, dead. The Lieutenant stood motionless for a while, then he whirled around to face the other gentlemen who, by this time, had stepped back farther from the soldiers. The Lieutenant rushed at them and stopped in front of his men. His face was distorted in an inhuman rage.

"Which one of you gentlemen wants to challenge me or the authority of Captain Smith now? You have all plotted against him since the infamous day you arrived here. You have scorned and ridiculed the laws that we have all prospered by. I will tell it to you again, gentlemen. He who does not work will not eat. You have lived off the good labor of the common folk for too long now and, by God's blood, you will work side by side with them or you will starve. Here, gentlemen, all men are equal in life as well as in death, so get you gone to your houses where I will come for you to work, or I will litter the ground with your opulent corpses."

The gentlemen looked at the Lieutenant with intense, almost

explosive, hatred, but none made a move against him. They all backed away a few steps and walked hurriedly back into the fort. The Lieutenant watched them until they all had re-entered the fort. Then he wiped the blood from his sword blade with a handful of grass and re-sheathed it. He ordered two of the soldiers to bury the dead man where he had fallen and then return to their posts. He turned to me.

"Matthew," he said, "we will distribute these horses where they are needed most. That will be your responsibility and see to it that they do only the work for which they belong. As of now, these animals are the property of the government and will be used only for the betterment of the people in our colony."

Two of the soldiers and I led the horses out of the stable. Guarded on each side by the rest of the soldiers, we went into the fort where the Lieutenant wrote a general announcement, saying that all those working men who required the use of horses were to come and see him and so state their need. He nailed this document onto the notice board, among a throng of people, and returned to his men, dismissing all of them except those holding their horses. He commanded them to stay with their charge and wait for him beside the President's House.

"Walk with me over to the blacksmiths, where the gentlemen deposited the harnesses that came with these animals. You can pick out the most suitable ones."

I thanked the Lieutenant and waited, knowing by the agitation on his face that he wished to say more.

"I have known about these horses for a long time."

His voice was apologetic.

"Because of my other duties I could not see to their proper use. With hundreds of mouths to feed, descending on us without warning, the disposition of six horses became a minor concern."

We led my two horses, tugging gently on their bridles, to the blacksmith's shop. The Lieutenant spoke briefly with the blacksmith, who subsequently fetched down two sturdy harnesses from pegs in the wall of his workplace. While the Lieutenant and I held the horses steady, he fitted them around the horses' necks, tying in the reins and pointing out to me the details of the various pads, eyes, and rings to be used.

When this was done, the Lieutenant thanked him generously and told him that the others would be coming to be fitted for whatever work they were to do, and that no horse was to be attended without his first seeing a signed authorization from him or Captain Smith. The blacksmith said that he understood and that the Lieutenant could count on him for support in his worthy endeavors.

The Lieutenant accompanied me and the two horses to the gate.

"I fear that what happened outside those wooden walls this afternoon is only the beginning of a most unfortunate civil strife. These so-called gentlemen are a proud, haughty lot. They have already tried to murder the Captain twice, once with the powder blast and just a few days ago with a paid assassin."

I was genuinely shocked. "I heard nothing about it," I said.

"You were still in your sick bed. I saw no reason to trouble you with that unhappy news."

"Who was it?"

"The Captain has refused to name the man, even to me, saying that he has forgiven him and that he wished to forget the incident. The Captain is the most noble man among us. Not a single one of these greedy dogs is capable of taking his place."

"What happened? How did the Captain escape? He is hardly able to move."

"The cowardly would-be assassin lost what little courage he

had when he came face to face with the Captain and could not bring himself to pull the trigger of his pistol."

"The Captain is going to spare the man?"

"Aye. Our Captain is a good man, a saintly man. These ingrates will see the day that they sorely miss him. Now take your horses. Do the work you must do with them and return them to me at the end of the day. If a gentleman comes and takes your horses, you are to come to me straight away and tell me of it. Don't try to resist him yourself. Those indolent exploiters of human efforts are well trained in the use of all weapons and would take it as their duty to murder a working man who would dare to defy them."

I told the Lieutenant that I would do as he instructed and took my leave of him. I led the horses outside the fort and along the wall, in the direction of our working site. I thought much about the Lieutenant on the way and was much puzzled. Some new and frightful force had taken charge of him. A long-buried hatred had released itself and had taken over his actions, pushing him beyond the restraints of his military duties. It was as though he was avenging a past wrong done to him, perhaps by a gentleman. But, as I told myself, he was right. The horses were needed for the necessary work of the colony and not for the pleasure of a few gentlemen. The Lieutenant had been right to take them but, as to killing a man over them, that seemed to me unnecessary.

I thought that had the Lieutenant spared the life of the gentleman, he might have won their respect with his show of mercy rather than solidify their resolve for fighting and revenge. I was worried, worried that the offended gentlemen would come and take my horses. I would be bound then to do as the Lieutenant had asked me. I feared great trouble from this and wanted to be no part of it.

CHAPTER 15

Sound The Alarm

The horses proved to be the quantity of labor that we needed. Our work progressed much faster after we had hitched them together and learned the proper use of them. We discovered that much of the dirt had to be cleared from around the tree stump first. Then a chain was threaded through several of the exposed roots and tied to the horse team with ropes. Two men, using strong poles to act as levers under the stump, and the horses pulling, would pry the stump out of the ground as cleanly as a barber would pull a tooth.

Using this method, we cleared our lot in half the time it would have taken us without the animals. Once our lot was cleared, we had to give up our team to those whose work lagged behind, and we moved on to another lot.

One of the men suggested that we clear the land the way the Indians did, with fire, and see to it that the stumps burned down into the ground. This was a good method, but it could only be used on land that could not be reclaimed until the next year or even two years hence. The colony needed cleared land in workable order, within weeks.

Another of our working men suggested that we use the cattle for this work, as well as horses. Serious consideration was given, but this notion was quickly dispensed with the cattle being more valuable for food production than for use as laboring animals.

It was toward the end of the week. I could hardly feel the presence of my wound anymore. We had just started to raise the timbers of the first house that we were building when the alarm sounded. Every man dropped his work, picked up his musket, and started running for the fort. I ran, hopping over logs and holes in the newly cleared lots, down the rows of one of our corn fields, all the while expecting an arrow to go singing past my ear.

I reached the gate with the others, and together we all poured back into the fort like a swift-moving human stream. I found Richard in our house, looking in vain for his musket. Anne stood in the corner, wringing her small hands. Her eyes pleaded for help, and there was an unmistakable joy in them when she saw me.

"Captain West's fort has been attacked by Powhatan's men in considerable strength, so I hear," Richard explained. "Some of his men who escaped have already arrived. They tell of unbelievable murders done by all the Indians. I'll wager, however, that the unfortunate savages were well provoked. I have not been deaf to the stories coming from that place. You said yourself that our men there used the Indians quite badly and that Captain Smith was unable to correct them."

"Then why has the alarm been sounded?"

"Someone here, an influential member of the council, fears a like attack, I suppose."

Wilcox ran into the house, cherry-faced, puffing his wine-smelling breath like an overheated bull, his clothes spotted with dark sweat.

"You've brought this down upon us, you goddamn Indian maven. Telling that painted savage in the jail all about us. Now that the devils think Captain Smith is dead, they are going to swarm over us like a horde of red ants, and it's all because of you!"

Wilcox pointed a shaking finger at Richard. A drop of thick saliva fell from his wet lower lip.

"And how in God's name could Tatahcoope tell his Indian brethren anything when he knows nothing of our situation, and he also knows that the Captain is alive? How could he speak to them, locked tight in prison as he is?"

It was the first time that I had heard Richard raise his voice in anger.

"They have ways, secret devilish ways, completely unknown to white men. But I, myself, have heard them speak to one another in all manner of bird calls, and they can see in the dark as well as any cat and can hear a twig snap for miles off."

"That's a confounded lie, you drunkard!" Richard shouted, getting to his feet.

Wilcox smiled, his watery eyes sparkled with glee.

"I suggest, sir," Richard said, gaining more control of himself, "that if the Indians attack us, it will be for the many wrongs that they have suffered at our hands. And if they use guns and powder against us, it will be those that you have stolen from us and sold to them to buy your accursed drink."

I readied my pistol. Wilcox saw it and eased his hand away from his dagger.

"I tell you, Mr. Scott, that if you are willing to step outside the fort and say those things to me, I will show you the worth of them with my sword," Wilcox said.

"The truth is not decided by a senseless duel, Mr. Wilcox. The truth stands by itself, forever. Every man here knows that you are a drunkard and a thief, but I know that you have been selling arms to the Indians," Richard protested.

I pulled back the cock on my pistol. The sound caused everyone in the house to wince.

"There is no way you can prove a charge like that, my lad," Wilcox said.

"I have seen you with my own eyes," Richard answered.

"Aye, you and who else? One of your Indian friends? Who's going to believe you? You've got to have more proof than the word of a savage."

Wilcox looked at Anne, who shuddered at the sight of him, then said, "You'd best take care of your future husband, ma'am, for he shan't have Master Matthew around to protect him always."

After an angry glance at me, Wilcox turned and left.

"Perhaps this time you went too far," Anne said.

"Did you truly see Wilcox selling arms to the Indians?" I asked Richard.

"Yes."

"How?"

"That is my concern, Matthew. When I am ready to expose him, I will do so."

"Supplying arms to the Indians is the concern of everyone in the settlement. The offense is punishable by death, you know."

"I know, Matthew. Either he stops his infamous dealings in arms, or I will present my charges against him and back them up with irrefutable proof."

"In the meantime, Richard, take care he does not shoot you in the back first. Stay here with Anne. Take my pistol. Wilcox will not return until the cause of the alarm has ended."

I readied my musket and ran back to the center of the fort, pushing my way through other hurrying men, to the Lieutenant's quarters. I was told that he had taken charge of the men on the palisades. I ran, holding my musket in front of me, up to the north bulwark where I knew the Lieutenant usually stationed himself.

The cannoneers were ready with flaming torches. The aimers had wedged their guns to fire over the block house. The Lieutenant nodded to me, then resumed his careful watch, scanning his keen eyes back and forth across the edge of the woods. All was quiet except for the muffled sounds of tramping feet and metal armor inside the fort walls. We waited, each man at his place, fingering his weapon, caressing it as tenderly as a precious lover.

The Lieutenant was about ready to call off the alarm and dismiss his men when shooting erupted in the forest to the north. I could hear distant screams and the unmistakable yells of the Indians. Our man posted in the block house leaped out into the pathway and started running for the fort. In a few minutes a group of our men ran from the woods, followed closely by yelling Indians, swinging clubs and hatchets. The Lieutenant ordered the cannons to be fired.

The sound was deafening and, for a while, the discharge of the cannon hid the whole scene before us in thick, billowing smoke. The smoke thinned, and through it, we could see our men still running toward us. The Indians were lying facedown on the ground. A great cheer went up from the men on the palisades, followed by many shouts, urging our men outside not to stop their dash for the fort.

The Lieutenant, knowing that the Indians were not hurt by the cannons but only lying down as was their defensive custom to escape our fire, ordered us to fire at the Indians lying on the ground. Several volleys of small shot were immediately begun. The bullets peppered the ground all around the Indians. Most of them jumped up and ran with all speed back to the protection of the woods. Two, however, lay motionless on the ground where they had fallen. The Lieutenant ordered us to continue firing into the woods for several minutes.

The gates to the fort were swung open and the flying men ran into the welcoming arms of the cheering, shouting people below on the fort grounds. They were some of the last stragglers from West's fort who had taken an overland course from the falls. There had originally been twelve in their party, but only five reached the fort in safety.

Once the men were inside, the Lieutenant ordered the firing to cease and a small company of those near him, including me, to come with him to where the Indians lay. We ran in double file, our muskets ready to be used, until we reached the Indians. The Lieutenant ordered half of our small company to go into the woods and pursue the Indians as far as the creek. If they encountered them, our men were to make all efforts to capture as many as possible. The men plunged into the woods, yelling like the Indians themselves, and soon disappeared into the dark interior of the forest.

The rest of us surrounded the two Indians on the ground. Both appeared to be mortally wounded, with bullet marks in their backs and much blood running onto the dusty ground. The Lieutenant nudged both with the barrel of his musket. One was clearly dead, but the other moaned and grabbed at the dirt with his hands. The Lieutenant turned him over gently. The man's face was twisted with pain. He said something in the Powhatan language that I could not fully understand, then exhaled and let his essence drift from his body. The Lieutenant looked at me for its meaning. I said that I did not know what he had meant, only that he had mentioned his werowance's name and a word that I did not know.

"Was he calling on his god?" one of the soldiers asked.

"It doesn't matter now what he was doing," the Lieutenant

said. "Take the rest of the men and bury these bodies in the swamp. Take the guns and powder from them, and any soldier who takes a scalp will be put in the stocks for a day and a night."

The Lieutenant and I waited as the soldiers removed the bodies of the dead Indians.

"Once they learn to use our guns, the colony is lost," he said. "Our supplies are running out. At the rate we are consuming them, there will be nothing left in three or four months. When Captain Smith leaves, we can expect no trade with the Indians. Our crops are not enough to feed us through the winter. We are forced to depend on supplies from home. All the Indians need do is capture the fort at Point Comfort and, if they know how to use the cannon, they can command the whole entrance of our river. Not a ship could pass there in daylight, and the river's shoals would prevent them from doing so at night. I am going to take a company and leave for Point Comfort within the hour to reinforce it."

I must have looked expectant, for the Lieutenant quickly added, "I am sorry, Matthew. I would like for you to come with us, but your skills are needed here more than ever. We must build strong houses for the winter. We want our people to live here and prosper, don't we?"

The men who had gone in pursuit of the Indians came out of the woods, trudging under the weight of their armor and weapons.

"We went after them as far as the creek, as you ordered, sir," said a sweaty, bearded sergeant. "But we did not see a sign of their presence, not even a footprint. We listened for them, but there weren't a sound. They vanished just as if they had been ghosts."

"Nonsense, Sergeant. They are there. It is hard to see in

these thick forests. There was probably a savage behind every tree."

"Sir," the Sergeant protested, "I swear to you on Christ's tomb that we saw and heard nothing."

"Nevertheless, Sergeant, keep on the alert. Now take your men and go to the swamp over there."

The Lieutenant pointed to the direction where the Indian bodies were taken.

"Guard well the men working there. When the tasks have been completed, return to your posts at the fort in good order."

The Sergeant saluted in the French manner and led his men toward the marsh. The Lieutenant and I walked back to the fort along the narrow causeway connecting our teardrop of land with the mainland of Virginia. It seemed like a narrow thread, ready to break under the slightest strain.

Muddy river water lapped steadily at the coarse sandy shore near where we walked. The sun glared white hot from its surface, even though it was now late afternoon. The Lieutenant stopped and looked out across the river to the distant opposite shore. He took several deep breaths.

"The air is sweet here," he said.

Breathing deeply, I agreed.

"I am always amazed at the vastness of this land. It is impossible for me to imagine it; not like England or Holland, which are small, confining places. Here there is much good for our English people, and more land than the Indians could ever use."

We walked on.

"The Captain has asked me to stay after he departs and see to the correct application of military discipline here."

"Will you?" I asked.

The Lieutenant nodded. "I must stay and see this task completed."

Once in the fort, the Lieutenant took his leave of me and I went straight to our house. Richard was sitting on the floor, reading the Latin poems of Virgil to Anne, who was seated in the chair, looking very weary. Richard jumped up as I entered. He wanted to know what had happened. I told him about the men from West's fort and the Indian attack.

"Aye, they were a sad lot, those men," Richard said, "half-starved and cut all over from their flight through the woods. We went out to greet them with the others."

"What do they say?"

"They blame Captain Smith for not staying to protect them. They have charged him with desertion and treason. There are men on the council who would welcome those charges against him."

"The damned scoundrels. I wish to God we had let the Indians have them. Once the Lieutenant has gone, nothing will stop them from murdering the Captain in his sick bed."

I left quickly to find the Lieutenant. My first assumption was correct. He was coming from the President's House where he had gone to seek permission for his march to Point Comfort. He turned toward the storehouse.

I called to him and he stopped. I ran up to him and, taking him by the arm, walked with him to the storehouse. I told him what Richard had said and suggested that for him to leave now would endanger the Captain and all of his loyal friends.

The Lieutenant stopped, his brow wrinkled in thought.

"I wasn't aware of this. I thought that men who had been pulled from under a falling ax would show more gratitude, but the entrance to the river must be protected."

"Sergeant Johnson seems a capable man."

"Aye, that he is, but . . . " The Lieutenant was silent while we walked the rest of the way to the storehouse.

He handed the store manager the requisition order, signed by Captain Smith, for twenty pounds of powder and a thousand rounds of shot, twenty pounds of lead and a hundred rounds of demi-culverin shot. The manager looked with unbelieving astonishment at this order. He reread it and twice examined the signature.

"You know, sir, that this request will deplete our present store of munitions by one quarter."

The Lieutenant's eyes flashed. His hand tightened on his sword pommel.

"Unless you want to see your supplies cut off altogether, then you had better have that order prepared within the hour," he said.

The clerk looked at the order again, nodded slightly to the Lieutenant, and disappeared back into the storehouse.

"Come," the Lieutenant said. "Let's see to the pinnace."

We walked down to where the ships were tied close to the shore. The pinnace in which we had returned from the falls was riding quietly at her mooring. We walked over the bending planks connecting the little ship to the land and went aboard.

The Lieutenant ignored the usual foul smell from the bilges and started to examine the condition of the vessel. There was some evidence of rot in the hull planking. All of the cordage for rigging was severely weakened. The mast and yard were lined with a multitude of cracks.

The Lieutenant shook his head. "God, how things decay in this climate. But she'll have to do."

We returned ashore and, before reaching the fort, met with a Captain Edwards of the ship *Virtue*. The Lieutenant told him of his need to move a detachment of his soldiers to the fort at Point Comfort and asked him for cordage to replace that which was rotted in the pinnace.

Captain Edwards laughed and said that we could have all the cordage we wanted, for the right price. His instruction from the owners was to show profit, and he could not afford the luxury of being generous.

The Lieutenant, instead of going for his sword as I thought he might, looked unaffected by the Captain's response. He further explained to Captain Edwards that if his men failed to reach Point Comfort in time because of damage to their pinnace, no ship would be able to pass to or from the bay.

Captain Edwards shook his head and said, in a much kinder tone, that he hardly had enough ship supplies to maintain his own vessel, and that he had to account to London for every foot of cordage used, every yard of sail, every crumb of bread. Even then his owners would not be satisfied with their profit.

"Many of these ships' owners are themselves investors in the London Company. Before my departure, they were speaking strongly of withdrawing their support, owing to the small returns from here and the tales of death and hardship from those returning from this place.

"You would do well," the Captain added, "to abandon this infectious swamp. God's blood! I don't believe even a bastard Spaniard could survive here."

The Lieutenant thanked the Captain for his advice and the time he took with us, and we went on our way to the fort. Just inside the gate we met with Captain Ratcliffe, who was hurrying to intercept us. He demanded to know where the Lieutenant had obtained the authority to move twenty soldiers to Point Comfort and to withdraw such a large quantity of supplies from the storehouse.

The Lieutenant showed him the authorization signed by Captain Smith. Ratcliffe looked it over quickly and, tearing it in half, threw it back at the Lieutenant.

"You dog, Captain Smith is a dead man. He has no more power here."

"He is not dead yet!" the Lieutenant replied in a loud voice.

I thought that the next move would be for their weapons, but Captain Ratcliffe drew back, suddenly realizing the danger of the situation. His face relaxed, his small, moist eyes revealed his nervousness.

"Lieutenant," he said in a much softer voice. "I should be the one to command these men. I have more experience in this country than the Sergeant you have placed in charge. I am the person most likely to lead them, and by virtue of my rank—"

"I will bring your request to the attention of Captain Smith," the Lieutenant said, cutting him short.

Ratcliffe's round, boyish face flushed. A wave of anger passed over it. He turned and left for his quarters.

"That man is too foolish to be a coward and too simple to lead men in battle. But nevertheless, I will ask the Captain about him," the Lieutenant said.

CHAPTER 16

Holy Wedlock

I t was the day of Richard's and Anne's wedding, one of those rare, bright summer days as can only be had in Virginia. The wind blew cool but gently from the north. The sky was washed clean and blue. Leaves fairly sparkled in the sunlight. On such a day, could anything evil happen?

Everyone not on watch in the fort or on the ships attended. It seemed a happy ceremony from the first. Everyone wore their finest, brightest clothes. The minister strode in among the guests with an air of pride and importance. He greeted everyone as though they were one of his lost sheep. Even the Captain attended, brought in his litter by the Lieutenant and three of his soldiers, and placed beside the first row of benches.

I was asked to stand with Richard since Sir Walter Fitzsimmons had asked to offer the bride in marriage. Even Wilcox arrived at the service and was among those, much to the approving eye of the minister, who were sober and sitting in the church. Lady Fitzsimmons, sitting in the front bench, seemed most distressed from the lack of a cushion. Those gentlemen who attended sat beside and behind her. They presented themselves, very austere and proper.

Richard stood beside me, happy and unusually tranquil. Anne came into the church accompanied by Sir Fitzsimmons and the slightly off-key music of our choir.

Anne looked at me once during the entire ceremony and, for one terrible moment, I fought with the insane desire to take her by the hand and rush out of the church with her. Had we been in England I might have done something foolish—perhaps not—but the temptation would have been harder to resist.

Anne made a very beautiful bride in one of Lady Fitzsimmons's gowns and, in spite of the heat, there wasn't a trace of perspiration on her face. She looked at me only that one time before the ceremony and our eyes never met again until the vows had been spoken and she turned to leave the church. Then it was only a glance, but it nearly stopped my heart.

Richard and Anne left the church amid the shouts and cheers of all those present. Music was played with military trumpets and drums. Cider and beer were poured liberally from the stock of newly arrived stores in the *Virtue*. Five pigs had been roasted over open fires and there were sweet cakes and fruits, pies of all kinds, slices of venison and turkeys. It was a feast such as no one in the colony had seen before.

Watching Richard's graceful, easy manner with the guests, seeing the abundance and how easily the few Indians, including Tatahcoope, mingled with the people in friendship and happiness, I began to believe that the meek would conquer the earth, that this was Richard's new and glorious beginning for humanity.

An inexplicable delirium came over me. I felt I had escaped a great crisis. I seemed as light as a hawk circling overhead. The terrors of the forest became insignificant. My past life in England was only a partially remembered dream.

I ate until I could hold no more. I drank and drank and drank, feeding this euphoria until I began to feel as invincible as Ulysses, as mighty as a god of Olympus. And throughout this debauchery, my desire for Anne seemed to reach into the very heights of the heavens. I wanted to shout her name to the sun, to every star in the night sky. Somehow, I restrained myself. She was now another man's wife and, to a considerable degree, the hope of the colony.

The revelry continued until sunset, by which time many of the men had passed out from the heat and overindulgence, and they were left where they had fallen. The center of the fort looked like a battleground with bodies strewn around in various grotesque ways. Some had thrown up the contents of their stomachs beside themselves. Others lay as if truly dead, with pale faces and shallow breaths, hardly perceptible from a distance.

I remember stumbling toward our house but recall nothing until the next morning. It was the Sabbath. The Lieutenant pushed open our door, letting in an explosion of white sunlight.

"Get up," the Lieutenant said. "The wages of sin is wishing you were dead."

I looked over at Wilcox's bed. It had not been slept in. I wondered, briefly, if Wilcox had survived the night.

"Time for services," the Lieutenant's voice boomed in the center of my head. And there is a new difficulty."

"Oh?" I asked, getting wearily to my feet and gulping from our water cast.

"The good Captain Edwards, who was so generous with his spirits at our wedding feast, weighed anchor at first light this morning and is now well on his way to the open sea."

"So, why should that be of importance to us?" I gulped more water until it ran down my chin onto my wrinkled shirt.

"The gentleman who offloaded the cargo and supervised its storage in the storehouse did not bother to examine its contents. And good Captain Edwards, not wishing to arouse suspicion by making a hasty departure, remained for the wedding and used his wine to render every man in the fort useless. He then took his leave."

"Yes, you've said so. I fail to see the harm in it."

"I looked at our new supplies brought by Captain Edwards and discovered that half of the grain is processed flour, already old when it left the dock in London. And now it is a comfortable home for thousands of worms the size of your trigger finger, not to mention the rats that greeted me when I opened the sacks of raw grain, which are half filled with pebbles harder than the head of a nail. The best wine and beer were served at the wedding while the other was put into the storehouse and is decidedly sour. I see now why he would not let us have cordage for our men to use in their journey to Point Comfort. There is hardly a strand that is not rotten and that is also true for the sail cloth. The weapons are rusted, and the gunpowder is of an inferior quality. The only items not worthless are the hats and gloves for the gentlemen."

"The damned scoundrel," I said, feeling a genuine rage against Captain Edwards.

"There is hope, however," the Lieutenant added. "We are not so cut off from the civilized world as those corrupt ship chandlers might think. Captain Smith will be returning within a fortnight. He intends to go straight away to the London Company and inform them of our true situation here. I daresay those swine who cheated us will find themselves before the King's justice with unaccustomed swiftness."

I attended services and spent the remainder of the day recovering my strength and repenting of my excesses. Wilcox stumbled in late in the afternoon, pursued by two soldiers who quickly dragged him off to answer for his failure to be at services. Later Richard came to collect his few belongings: his pens, paper, books, and sword. The bed would remain for the next occupant. He invited me to attend supper with him and I, against my better judgement, accepted.

I washed the grime of the fort's dirt from my face and hands with the remains of our water from the water cast, and put on the suit of clothes Richard had given me. My hair had grown overly long without the services of a barber, and I tied it back in the manner of the Indians. My reflection in the water showed the mature face of a frontier gentleman, tough and sunburned, without a trace of beefy softness.

Richard's house was not far from the fort and a pleasant walk in the twilight of a summer evening. I took my sword and pistol since there were still hostile Indians about, and walked down the newly cleared road, among the trees and singing birds and the dizzying smells of our near island.

Richard's house was a short distance to the other constructions that I had been working on since my return from the falls and, in form, it was much like them. He had done much of the work himself, and his lack of skill showed. Many of the boards were poorly fitted, nails and spikes had been driven improperly. The house itself had an unfinished, fragile appearance.

I knocked on the door and Richard greeted me with a smile and a friendly clasp around the shoulders. Inside, I realized how much I had missed a boarded floor. I had the immediate sense that I was in a true house again, like those in England. The place had three spacious rooms, and Richard had pieced together several crude chairs and a shaky bench seat. The fading yellow sunlight peeked in through the windows which had real glass in them. There was no finished wall inside, and Richard said enthusiastically that he planned to use local materials for the plaster.

"The Captain has excused me from all common labor so that I can finish this house before winter and clear the rest of the land for next spring's planting," he said.

The place was little better than what many of the poorest peasants have in England, yet it was all new, like our Virginia, and smelled of freshness and hope.

Richard seemed to bubble over with joy. He even appeared physically stronger and more energetic. He led me into the small kitchen where Anne was preparing a large meal of venison and fish with corn and some other green vegetable that I did not know.

"The metal skillet I made myself, and Tatahcoope showed me how to make earthenware pots. The forks and knives are a gift from Mrs. Fitzsimmons. Captain Smith and his men gave us a month's supply of candles, taking them from their own rations. That was kind of them, don't you think?"

I said that it was and, regretting that I did not have something to offer, handed him my pistol.

"To replace the one that you lost," I said.

Richard smiled. I knew he was going to refuse it.

"We have no need of that now," he said.

He walked over to a chest where he kept his papers and took out the stuffed body of a small blackbird, with its wings outspread.

"Tatahcoope gave this to me and said that if I place it outside my door, no Indian would dare to harm us. It is a part of their religion and is believed by them to have supernatural powers, especially when worn by one of their conjurers."

"Please take the pistol anyway," I said. "There are renegades even among the Indians."

"No, thank you, my friend. You will have greater need of it than I. I don't believe I could truly use it for the purpose that it is intended. I am a peace-loving, God-loving farmer now, without the desire or intention of hurting any one of God's creatures."

"You should think about your wife, Richard, and your future children."

"Should I bring the mark of Cain down upon my children? No, Matthew, I will not lift my hand against my brother. It is most important that we begin this new life in this new world observing God's laws. If we do, he will protect us from harm. If we succumb, if we sin again, we will know death as our original parents did. We have lessons to go by, and this time we should not fail."

Anne looked with fear at the pistol I held out to Richard. I wondered if she was afraid of the pistol or afraid that Richard would not take it. Richard turned away and started out the back door. He signaled for me to follow. I started to replace the weapon in my belt, when Anne reached out and stayed my hand. She snatched the pistol away and tucked it into a pocket behind her apron. She flashed a quick smile at me and turned to the cooking. Richard called for me and, after a moment's hesitation thinking of what I should say to her, I went out to him.

We walked over his four allotted acres. Only one acre had been cleared, and it lay still littered with dead brush and the twisted remains of tree stumps, bleeding clear sap from their broken trunks. Richard estimated that most of the ground would be cleared by planting time. I disagreed, unless more work animals arrived, more tools and more men. He would be fortunate to have half the work completed by that time.

Richard did not comment. His face glowed with trust and confidence. He looked happily at his hands, turned them over several times in front of his eyes.

"These will be enough," he said, smiling like one who has

no doubts about the best outcome.

We talked for a while longer about the business of the colony, and then returned to the house where Anne had laid out a very attractive supper. Richard and I ate heartily, but Anne took only small portions and did little but dabble at those. It was the heat, she said, and left for the bedroom as soon as we had eaten. I asked if Anne was ill.

"The newness of the married state," Richard said, "and too, she is right, it is the heat. Many of our people find the tropical heat difficult adjusting to after the temperate climate of England."

After supper, Richard lit his precious candles, and we sat in the crude chairs, talking of our school days in England. Richard informed me that the minister in the colony had disclosed plans of the council to build a university, possibly at the falls, and that if he wished, he could have a position as Headmaster.

"It's far away into the future," Richard said. "We must first have more people, more families. There is room in this land for children, as many as a man desires, and there are the Indian children. What better place for them to learn the best of our knowledge and our religion? We have the opportunity and the chance to create a world of equals, unknown since the days of ancient Athens."

We talked for a while longer about this. That is to say, Richard, who knew more about such matters than I, did most of the talking. I concluded my visit, since it was getting late for returning to the fort, by saying that it was most important, at the present, to clear his remaining acres and that I would try to send the horses and men to help him in the morning. He thanked me for my genuine friendship and invited me to return at any time.

I asked if I should get the doctor for Anne, and he said no, that he was sure her malady would pass.

"She thinks much of England and, as the time draws near for the Fitzsimmons's departure, she grows even more melancholy."

We shook hands like two old friends should, and I went down the narrow road to the fort. It was pitch black on the road, and I walked with my musket ready and the cock locked back in the firing position. It was a dangerous thing to do since there were many obstructions in the road and often I stumbled over them, twice falling to the ground. I was challenged at the gate, and I called out my name with surprising loudness. I wanted no mistakes about my identity and the fact that I could speak English like an Englishman. The gates were swung open. I thanked the guard for his restraint and returned along the second street to my house.

I passed one of the gentlemen's houses, which was well lit with candles and burning torches. There were many gentlemen present, playing dice, all drinking and talking in loud voices. I stayed out of the light, and they did not see me pass. The rest of the fort was quiet, however. A few torches burned near the palisades, and one lit the storehouse where a guard stood, resting sleepily on his musket.

Wilcox had not returned, and I wondered where he could be. How could he survive outside the fort at night, unless he was in one of the ships? The pleasing thought occurred to me that he might have departed with Captain Edwards. They seemed to be brethren of the same stripe. The more I thought about it, the more I was sure that was what had happened. I went to bed exceedingly pleased with this possibility, and slept soundly all night.

The next day more of our men arrived from upriver, saying that the Indians had increased their attacks and had killed a large number of our people. All of their supplies were stolen, and they said that our settlements must be abandoned or we would be starved out. I only heard these reports secondhand, since I left early with my men to work at the building site. The corn harvest would be upon us soon and the building must either be completed by then or abandoned until after the harvest, which meant the work would continue into the short days of winter.

We worked like a colony of ants during the day, and it was often dark before I ate my supper and fell into a sweet sleep. I did manage to send the horses over to Richard's farm, and several of my men volunteered to go. I was unable to accompany them because of the great quantity of work to be done. I had to wait until the latter part of the week to pay a call on Richard.

I hurriedly bathed in the river and arrived at Richard's house about dusk. After a long wait, Anne greeted me at the door. Her eyes were still sunken, her face drawn and pale. I asked if Richard was about.

"He has gone to the jail to speak with his Indian. He works much on his lexicon."

"Did he use the horses well?"

"Yes, very well. We are thankful to you for them. Several of the gentlemen from the fort came this afternoon and took them."

"Do you know them?"

"I do not know their names, but I know them on sight."

"Then you must point them out to me."

She turned away. "Not today. Our allotted time for the

horses ended today anyway, and it would be pointless to fight over them now."

"I must inform the Lieutenant."

"Then do so if you must. I am not concerned with it."

Her tone was sharp and biting.

"Anne, may I fetch the doctor for you?"

"No. No doctor can help me." She turned to face me. "I am not sick in body."

"Then what is the matter? Has Richard been too demanding in his affections?"

"Richard has demanded nothing. He studies, he works in the fields, he says his prayers at night, and kisses me before going to bed. He demands nothing. It is I. I have not given. I cannot give."

"Surely there is something the minister can do," I said.

"The minister—that man is a stammering fool, quoting Bible verses to fend off the real troubles of life."

"But—"

"Oh God!" she screamed at me. "You are as great a fool as he. Do you remember that day, before you left for the falls. You walked down the riverbank out of sight of the fort and bathed your body. You swam in the river and seemed as happy as a young boy."

I thought back, remembering vaguely.

"You passed a group of us washing our clothes. You spoke very civilly to me and walked on."

I remembered the incident but did not remember Anne.

"I watched you secretly then. At the first opportunity I pretended to return to the fort for more clothes, but instead I followed you, unseen of course. I kept to the woods and watched as you took off your clothes and went into the water.

Then, as you came out, you looked to me as beautiful as a pagan god. Never have I felt such passion for a man. Once I thought that you would discover me when I slipped from a small bush, but you decided that it was nothing to be concerned about. I crept away before you dressed and returned to the washing. You never knew, did you?"

"Good Lord, Anne. Do you know what you are saying?"

"Yes. Yes. And I feel so much at ease for having said it. I wanted you from the first moment that I saw you in the fort, that day we all assembled after our arrival here."

"You fainted that day."

"Yes, I did feel truly faint, but I only pretended to faint to attract your attention. But Richard came to me. Poor Richard, with his heart and eyes so glowing with strangeness—why did you never come to court me?"

"I thought of it many times, but Richard told me that he wanted to take you for his wife. You know his hopes for the future. His reasons for wanting to marry you are far nobler than mine. You know why he is here. He is a man of learning and vision. I knew that if God would favor anyone, it would be Richard. I came here only to escape the law, and if it becomes safe for me to return to England, that is what I will probably do."

She seemed not to hear what I had said but stood in front of me, wringing her tiny hands.

"I know he is a good man," she said. "A learned man. And that his reasons are pure, but his dreams and hopes are not mine."

"Then why, in God's name, did you marry him?"

"Don't you know? Can you not guess? I married him to be near you. I . . . "

I will never know what came over me then. What unearthly

power seized hold of me? My mind, my very soul, seemed possessed. Right and wrong were completely obliterated from my conscience. I did not care for honor, friendship, duty, respect, Heaven, or eternal damnation. Nothing mattered but having her. I took her in my arms. Our lips rushed together and mingled, hungry and burning. I led her to the bedroom and, knowing full well what I was doing, leaped joyfully into the fires of hell.

Once the deed is done, the abominable act committed, there is no turning back. There is no reversing the order of time and undoing what we would rather not have done under more lucid influences. History does not go full circle, allowing us to correct our mistakes. Once the event occurs, it changes the course of life until the end. Each event diverts us, like a ball that is set to rolling down a hill. Each obstacle it bumps into diverts it into some other direction. Each deflection is another unknown path. Some complete the journey to the bottom of the hill, others do not.

The Reverend Albright had said that we are free to choose, that unlike the mindless ball, we can avoid the trees and bumps, but I doubt that. He has never been gripped by the sharp talons of passion, real passion that goes to the depths of the earth or shoots toward the stars. If he has known such passion and still believes a man can choose, he is being false to himself and to his flock.

The complexion of the world had changed around me. The infamous word ADULTERER seemed branded into my forehead. Everyone who looked at me saw it, and saw also that I was not an ordinary adulterer. I had not seduced some sailor's wife or a titled lady, long neglected by her husband. I had lain with my best friend's wife. I had uncovered her nakedness and I had drunk deeply of my passion for her, without shame, without discretion. I was the first man she had ever known in such a way. She had feigned sickness since her marriage night to prevent Richard's caresses.

"And now," as she spoke to me after we had lain together silently for a long time, "when he takes me, I will see only your face, feel only your body with mine."

God knows how I trembled at those words. I would go on deceiving Richard, even if I denied my love for his wife and denied my longings for her body. I would continue to make a cuckold of him in spirit as well as in body—yet the spirit does not offend nearly so much as the body. A man may desire many things, even another man's wife, but if he does not commit his body to the act, he can overcome his wild and rapacious spirit without offending.

CHAPTER 17

The Demise of Decorum

I did not see Richard again until the day before the Captain was to depart for England. I went with the Lieutenant and Captain Ratcliffe to greet the arriving pinnace, commanded by Captain Davis, that was being pulled into shore. She had sixteen men aboard as passengers for Virginia, some laborers and some soldiers, and a quantity of supplies for our storehouse.

Captain Ratcliffe greeted Captain Davis like a long, lost friend and asked that the sixteen men brought on his ship be placed under his charge to strengthen the force bound for Point Comfort. Captain Davis seemed a bit distracted and confused by Ratcliffe's overly friendly manner and said that he could do what he liked with the men, that by bringing them in good health to Virginia, he had discharged his obligations. The Lieutenant said that it made little difference to him so long as they left for the Point as soon as possible.

Captain Ratcliffe assembled the weary, confused newcomers into his company and marched them off to the fort. The Lieutenant and I escorted Captain Davis, along with several of his sailors walking on wobbly sea legs, to the fort where Captain Davis was to deliver a bundle of letters to Captain Smith.

On the way, Captain Davis inquired as to who Ratcliffe was, and said that although he looked familiar, he could not place him. The Lieutenant said that Ratcliffe used to be called

Sicklemore, but that he had changed his name to avoid trouble back in England.

"He certainly seems like a man in much haste," said Captain Davis.

"He is," the Lieutenant answered. "He wants the world conquered in his name, or names, before he turns thirty, something like Alexander of Macedon."

Captain Davis laughed and ordered his sailors to wait for him outside the door of the President's House. The Lieutenant led the sea captain inside.

Captain Smith lay in his bed on one side, his head propped up on pillows. There was a terrible stench of rot and excrement in the room. Captain Smith had been a man in his thirties with a strong body and clear, bright eyes. But when I saw him with Captain Davis, he looked like a man twenty years older. He was pale, drawn, and weak from constant pain. It was indeed a miracle that he had lived so long, but I gave up hope at that moment thinking of him surviving a sea voyage of many weeks.

Captain Smith acknowledged us with a nod and bid us, with his hand, to come closer. He asked me how I fared with the building. His voice was weak, and he seemed hardly able to get the words out. I gave him a brief report of the present constructions and said that with the horses, we should have much of the work finished before winter. He smiled and spoke at some length with Captain Davis, thanking him for the letters.

He spoke also with the Lieutenant and, before we departed, handed him a large paper folded in quarto, on which he had written his report for the new President and Governor when they should arrive. The Lieutenant was to copy and present this report to all those in authority in the present colony. The Captain apologized for his inability to speak further with us and bid us to remember him in our prayers. We took our sad leave of the Captain and said that we would be present to wish him a safe journey at his departure.

I passed Richard on the way back to my house. He was returning from the storehouse with his week's rations and called to me several times. At first, I pretended not to hear him and then, when his calls became so loud that I could not possibly ignore them any longer, I stopped. He seemed very light-hearted and happy. He wanted to know why I had not come to visit. He said that he had looked for me daily, and could not imagine why I stayed away.

"Marriage," he said, "has not altered our friendship. Please stop by for supper, any night."

I said that I was working over hours to finish the buildings, and that I would visit him and his wife at my very first opportunity. I asked if Anne was happy.

"Yes, extremely. She has gotten over her fears of the married state, and she asks for you."

I said that it was most kind of her. I tried not to present a formal and austere manner but I feared, in spite of my efforts, I must have seemed cold and distant. Richard's dark eyes studied me. He sensed an unnatural reserve in my manner and was puzzled by it. I said that he should forgive me for my apparent distance, since I had only that minute returned from seeing Captain Smith and was much distressed at his state of health.

He accepted this answer and, taking my hand, shook it vigorously, making me promise to call at his house within the next week. I promised, although it was much against my constitution to do so. I had made a vow to myself never to enter his house again and never to look upon his wife with my eyes. I had sworn also to attend services every day and pray for forgiveness, which I had not yet done.

That night I slept little. I felt that I was in the grip of an incurable disease. I continually saw Anne before my face. I kept remembering the last moments in her arms—the smells, the sounds, the words of love she spoke into my ear. I was feverish and filled with desire for her. I thought of nothing else. Not even Wilcox's continual snoring and stench disturbed my hot desire.

Twice I rose, thinking to steal secretly to Richard's. In my nocturnal madness, I thought that somehow Anne would also be awake and would see me at her window. I entertained such insane thoughts and schemes seriously for a long time before realizing them as complete folly, the acts of a madman and a fool.

Dawn came, a misty quiet dawn as only Virginia can have. Birds broke into song and fluttering. My fever vanished. My thoughts turned to what I would have for breakfast, something hearty and filling. I prepared a double portion of the rations I usually ate and even included my last two duck eggs. Wilcox preferred his drink to meat, although two days hanging in the stocks had turned his eyes elsewhere. There was still enough after I had finished for him to enjoy a good breakfast.

This was the day of the Captain's departure. The ship would be leaving with the falling tide later in the morning. I decided that I would see the Captain off in the new clothes I had bought with my meager earnings as a carpenter and builder.

I washed my face and neck, brushed my hair and tied it into an orderly fashion, and trimmed my new beard. I went alone to morning prayers. Richard and Anne were there but did not see me. I waited until they were seated, and then I moved in and stood at the back of the church with the rest of the men. The Reverend Albright gave his usual blessing and prayed desultorily for the Captain's safe voyage.

The service ended quickly. Most of the people walked down to the ship and waited in a quiet group while the sailors finished loading the ship and making their mysterious preparations for sea. Those gentlemen and gentlewomen returning to England on the ship were saying their farewells to their equals.

Mrs. Fitzsimmons stole over to where Richard and Anne were standing and spoke a few words to her. She kissed her on the cheek and returned to her husband. Anne, upset by Mrs. Fitzsimmons's words, dabbed at her eyes with the hem of her apron. Richard stood by, conversing with many of the people around him. The minister walked up to him and began a conversation which included much laughter and many friendly pats on the shoulder.

Even Wilcox was there, unwashed, unkempt, and suffering from a two-day ordeal in the stocks and deprivation of his wine. He seemed completely unashamed of his appearance and would walk boldly to this person or that and speak as though he was the greatest authority on whatever subject happened to be currently under discussion. Once he approached the minister, took his hand and shook it vigorously.

Reverend Albright was visibly repelled and made no attempt to mask his feelings. Wilcox, with total disregard for the minister's feelings, was congratulating him for his God-sent messages and that he, the minister, had given him the courage to cast away the evils of wine and sloth, and to embrace the sanctity of sobriety and duty. The minister tried valiantly to appear interested in what Wilcox was saying, but on occasion would turn his head away as if to avoid the overpowering stench.

The arrival of Captain Smith stopped all other activities. He lay on his side, covered with a thin linen sheet, and was borne gently on his litter by eight of his soldiers. He was extremely pale and weak, and many who were close to him gasped as he was carried past. The Captain waved to all those near him. I tried to get closer to give him my last farewell, but the crowd resisted my efforts and the Captain passed by without seeing me.

The Lieutenant, dressed in full armor, led the way with a drawn sword. His face was tense and his eyes swept quickly over the people lining the path to the ship.

The Captain was carried aboard the ship with the utmost caution and gentleness. Yet, in spite of their efforts, one of the soldiers stumbled while boarding the ship and jostled the litter, causing the Captain to wince with pain. We all knew that he would never survive the voyage, yet no one spoke of it. It seemed forbidden, like inviting the powers of death into one's own presence.

Once on board the ship, the soldiers held onto the Captain's stretcher while the Lieutenant disappeared below deck. In a few minutes the Lieutenant returned and had a great argument with the ship's captain over the accommodations for Captain Smith. I could hear the Lieutenant's voice above that of the ship's captain, but I could not hear what agreement they reached.

The Lieutenant signaled for his men to follow, and together they bore Captain Smith into the ship's bowels, out of sight of those of us on shore. The Lieutenant returned with his soldiers in good order and left the ship, looking exceedingly agitated.

The boarding planks were pulled away at the order of the ship's captain, and the lines loosened from the tree stumps on shore. Most of the passengers who could find an uncluttered place at the gunwale waved happily to us who were standing ashore, and we shouted "Good Voyage" and "Godspeed" until the anchor, holding the ship out from shore, was raised and the sails were hoisted.

It was not a happy sight to see that ship moving out into the river, separating itself from us with each minute of time. I had an uneasy feeling as I stood watching it glide down the James toward the sea. The villain who tried to murder Captain Smith had succeeded and there was no man, save the Lieutenant, who was strong enough to resist a rebellion if one should come. That ship, as strong as it was, could be swallowed by an ocean wave and leave not a trace. It was such a fragile link with England, not even as direct or continuous as a single strand of spider's silk. It was a miracle that any ship made the crossing safely.

I saw Richard and Anne coming toward me. There was no use pretending that I had not seen them. There was no escape. Richard was calling, asking for me to wait. By the most supreme effort, I managed to look him straight in the eye while we talked about the unfortunate departure of Captain Smith. It was not a serious conversation, but more like the typical exchanges of superficialities that one does with acquaintances after church services.

I would now and then exchange glances with Anne. A normal man would have sensed, if not seen, the fire between us. But not Richard. He would never have suspected his loyal friend of making love to his wife. And, most certainly, he would never have suspected his wife.

"Why haven't you called on us?" Richard asked as we walked back to the fort. I explained that with the building and the advancing season, I had not had the time.

"Then don't be surprised if we call upon you. Would that be agreeable to you?"

"Richard, you know how rude my condition is."

He agreed, but protested. "Old friends should not be apart for so long."

In order to satisfy him, I said that I would stop by soon to sup with him, but that he should forgive me if I could not remain long.

We parted with a hand clasp and smiles. Anne suddenly kissed me on the cheek. It was like the touch of a hot coal. I turned quickly away, lest Richard see the red flush that had come into my face, and headed toward the President's House. I hoped to find the Lieutenant there. I had made up my mind to enlist as one of his soldiers and go as far away from Jamestown as I could.

On the way, I sensed the mood of the fort had already changed. There was much noise and laughter coming from several of the gentlemen's houses. Everyone I met seemed festive and free spirited. The blacksmith had closed his shop. The sawmill was not in operation. Barrels of wine had been brought into the fort from somewhere—they had been kept in hiding until an occasion arose for their use—and cups of wine were being sold openly to anyone with a shilling or rations to offer in barter. There was dancing in the street, and love offered shamelessly from men and women. It was a contemptible sight to behold, as though all of the colony, in the wink of an eye, became as pagan and as full of debauchery as ancient Rome.

Captain Pierce, the captain of the fort, shouted for me to enter, when I knocked on the door of the President's House. The Lieutenant was with him, as I had guessed. Both men were bent over several documents which were laying on the desk.

"Well?" Captain Pierce demanded. "State your business and be gone."

"I wish to enlist in the Lieutenant's service and go with the next detachment of men to the fort at Point Comfort, or to the falls."

"That is for you and the Lieutenant to decide. I have no time for such things. You may go, Lieutenant," the Captain said to him. "Come to see me in the morning and we will think on this further."

The Lieutenant saluted, and I followed him out of the house. We stopped just outside the door.

"No," he said, not giving me time to repeat my request. "Your services are needed here in the building. Any of these laborers can be trained as soldiers, but few people here have a carpenter's hands and eyes. We must prepare for the winter. At least we can provide for shelter, but I fear many of these people will go hungry."

"Is that what you and Captain Pierce were discussing?"

"Yes. The way our supplies are being consumed, they will be exhausted in three months' time unless a ship arrives from England. We cannot expect trade from the Indians now that Captain Smith is gone, although we must try."

The Lieutenant looked around at all of the people dancing and drinking.

"God's blood, would you look at that!"

One of the wine barrels had been mounted on a platform near the center of the fort and had been draped with strips of gold cloth. People danced around the barrel and, as fast as wine was poured into it, they fought over who would be first at the tap.

"The fools! The silly children! They believe they have been delivered from the hands of a tyrant and now Utopia is within their grasp. Manna will rain from Heaven. Water will be turned into wine by their new messiah."

I saw what the Lieutenant meant. Wilcox danced around on the platform and drank portions of the wine passed up to him, before pouring it into the barrel. The Lieutenant threw his head back in a great peal of laughter, as Wilcox danced his drunken, whirling dance round and round the wine barrel.

CHAPTER 18

Betrayal

I do not believe that the children of Israel suffered as harshly under the bondage of slavery as we suffered that winter in Jamestown. Captain Smith's ship was hardly out of sight when a band of the gentlemen, led by one Sir Henry, sent longboats to Hog Island and there captured twenty hogs, six lambs, and many hens. All were slaughtered and prepared for cooking that day.

A single soldier remained on guard in front of the storehouse. The storekeeper had joined the revelers and had handed over his keys to Sir Henry, who led a party of men and women straight to the storehouse. They demanded that the guard step aside. He refused, and several men rushed upon him, took his musket and threw him to the ground. They then unlocked the door to the storehouse and poured in to take what they pleased. A table full of various cakes was prepared from the stores and many appealing dishes were made from the fruits and greens to be found. One woman had even discovered a cache of sweetmeats, well concealed under a pile of old lumber.

A great feast was held that night. Everyone in the Jamestown colony came and stuffed themselves with meats and fruits and drank wine to near drunken oblivion. And I, I did not remain an innocent onlooker. The smell of the roasting meat, the laughter, the artificial joy infected me and drew me, irresistibly, into its fold. I ate the meat and drank deeply of the wine and joined hands with men whom I would ordinarily have despised, and called them friend.

There were only a few who did not partake of this unholy rite—Richard, Anne, the Lieutenant, Captain Pierce, and the minister, although I learned later that he paid well for large portions of the best cuts of meat and other victuals prepared that night, and had them delivered secretly to his house.

Once, while I was lifting the wine cup to my mouth, I saw the Lieutenant standing, in his armor, upon the raised bulwark. The light from the cooking fires lit the prominences of his face: his nose, cheeks, and chin. The firelight on his helmet and breastplate made them seem to glow with fear and rage. He was a fearful spectacle to behold and I, half in fear, half in wonder, lowered my wine cup and left the merrymaking for the refuge of my house.

The next morning, the fort appeared to be in ruin. Smoke rose from every corner. Men and women lay on the ground where they had fallen in a drunken stupor. Some were still entwined from the night's debauchery and fornications. The sickening stench of meat and stale wine corrupted the air. My head swam with each breath, and I was in haste to get about my work. I walked over to the church, but it was empty and there was no sign that services would be held that day. I waited, nevertheless, until the time appointed for them. When it became evident that the minister would not arrive, I left for my work at the building site.

Even the building site had an unusual look of ruin about it. The houses, in the early stages of their construction, appeared more like they were falling down from neglect. The others, although claimed with people living in them, seemed empty and abandoned. I did what I could until around noon, but could not do further without the help of my men. I decided to locate them and see if I could not bring them back to work.

Lucas, my best man, was in his house eating his breakfast. He was dressed only in a long shirt, and greeted me civilly. I went straight to the issue and asked why he was not at work. He seemed truly surprised by this and said that today had been declared a holiday. I asked him who had made such a declaration.

"One of the gentlemen. The adjutant to the Governor, now lost at sea with Captain Newport."

I told him that it was nonsense. "None of the gentlemen had authority to make such a decree. Only Captain Pierce could order a holiday. You had best return to work with me."

Lucas became indignant. "I didn't come to Virginia to build houses for other folks to live in, Master James. Me family back in England is poor and countin' on me becoming a man of wealth. I cannot afford to waste more time."

"And how do you propose to gain the wealth you believe to be here?"

"Sir, there is gold close by the falls. Many of the gentlemen have assured us of it. The gentlemen of the London Company said that the samples returned to them prove it positive."

"You know, Lucas, that I have gone with the Lieutenant all the way to the mountains and found no gold or any mineral of value."

Lucas squinted. "I'm not saying that you would tell an untruth, sir, but maybe you didn't look too good, or maybe you're not too anxious to have others know what you and the Lieutenant found. I can understand that, sir. A man loses—"

His remark feeling like a slap in the face, I cut him short.

"The only gold in this country is fool's gold and you, Lucas, deserve all you can find of it."

His eyes glazed over, and I knew that his next move might

be for my throat. I put my hand on my pistol. He saw the move with a flick of his eye. I backed farther away, out of lunging distance, and waited until Lucas thought better of it. I left, slamming the door of his house behind me.

I then went straight to the President's House, where I found Sir Percy, Captain Smith's replacement, down with a fever but not too ill to converse with me. He said there was little he could do, that the conduct of the people was out of his hands and he could not risk fighting among his own people, with the Indians growing more hostile every day. He spoke with assurance and seemed truly convinced that the gentlemen and common people would come to their senses and see that we were all dependent upon one another. I asked the whereabouts of the Lieutenant.

"He has gone upriver to trade with the Chickahominys and should return in three days or less."

"What am I supposed to do?" I asked.

"Do what you wish or what you can. Take your rest today. I'm certain that tomorrow Jamestown will be working again."

I left the President's House and, not knowing what to do next, started toward my house. I was halfway there when I heard the sound of horses' hooves approaching. Three gentlemen swept past me. They had ridden through the open gate which was without a guard. One had the body of a deer slung over the pommel of his saddle. The other two were leading a captured Indian, bound by the hands and neck.

They reined to a stop in front of me. I recognized the gentleman from the ship that I had crossed on, but I did not know his name.

"You see," said the gentleman, with a broad smile to show his handsome teeth, "these horses were meant for better work than the crude labor to which you and that upstart Lieutenant have put them. We have good meat now."

He pointed with his riding whip to the deer, which was being pulled from the horse's back and dropped onto the dusty ground.

"And a prisoner, a prize of war," he said, motioning to the bound Indian who could not have been more than sixteen years.

The young native boy was covered with dust and bloody scratches, apparently caused from many falls. He kept his eyes cast down and could not suppress the trembling in his body. The other gentleman sat astride his horse next to the captured Indian and smiled with unrestrained pride.

"Why is he bound by the neck as well?" I asked, thinking it a particularly cruel measure.

"A method learned from the Turks. Keep the prisoner running so that he is pulled along by his hands. If he should work them free or if the rope should slip from them, the neck line will pull taut and teach him a valuable lesson. You see, it is much to his advantage to keep a hold on the line with his hands. Very clever, don't you think?" The gentleman leaned forward on his pommel and looked down at me. "I imagine that you would as any good carpenter should. Commanding and governing are best left to the intelligence of the better sort among us. Try to remember that and see to it that the tradesman's son masquerading as a gentleman is reminded of it, should he ever return."

The gentleman then spurred the horse, causing it to leap forward and jerk the Indian off his feet. The boy hit the ground with his body, hard enough to break every bone in it. He hung on to the rope, gritting his teeth to keep from crying out as the gentleman dragged him across the open square to the jail.

That night the gentlemen, along with some of the officers, conducted another bacchanalian rite, which I observed from my post at the bulwarks. The dark outside of the palisades was pitch black. The air was still. In my mind, I could see hundreds of Powhatan Indians creeping around the fort, but I would not have been able to hear them for the noise the revelers made.

Down inside the fort was a den of hell with all of hell's demons dancing and parading around and around, totally giving themselves up to the pleasures of the flesh, eating until they vomited, drinking until they were driven mad. And I was no better than the worst of them. Did I not covet my neighbor's wife? Had I not slept with her and uncovered my brother's nakedness? My sin was greater than all of theirs, for I knew, even as I stood there apart from their revelry, I would have her again.

I stood on the raised bulwark for a long time, feeling nothing but despair, when my attention was drawn to the center of the activity below. The gentleman who had captured the Indian went to the jail and took out his prisoner. The Indian boy was led to the square and there tied to several wood stakes by his arms, which were stretched out to each pole. Two doors had been nailed together and propped up behind the boy. One of the men drew a chalk outline of the boy's torso on the backboard and walked away, laughing. I could see the Indian's black eyes glistening with fear. His head jerked from side to side as he glared out at the cheering crowd.

A circle was cleared around the boy, and the gentleman responsible for his capture stepped into the circle and drew a line in the dust with his foot. He bowed to the other gentlemen, who laughed uproariously, then bowed to the rest of the crowd, who cheered and applauded. He then assumed the en garde position, left arm tucked behind his back, rapier at the ready with his right.

The Indian boy, seeing what was about to take place, tested and tore at his bonds like a captured lion. The gentleman waited until his captive had calmed down, then lunged at him. The Indian boy jerked his body wildly to one side, and the gentleman's sword thudded into the wooden backboard, an inch outside the chalk outline. He assumed the en garde position again and immediately thrust to the other side. The Indian jerked away, and I heard his body slam against the backboard when the cords around his wrists pulled tight. Waves of laughter ran through the crowd, and people pushed one another aside for the best view. Not even the Turks could invent such cruelty. I resolved to try and rescue the boy if I could. I jumped down from the bulwark and moved as quickly as I could to the inner ring of the circle.

Another gentleman was taking his turn with the Indian boy. It soon became clear that they did not intend to kill the boy immediately. They were having their hideous fun torturing him by seeing how close they could bring their sword thrusts to his body without striking him. The sword point in the backboard image closest to the center would mark the winner. The boy was bleeding a little from his right side where a blade had cut through the skin.

Freeing the boy seemed nearly impossible in the crowd. If I took their amusement away from them, they would not think twice about stoning me to death and killing the Indian boy as well. But I didn't know how long this terrible game could go on before something went wrong, and a sword would be run through the boy's vitals.

I made haste back to the bulwark and charged the cannon with enough powder to create a considerable noise. I then attached a long fuse to the touch hole and, finding a loose board, I hid the fuse from sight behind it. I managed to light it with the flints from my match box, then hurried back to the crowd and moved unnoticed as close to the Indian boy as I could. The best place was behind the backboard. It wasn't well lit, and there were fewer people. I reached this position just as the cannon fired, making a terrific noise and creating a brilliant flash of light that momentarily lit up the whole fort.

A scream rose from the crowd, and they scattered into the streets like a flock of birds startled by a fowling piece. The gentlemen, temporarily confused by the disruption, looked to one another for a few moments, then ran toward the sound of the explosion with torches in one hand and drawn swords in the other.

After they had departed, fortunately with most of the light, I leapt up next to the Indian boy and, in a few seconds, had cut him down. His chin was covered with saliva, and he nattered repeatedly the name of his god and other words that I did not understand. I grabbed him around the waist and ran, crouching low, to the opposite end of the fort.

I waited in total darkness beneath the palisade for the boy to catch his breath. He asked my name. I told him. He said his name was Nanquoto and that he would be forever in my debt. I said that there was no time for talk and, taking him by the hand, I led him up to the raised bulwark. All of the gentlemen were searching the north bulwark and examining the cannon with their torches.

I helped Nanquoto over the sharpened ends of the palisade. While he hung there, I wished him Godspeed in his escape. He pushed away from the wall with his body and let go. An instant later I heard him hit the ground below and scurry off toward the trees. I wondered briefly how he would escape from our little peninsula. Whatever course he took, no difficulty would be too great for him. The Indians thought nothing of enduring hardships that an Englishman would absolutely refuse. He would swim the river and walk up to his chest in slime to reach safety.

I crept down from the bulwark and made my way back to the center of the fort. People had already begun to reassemble there. The gentlemen were returning, laughing until they saw that their prey was missing. The gentleman who had captured Nanquoto flew into a rage and promised to put everyone present to the sword, unless the perpetrator of this theft be handed over to him by morning. The other gentlemen stood by him with drawn swords. One of them shouted,

"You will learn who is in charge here and not to taunt your betters."

Having said this, they pushed their way through the crowd and returned to their lodgings. Most of the people immediately began accusing one another. They lamented that the Indians were not bad enough. Now they had to bear the wrath of the gentlemen. I was tempted to own up to my guilt, but I knew the crowd would have torn me to pieces.

———— •◦• ————

The next day nothing was said of the matter. I went to my work at the building site and found no one there. I did what I could without help or horses until about noon. I was also out of nails. My tools needed sharpening. I needed saws to replace those worn out. Nothing could be done to advance the building unless discipline was restored to the town.

I resolved to visit Captain Pierce once again to see what he could do to establish order in the town. On the way, I stopped by Richard's house. My intention, I told myself, was to see how his work was going on, and if people in the fields had stopped their labors as they had in building.

The truth was that I had scarcely had Anne out of my mind, waking or sleeping. Even when I tried to force myself not to think about her, images of her came back to me all the stronger.

I knocked on the door, hoping she would not be home, hoping that no one would answer, and hoping even stronger that she would greet me with smiles and kisses. I was on the point of turning and leaving when the door swung open and Anne stood before me.

She did not look pleased to see me. I asked if Richard was home and added quickly that I wished to talk to him about the state of the colony. She stared at me for a long time, the way an angry mother looked toward a disappointing child. Without saying a word, she took me by the hand and pulled me into the house.

"Where have you been?" she demanded. "It's been days. I have looked for you by the hour. I hate you!" she said, throwing her arms around me. "I love you," she said. "Nothing else matters."

I held her in my arms for a long moment and kissed her gently.

"Anne," I said, "the colony is in a bad way. The people have given themselves up to idleness and reveling. The government is in the hands of half-madmen. Something must be done."

She shook her head. "I don't care about any of that. Come with me. Oh, come."

She led me hurriedly to the bedroom.

"But Richard?" I asked.

"Gone to be with that Indian, Tatahcoope. He fears for the brute's life. He has not finished his lexicon yet."

We said no more after this except for the sweet murmurings of lovers. We lay on the bed Richard had built with his own hands, naked as the first children upon earth. We drank deeply of each other's body, and whispered words of passion that flamed and burned our minds and hearts and seemed to scorch the very straw we loved upon.

When we had finished and were dressing, she told me that she could not bear it if I did not come to her every day. I asked her if we were to compound our sin and not seek forgiveness.

"Once we committed the act," she said, "the sin of adultery could not become the greater, save by murder. No matter how often we meet as lovers, the offense will be the same."

"Perhaps you are right," I said, "but nothing good can come of this, you know."

She put her fingers to my lips.

"What we are at this moment is good. We are true lovers, sharers in one soul. Nothing else is important."

I wanted to agree with her. I wanted to say it openly and believe it as she did, but I knew that if we were lovers, as she said, then we were also liars and deceivers. I said nothing. The force drawing me to her was stronger than the force of my conscience. I put away that chastising voice. The part of me that yearned for Anne did not care that my moments with her were the only moments in the time of my existence. They were real and memorable. To be in love was the one great destiny of every person.

I returned to town about supper time and discovered from Wilcox that Richard had been seized by various gentlemen and thrown into jail. I went straight away to that terrible place and found Richard sitting and talking with Tatahcoope. He smiled upon seeing me enter. Then he rose and walked toward me with an extended hand. The Indian stood up also, and I noticed that they both looked somewhat sickly, especially Richard.

Both had deep coughs and watery eyes. The Indians were more susceptible to our colds and pneumonia than were the English. Many of them died from these diseases.

I asked Richard why he had been placed in jail and what were the charges?

Richard looked puzzled. "Sir Henry accuses me of setting free one of the prisoners last night." There was a tone of despair in his voice. "I tell you, Matthew, I know nothing of the matter. I was at home reading most of the night. Everyone appears to be very angry at me. Some are even calling for my head. They say I have chosen the Indians over them and am therefore a danger to the whole colony. This was never my mind at all, but no one will listen to me. They seem convinced that I am a spy for the Indians. Tatahcoope knows that this is not so, but he is not allowed to speak."

I took Richard's hands in both of mine and felt a shudder run through my body.

"I will go to the President about this, and I will see the Lieutenant as soon as he returns."

"One other request, Matthew. I know that you have much to do in the work of the colony, but would you inform Anne of what has happened? Tell her that this occurrence is an unhappy mistake and that I will return soon. I would not have her worry. She is not well, you know, and suffers much from women's complaints."

"I will tell her," I said, forcing myself to look into his troubled eyes, denying in myself the shame that was spreading through my body like a poison.

I started for the President's House and was about to knock upon the door. The Lieutenant was not returned yet. The President was ill with fever. Nothing could be done in the way of a trial for many days, possibly months, and Richard's innocence could easily be established as soon as the force of Sir Henry's passion cooled.

Once a trust has been betrayed, responsibility is negated. I betrayed Richard for my own selfish reasons, and his imprisonment would give me freedom.

I turned away from the President's door and went straight to Anne. I told her what had happened and, although she at first expressed concern for Richard's fate, she knew instantly what it would mean for us.

That night we slept in each other's arms; unhurried, unafraid, making love and being soothed into sleep by the strange harmony of crickets and the quiet call of night birds. A gentle wind from the river brought the scents of water and reminders of home.

———•◦•———

I did not go to the building sites or into Jamestown for the next several days. Anne and I romped and played like Pan and his wood nymphs, giving no thought to where we were or to danger. Richard's Garden of Eden had become for me the pleasure garden of an Oriental king. We joyfully and eagerly committed our sin in the woods, on the shore of the river after bathing, in every room of the house, once on the dining table, once on the bench. We would have satisfied our passion on the roof if it had been convenient. No place was too sacred to receive the milk of our lust. We were as wasteful and without care as soldiers after a battle.

It was while I was in town to collect rations that I heard Richard was about to be executed. The news stunned me, especially coming as it did from a conversation I overheard while standing in line at the storehouse. I left my place and ran straight to the President's House. I pushed open the door without knocking. There was no guard. The Lieutenant was talking with Sir Percy at his bedside. They both looked at me.

I apologized for interrupting but said that my business was of the most urgent matter and, without waiting for permission to speak, asked if an order for Richard's execution had been submitted.

Sir Percy nodded.

"Without the right of a trial?" I said with considerable heat.

"There was a trial," the Lieutenant said, standing up and walking toward me. "We have only learned of it, but why is it news to you?"

"I have been busy with the building and haven't had the time for town politics."

"Then you must have been very busy indeed. It was the first news I heard upon my return from upriver."

"How does the President fare?" I murmured. "Will he sign it?"

"They are bringing a lot of pressure to bear on him. Sir Henry has already dispatched a report on the state of the colony to friends of his in London, hoping to prejudice the company against him and Captain Pierce. One more report with more of Sir Henry's lies, and Sir Percy may find himself returning to England in chains like the Italian, Columbus."

"The whole affair is a farce and you know it, sir. What witnesses did they have? They didn't call me or his wife."

"And how would you know about his wife?" Webster snapped.

"Because I was lying in her bed," I shouted back.

I might as well have said that I had leprosy from the way the Lieutenant responded. Sir Percy rose from his sickbed and sat up on his elbows.

"Good God, Matthew!" The Lieutenant said, turning away from me as he would have turned away from a pit viper.

"And that is not all." I continued. "I was the one who freed the Indian. Sir Henry's gentlemen friends captured the wretched creature, stole his game, and brought him back to the fort to torture him for their sport and, I might add, to the delight of the good people of Jamestown. The Indian would have died horribly and most unjustly if I had not come to his aid."

Sir Percy fell back on his bed, exhausted.

"I was informed of the Indian's treatment. And I dare say, young man, that you played right into his scheme. He was probably planning to let the Indian escape after working up the bloodlust of the mob. Then he would claim that Jamestown had been betrayed by spies and conspirators, naming me as the head. Unfortunately, his plan worked too well. The people are demanding that I step down before my term has expired and that Sir Henry assume the government. I don't think he has any intention of executing your friend, but if it suits his purpose, he will not hesitate to do it. The trial he conducted was irregular and, of course, illegal. But the laws are not necessarily rules of just or fair behavior. They are the results of conflicts between powerful forces, and reflect the will and desires of those who win those conflicts."

He looked at the Lieutenant.

"I will not sign the order for Mister Scott's execution, but that means nothing unless Sir Henry and his faction can be broken up."

Sir Percy's voice was very weak. Lieutenant Webster knelt beside him and, taking his hand, assured him that he would do all in his power to thwart Sir Henry's ambitions. The Lieutenant stood up and motioned for me to follow him outside.

"Would you be willing to admit to freeing the Indian?" the Lieutenant asked me directly.

"Yes."

"And what about sleeping with Master Scott's wife?"

"Yes, if such an admission became necessary. But to make a thing like that known would hurt both Anne and Richard, as well as myself. If it's any comfort to you, sir, I have decided that, regardless of how much I love the woman, I will keep myself away from her. Our sin can only bring destruction upon us both."

"Aye, and, not to mention her innocent husband."

"That is true, sir."

"Lord knows, the way this town has been, it would not surprise me if the whole wrath of God came down upon this place. Oh, speaking of God's wrath, did you hear about Ratcliffe?"

"No, I haven't."

"He and most of his men were killed in an Indian ambush while trading on the Pamunkey River. Ratcliffe's demise was particularly grizzly—skinned alive, then burned."

"By God's wounds, I had not heard a word of it."

"It doesn't surprise me. Everyone is properly happy that there are fourteen less to share in the mythical gold they all hope to find. I, myself, was attacked several times and, what was worse, I was unable to trade for a single bushel of corn. All of the people along the Chickahominy refused us a landing and shot arrows at us every time we approached the shore. I fear that shortly they'll overcome their fear of our guns and attack us in strength and drive us into the river."

"What do you propose to do about Sir Henry?"

"Sir Percy has given me an order for his arrest on the charge of mutiny. I am not too sure that I will be strong enough to enforce it. Such is the popular feeling in favor of Sir Henry. Nevertheless, go and fetch your musket and meet me in the square. I will have a detachment of men ready for the work."

I ran back to Richard's house and told Anne what had occurred. I grabbed my musket, powder, and ball, and ran, out of breath, to meet the Lieutenant who had already assembled his men, about fourteen in number, in two ranks. We marched to Sir Henry's house with our arms at the ready. People gathered quickly around us, some voicing their disapproval, others glaring at us with unmasked hatred.

The Lieutenant, unperturbed, knocked politely on Sir Henry's door. There were several other gentlemen sharing the house with Sir Henry. I recognized the man who answered the door as being one of Sir Henry's band of hunters. The gentleman looked us over from head to foot, smiled, and asked what our business was.

The Lieutenant asked if he could speak to Sir Henry.

The gentleman said that he was presently asleep and could not be disturbed. The gathering crowd had become noisier. A few loudly demanded that the Lieutenant withdraw. Others shouted that Sir Henry was the rightful governor. The Lieutenant advised the gentleman in the doorway that he had better awaken Sir Henry as he had an order for his arrest.

The gentleman laughed and made as if to close the door, but the Lieutenant jammed his boot down against it and, leaning closer to the gentleman, said in a low voice, "I don't want to hurt any of these good people here, but if you don't go and fetch Sir Henry straight away, there will be more blood spilled here than at any time since the establishment of the town."

The gentleman's smile faded. His full lips disappeared behind his beard and mustache. His eyes glinted like two pieces of broken crystal.

"I'll attend to this," a voice said from behind him.

The gentleman stepped aside, and Sir Henry moved into the doorway. A few cheers rose from the crowd.

"Long live Sir Henry!" someone shouted louder than the others.

Sir Henry, red-faced and with bloodshot eyes, smelled of soured beer and tobacco. He was half dressed in breeches and shirt and looked as though he had been sleeping in his clothes.

"Is it necessary to bring an army with you, Lieutenant? Surely justice needs only the good conscience of men."

More cheers came from the people surrounding us.

"The good conscience of men may differ, depending on their wants, Sir Henry," the Lieutenant said. "In such cases the law, as it is written, must be enforced."

"And what is the reason you come hither? What law do you enforce? What charge is being made against me?"

The Lieutenant handed him the order of arrest.

"The charge is mutiny, sir," the Lieutenant said without blinking an eye.

Sir Henry read the order quickly, then looked at the Lieutenant. His eyes played over the Lieutenant's face for a long while. He stepped closer and said in a low voice, "What if I refuse to accept this?"

"Then I will order my men to seize you."

"Do you think they," Sir Henry glanced around at the people, "will let you?"

The Lieutenant looked straight into Sir Henry's eyes.

"We are prepared to see that the law is carried out."

Without taking his eyes from Sir Henry, the Lieutenant ordered our muskets to be made ready. This was promptly done. The people surged back, then forward again, as though a great breath had been drawn by the crowd and expelled.

Sir Henry gritted his teeth. "So be it then. I will go with you, but be warned that I will not forget this incident."

The Lieutenant stepped back, and Sir Henry walked out between our two ranks where we escorted him to the President's House. The crowd followed for a short distance but soon dispersed after the soldiers had taken their positions around the house.

Sir Percy was sitting at his table, breathing hard, and he seemed barely able to hold up his head. Captain Pierce stood next to him. Without giving Sir Henry a chance to speak, Captain Pierce explained the charges and asked if he could defend them. Sir Henry said that he had no need to defend himself against them, since he was not guilty, and that he demanded to be set free on his own word as was his right as a gentleman.

Captain Pierce said that for Sir Henry's personal safety, he thought it best that Sir Henry be confined to the jail until passage could be arranged back to England. There he could stand fair trial away from his enemies in Jamestown.

The Lieutenant withdrew Sir Henry's sword and dagger and handed them over to Captain Pierce. Sir Henry wheeled around like a trapped beast, and the Lieutenant leveled his pistol at him.

"One more step and you will save us the trouble of holding you, sir," the Lieutenant said, calmly and deliberately.

"You're not going to put me in with that savage and his friend? They'll murder me within the hour."

"That may be true, sir," said the Lieutenant.

"Then confine him in one of the pinnaces and put a strong guard over him," the Captain said.

We marched Sir Henry down to a pinnace and put him aboard it, placing three of the soldiers on the pinnace as guards, to be relieved every four hours. The Lieutenant ordered sufficient victuals to be stored for Sir Henry, and we returned to the fort in good marching order.

Inside the fort, I left the company and went to the jail to see Richard, but discovered that he had already been released. I was seized by a moment of fear, thinking that I might have left something of mine in his house. I couldn't remember anything and so returned to the storehouse and drew my rations.

CHAPTER 19

The Well Has Run Dry

I t was shortly after this time that the Indian attacks began. At first, they were directed against our foraging parties and hunting groups, usually ambushes from behind trees and bushes. Then our fields were attacked, and the crops burned. Word came still later that all of our livestock on Hog Island had been killed by the Indians and taken from there to be used for their own meals.

An unspoken, unreasoned fear swept through the people, and one day I awoke to the sounds of a general riot in the town square. I dressed and went outside. Everyone in the fort and almost everyone in the entire colony was gathered around the storehouse, demanding their rations for the year. Soldiers had left their posts and had joined the riot, all surging and swirling around the square in a whirl of disturbed, faceless humanity.

The sound of horses' hooves pounding on the packed dirt of the fort drew my attention to the nearest gate. The gentlemen of Sir Henry's faction entered the fort on horseback, two abreast, and, without slowing their pace, rode straight into the crowd. Human screams rose from the melee. Horses trod on the people as if they were running through a wheat field. Several of the horses reared and kicked at the people ahead of them who, desperate as ants under the shadow of a man's foot, crawled headlong over one another, tearing away clothes, hair, and grabbing at ethereal air.

The horses passed, leaving no fewer than twenty injured on the ground. Their pain and suffering were ignored by the rest. Shoes, boots, and bare feet stepped on their heads or trampled their bloody limbs.

The gentlemen kicked in the door of the storehouse with their horses, dismounted, and entered. The crowd followed, and soon, wild shrieks came from the beleaguered place. People began leaping from the windows, their hands clutching the last of the rations. Few escaped with more than a handful of grain. Even the gentlemen fared no better. There was simply nothing in the storehouse to eat.

The gentlemen rode away as before, not caring who they trampled. The rest of the crowd rushed upon the empty storehouse until nothing was left of it but the four walls. The explosion of a powder cask could not have done more damage.

There was an eruption of musket fire from the river that sent the few remaining scavengers scurrying back to their quarters. Following that, there was more musket fire. This time it was the orderly firing of soldiers.

I ran toward the gate, jumping over the writhing bodies of those trampled by the horses. I reached the opening in time to see most of the gentlemen spurring their horses toward the building site. One of the horses had been wounded. Its hind legs had collapsed, and it stood on its front legs, pulling at the ground. The animal's rider spurred the horse until the beast screamed in pain and desperation. The guards at Sir Henry's pinnace stood in an orderly file, reloading their muskets.

A group of people, perhaps as many as twenty or thirty, ran past me, out of the gate, toward the stricken horse. The sun glinted brilliantly from some of the objects they held in their hands. They were all carrying either knives, hatchets, or swords, and all were running as silently as an attacking predator, as swift as vultures, to the wounded horse.

The gentleman rider, seeing these people running toward him and guessing their intent, leapt from the broken horse and ran toward the building site. The soldiers guarding the pinnace lowered their muskets at the people who had, by then, reached the horse, surrounded it, and were hacking away at it.

I heard the voice of the Lieutenant order his men not to fire, and they lowered their muskets but remained standing together, watching the people carve away the living flesh of the horse.

I had seen enough and returned to the center of the fort where I helped the physician and the minister carry the wounded into the church where their wounds were treated. None of the people appeared to be mortally wounded. There were a few broken arms and legs. Some were badly cut, and others were worked up into such a state of fear that they were unable to do little but babble unintelligibly.

I had no notion of what the gentlemen intended for the new buildings, but I knew that little would be done there that day in the way of construction. I was determined, however, to go there and see what was taking place. I finished with the wounded after about four hours of labor and walked to the common well to wash the blood and dust from my clothes and body. I walked in my wet clothes back to my house, threw open the door, and was met by Richard and Anne, standing next to their chests. They looked worried and hesitant.

Richard explained that the gentlemen had ridden up to his house and had ordered him and Anne out at gun point, allowing them to take only his books, writing material, and a few clothes. Richard sat down on his chest and buried his face in his hands.

"What to do? What to do?" he repeated.

"We will go straight to the President," I said, "and acquaint him with this injustice."

I quickly changed into dry clothes while Richard and Anne waited outside. When I was ready, Anne went in the house to wait. Richard and I went to the President's House. The guard on duty refused us admittance, saying that the President was too sick to see any callers and that he doubted our chances would be any better the next day.

I advised Richard that we should see the Lieutenant and inquired of the guard where he might be found. The guard said that he had seen him going to his quarters not long before we arrived. We then went straight away to the Lieutenant's house and knocked upon the door. A voice commanded us to enter.

We found the Lieutenant seated at his table, alone, drinking a cup of water and still dressed in his armor. His black hair was greatly disheveled. His face was smeared with dirt and gunpowder. He looked at both of us wearily and motioned for us to take a seat at the table. I told him about the gentleman taking over Richard's home and property and putting them out on the street.

The Lieutenant gulped the last of his water and placed the empty cup on the table in front of us.

"You see that cup?" he said.

We said that we did.

"It is empty, isn't it? There is nothing in it. If I want to fill it again, I go to the water cask and fill it from that. If the water cask is empty, which it is, I go to the well and fill the cask. But suppose the well has gone dry? I still need the water, and I know that if I don't get it, I will die of thirst. And I know that if I drink the foul liquid from the swamp or the river, I will die of the bloody flux. That is what has happened here, my good men. The well has run dry."

I was a little confused, having just washed myself with water from the common well, so I asked the lieutenant to explain further.

"Each man is a well," he said, "from which he draws the substance for his life. He takes his courage from this well. His sense of justice comes from it, his understanding, his honor, and whatever goodness there is. Some of us have deep wells with sweet water. Others have shallow wells with foul, bitter water. We all drink from our own wells as long as there is water available. Those with deep wells among us share their water. No one wants to drink foul, bitter water. Now, because the wells have been cut off from their sources of water, the deep wells from which everybody drinks runs dry quickly, and there is nothing left but bitter, filthy, unhealthy water.

"That is what has happened here. The best water has been taken from us, and there is nothing left but foulness and bitterness."

He looked at Richard. "I cannot get your house and property back for you. I have no more resources. The people have given themselves over to the worst of us. The well is dry. The horn of plenty is empty. Only my most faithful few soldiers remain trustworthy, and we are fast running out of gunpowder. When that is gone, Sir Henry's men will ride over us and give us a taste of their steel. The future of this colony is out of my hands."

He wiped his dry lips with the back of his hand.

"However, there is one more act I shall perform in the name of justice. Before first light tomorrow, I am going to send Sir Henry back to England in the pinnace, along with such people as I choose who are worth saving. You are welcome to go on that ship if you wish. If you do not wish to, then I must ask you to keep this plan to yourselves."

The Lieutenant looked at us with hard eyes.

"Do I have your word on it?"

We both swore that we would keep our silence.

"Will you go then?" The Lieutenant wanted to know immediately.

My first inclination was to say yes and perhaps I would have if Richard had not voiced his opposition to leaving— abandoning the colony, as he put it.

"And you, Matthew? What do you say?"

"The only thing waiting for me in England is prison, sir," I said. "It's against my inclination to return and risk even that."

"So be it," said the Lieutenant. "Most likely we will all end our days here in Virginia. My own sense of duty requires me to also remain here when I would rather go. And who is to say? The situation may not be as bad as it appears. Our supply of victuals is gone. Our animals are gone except for the horses, and I dare say they will not last another month. There is nothing for us to eat but roots, berries and acorns, but we still have a good water supply. We still have some Indians who are friendly with us and, God knows, we still have hope."

CHAPTER 20

The Starving Time

In the coming months I was to think of that word, *hope*, often and all of the other important words Englishmen were fond of using. For the Lieutenant, they were honor, duty, courage. For Richard: justice, truth, and beauty. These words had always been held in great esteem. Their meanings have been debated and fought over but never fully understood or explained. The English say they live by these words and perhaps it is so, for that winter of 1610 we were to learn, firsthand, what they did not mean.

As for me, the one word I seemed to live by was *adulterer*. It seemed to be carved in stone and hung about my neck, yet I would not have changed it. I would not have denied the black truth of it. Neither would I have denied my love for her. Such was my cowardice, however, that when I thought of approaching Richard on the matter, I would always find a way of avoiding it. Perverse as it might be, I wanted him to know.

Winter came, howling and blasting its cold breath through Jamestown, ripping the remaining dried leaves from the trees, tearing at our thin clothes and drawing vital heat out of everything alive. It was then that the first of the deaths began; at first, two or three a day from cold and hunger. We conducted funeral services for them until they became too numerous and the services no longer seemed important. Men who helped to bury their friends one day would themselves be dead the next.

The dying were stripped of their clothes before they had breathed their last. Their quarters were stripped of anything that could be eaten or worn. They were buried at night outside of the fort, quickly, often flung in their graves with little more care than if they had been stray dogs.

The Lieutenant made many attempts to leave the fort and trade with the Indians, but he was always attacked before he could get more than a mile away. His men were often too weak to walk, much less fight.

Powhatan's men had the place under perpetual watch, a lesson learned by the six gentlemen of Sir Henry's who had taken over Richard's house. They were all killed in the first of the Indian attacks, slain while they lay in their drunken sleep, not one of them ever knowing the cause of his sudden thrust into eternity.

No one dared to leave the fort during the day but at night, under the cover of darkness, we learned to creep out through the palisades and forage for what roots we could find. We would make an edible broth from this, adding grass, wild onions, and various tree leaves, mostly bay.

It was not uncommon to see men and women eating a broth made from the mud of the fort and eating it as though it were as tasty as a dripping roast. Our days became absorbed in the constant search for warmth and sustenance. Many of our people became so weak they could not even crawl upon the ground. They simply lay in their beds and waited for death, which was never slow in coming to Jamestown.

Each night the death patrol made the rounds of the houses in the fort, and each night they hauled out two or three, sometimes five to the cemetery. Those of us who could still work spent many hours digging graves. Death became so common that often the dead were left where they had fallen, until the stench became so nauseating that a shallow hole was sometimes dug beside their bodies and they were rolled into it and quickly covered up.

On one of those nights, Richard and I foraged further away from the fort than we reckoned on. We stumbled upon two Indians sitting around a small fire, talking and roasting a leg of venison. The rest of the deer carcass hung on a rack near them.

The delicious smell of the roasting venison overcame all of our other senses. The power of it seized control of my thinking and before I knew it, I had jerked my knife from my belt and had started to charge for the meat. Richard grabbed my arm. He was trembling. He moistened his lips with his tongue.

"We must not kill them," he whispered.

"You don't expect them to hand over their meat out of kindness, do you?"

"No. We should offer to trade."

"With what?" I said, feeling my stomach quiver with want and expectation.

"We have knives and pistols," Richard said with conviction.

"Don't be ridiculous. The pistols are worthless, and how do you expect us to get along without knives?"

He hesitated. His eyes, shadowed by the dim firelight, made him look skeletal and sightless.

"All right," I said. "We will offer to trade, but stay by my side."

I stepped into the small clearing and, at once, the Indians spun around on their heels to face me. They were terrified.

"Netoppew, Netoppew." *Friends, Friends,* I shouted.

Both Indians ran for their bows. I pursued one and, in an instant, caught up with him. I don't know where my strength came from, for I had not had anything of substance to eat in many weeks. Just before he reached his bow, I caught him by a lock of his black hair and pulled him off his feet. The fall stunned him for a moment. He was very frightened.

He pulled a knife from a deer skin sheath at his side. I kicked it from his hand. He rolled over, jumped to his feet, and tried for his bow again. I was on him in an instant, holding him around the neck with my left arm and plunging my knife into the small of his back. His body stiffened, then went limp. A sound came from deep within him, a sound like the tiny scream of a mouse caught in the jaw of a cat. I let him fall and only then did I think about the other Indian. I looked quickly around and saw him lying near the fire, his eyes opened in death. Richard stood over him, still holding the bloody knife. I walked over to him.

Tears were running down his cheeks. He saw me and opened his mouth to speak, but no words came. I felt a great pity for him. There was nothing I could say of comfort, no words that meant anything. We who were still alive in the fort had moved beyond the power of words.

I wiped the blood from my knife and sheathed it. Then I walked over to where the venison was roasting, sat down beside it, and started to eat. That was the most delicious meal that I had ever had in my life. I knew then why a ravenous animal eats the way it does, greedily, without regard to niceties. I gorged myself on the leg of venison until I could not stuff another morsel. Richard tried to eat but spat the meat out in disgust and went and knelt beside the young Indian he had killed and offered prayers for the boy's soul.

I finished and threw the gnawed bone aside; then went over to the body of the Indian that I had killed and hurriedly removed his deer skins. The longer we remained there, the greater the chance that we would meet with more Indians, possibly friends of the deceased, bent upon revenge. I started to strip the other body when Richard grabbed my arm.

"Must we rob them too?" he said.

"The hour may come when this Indian's deer skin will mean the difference between freezing to death and living until next spring."

"If this is what must be done to stay alive, I would prefer death," Richard said.

"Richard, death comes too easily. You have already seen how it has perched in Jamestown. How it takes the good and the bad. We must struggle with all of our strengths to stay alive this winter. And even then, death may come, despite all our efforts. If I have to kill and steal to stay alive, I will do it, and if the first flowers of spring find me yet alive, I will ask forgiveness then."

Richard shook his head. "No. No, I will not do it," he said.

I shook his hand from my arm and quickly untied the bindings of the dead Indian's clothes and pulled them from him. This one was also wearing moccasins, which I removed and stuffed into my belt.

"Will you come back with me?" I asked him.

He nodded.

I wrapped the deer skins around my waist and shoulders. Cutting down the remainder of the deer, I hoisted it over my shoulders. We made our way slowly back to the fort, stopping once close to the fort as a group of eight to ten Indians, speaking in low tones, passed nearby us. We moved on and slipped back through the unguarded gate. We crept back to our house without being seen and found Anne awake, wrapped in a blanket and shivering with the cold.

I was attempting to hide our spoils when Wilcox entered, bearing a torch. He saw the venison and the deer skins and the blood on us and laughed. He announced that he was moving into one of the houses that had recently been vacated so that he could conduct his business there without interruption.

"Will you share your meat with me, or should I announce it to the whole fort? That is, those of us who are still alive."

"Wait," I said and cut off a large chunk of the deer and gave it to him. "Will this buy your cooperation?" I asked.

"Please, Matthew, my friend. We must be generous with one another in this time of trial. If I can be of service to you and these good people here, please let me know. But meat is something I am short of."

"What about salt? We need salt to preserve this meat," I said.

"Salt?" Wilcox repeated, scratching his beard. "I can get you salt, but it will not be easy."

I took out one of the deer skins that I had hidden under the bed and gave it to him. He held it up to the torchlight and examined it carefully.

"A good hide," he said, rubbing it with his fingers. "And not old. I will have the salt here before dawn. Be ready. I will not have much time."

Wilcox had never lived much in our house after our return from the falls, and now that the ships and mariners were gone, I wondered where he procured his goods to offer in trade.

"From the dead," Richard said, "but he doesn't kill them to get it. He goes nightly with the death patrol to those houses where all have died or where they are dying and too weak to resist. He robs the house of all its goods. It has become a common practice with the men on that duty. He knows that everyone has something of worth, even if it's only a piece of hard biscuit, stored in a secret place as a last hope. There is always something: a gold ring from a loved one back in England, a thin blanket, worn clothes, oil for lamps, the lamps themselves, their weapons, and yes, salt. Wilcox, if he survives, will be the wealthiest merchant in the colony."

I took the other deer skin and wrapped it around Anne's shoulders. Her shivering eased a little.

There was no wood for fire. Anne burst into tears.

"I'm sorry," she cried. "I burnt it all. I was so cold. I burnt it all. I know that I should not have done so, but I was so cold."

I looked at Richard, who glared at her without sympathy, without even seeming to see her condition.

"Richard," I said, "we need wood to cook a portion of this meat."

He glanced at his book chest, knowing what I meant.

"Take it then. Use it to preserve your miserable, pointless lives a little longer."

Then he left, slamming the door behind him.

I removed the heavy volumes quickly and, with the heel of my shoe, broke the box up into splinters of firewood, and fed them into the fire until a cheery red blaze was going. The heat made a difference immediately. Anne stopped shivering. The cold that had chilled me to the very core of my body gave way to a comfortable, fluid warmth.

I cut a portion of the venison large enough to feed Anne. Using my musket rod for a spit, I situated the meat over the fire so as not to char it, and turned it slowly.

Anne came over next to me and wrapped us both in the blanket and deer skin. She slipped both arms around my waist and nestled her head on my shoulder. Her breath was like that of a small child's on my neck. We both stared into the fire, the consumption of Richard's book chest.

I turned the meat slowly. Thoughts of hunger again rose to my mind, but quickly vanished. Anne's body was warm beside me and felt as frail as a sparrow's. Her throat and face were more delicate than the finest china. Each time I looked at her I wondered how nature could create such perfection and set it amidst a rude and ugly world.

"Does Richard know?" I asked.

"No," she said in a voice so gentle as to be almost inaudible, "but he suspects something is wrong."

"Perhaps he does know."

"What does it matter now?"

"Have you done your wifely duty toward him?"

She looked up at me with a slight smile.

"I was forced to," she said. "For the first time, last week, before we came here."

"Forced to? Richard forced you?" I said, feeling a surge of anger.

She laughed, giggling in a girlish way.

"No. He would never do a thing like that." She hesitated, still smiling. I waited.

"You forced me," she said.

"I don't understand," I said.

"I am with child," she said, almost in a whisper. "Your child. I had to do something, or he would know for sure. It seemed important then."

"My God! With child? My child?"

"Yes. Does it make you happy?"

"I don't know. If we were back in England or almost anywhere else in the world, I should be dizzy with happiness. But here in Jamestown, in the company of death itself . . . How can I be happy?"

"But there is also life, new life, the wonderful life I now have within me. It is a good sign. God approves."

"It was a life begot in sin, Anne."

"But the child is not guilty of our wrongdoing. It was

conceived in love, and that is greater than all of our sins, isn't it?"

I held her next to me.

"I don't know," I said. "I honestly don't know. But you and the child will live, Anne. I will see to it if I have to steal or kill or take the last morsel of food from my mouth. I will see to it that you live through this."

We held each other, wrapped in our crude coverings, in front of the fire for a long while. When the meat was ready, I served it to Anne and she ate it hungrily, licking the grease and fat from her small fingers and sighing with the pleasure of it. I put more of Richard's book chest on the fire and then we made love before it, sweetly, deeply, with unrestrained passion, and not caring if Richard returned to find us or not.

Richard did not return, however, and late in the night we were awakened by what seemed to be the noise of men in battle. I fastened my breeches and Anne prepared herself. Light shone in from the window as from a large bonfire. I opened the door cautiously.

The entire land around the fort appeared to be on fire. People had run to the palisades and were watching it through the cracks in the fortress's wall.

Anne and I ran to the nearest bulwark, where it looked as though the whole fort had been transported to the center of hell itself. The woods and fields were all burning. In the river, our last ship had been turned into an island of fire. Flames climbed up the tarred shrouds like candle wicks. Fire shot from every port and crack in the small ship, consuming it until there was nothing left but an unidentifiable red mass drifting on the water.

Richard came up to where we were standing.

"This is only the beginning," he said, looking with wide, feverish eyes at the holocaust. "I have released Tatahcoope."

"Is he responsible for this?" I asked, sweeping my arms around at the destruction.

"I don't think so. He could hardly walk, he was so weak. He asked me to join him and become a member of his tribe. He wanted me to show them how to use English weapons.".

"What will you do?" I asked.

Anne looked at Richard with profound expectation.

"I cannot go with him. My life and duty are here. There is still hope." He took Anne's hand and kissed it gently. She withdrew it brusquely and slipped it into mine. Richard looked wounded to the core. In one terrible instant he knew, positively, what no man or woman wishes to know. The knowledge would not have been more devastating than a musket ball placed through his vitals. He turned slowly and, staggering slightly, made his way through the fiery shadows of running men.

———————

Richard took to his bed shortly after, with severe fever. He refused what nourishment and care we could provide. I moved my bed to the part of the house where Wilcox had slept and Anne moved with me, taking the few things she had managed to save from her house. There, before the very eyes of her husband and my boyhood friend, we slept together as man and wife would sleep.

We did not care if he saw or heard us. We shamelessly partook of each other whenever the passion moved us, whether at night or in daylight. Richard, if he was conscious at such times, put his hands to his ears and squeezed his eyes shut to block out this hideous crime. We hardly gave his presence a thought. To us, he was already dead.

It happened that one night, about Christmas, Richard called me out of a deep sleep. It was like a voice from the beginning of time, calling me out of a black pit. There was no earth, no sky. I seemed to be floating upward, faster and faster, until I sat up in my bed and heard Richard calling in a weak voice. I went over to him and knelt beside him.

He took my hand. I could see its pale, thin form in the shaft of moonlight slanting down from the window. I could not see his face and that was just as well, for I feared that I might not have had the courage to look at it.

"Matthew," he said in the wheezy breath of an old man. "I am dying at last. Take all of my books and whatever else of mine that you can make use of, even these clothes from my body."

He rolled a bundle of clothes into the square of moonlight on the floor.

"You have all that was mine now. That is the way it should be. You were meant to survive in this land. I have been the greatest of fools. How you must have lost patience with me—my silly prattling, my blindness to all except my own view of living. I am dying, Matthew. Life is slipping from me like smoke disappearing into the night."

He gripped my band a little tighter.

"I tell you, Matthew, I do not know what is beyond and, for the first time, I do not even know if there is a God. Nevertheless, forgive me, my friend."

"Richard, it is I who should beg your forgiveness."

"No, no, you have only followed the naturalness that is within you, while I forever sought to deny it within myself. I perverted it into the pedantic notions of an English schoolmaster. I knew Anne's heart was not mine, yet I forced her, being so convinced of my own righteousness. I see now that I gave no thought to anyone else, and it is fitting that I learn the truth in my last moments on this earth. Matthew, this is not the home I would have had in Virginia, but it is good enough."

He stopped and struggled for breath.

"Finish my lexicon, Matthew. That was good work. Keep the language of Powhatan alive."

He slipped his hand from mine and lay struggling for breath. Then his breathing eased, and he spoke in a voice hardly audible. "Lord, have mercy on my soul." And with that, he exhaled the last breath he would ever take.

An intense cold descended upon me. It chilled me to the heart. I began shivering uncontrollably. The quiet was even more intense, like the quiet of earth before the first animal voice was ever heard, the terrifying quiet of a barren mountain or an open sea. I wanted the tears to come, but they would not. I wanted to take Richard's pain to myself, but it would not come. Pain, blood, feeling, all seemed to have gone from me. I could only stay in my place, kneeling beside him, until I heard the death wagon coming.

I forced myself to my feet and stepped outside. The ghoulish men stopped the cart. Four shriveled bodies lay in it, with their heads dangling over the rear. They were as naked as the day they had come into this world.

Two of the men went into my house. I followed and drew my sword.

"Take his shirt," I said.

"We want the shoes. And had he no food, no money?"

"He had nothing but the clothes you see there and a few books."

"We will not take him unless we get the shoes."

"Is Wilcox with you tonight?"

"He waits at the gate."

"Then take the shoes. Take it all. But tell Wilcox where you got them or, God knows, both of you will be the next passengers in that infamous wagon."

One of the men tossed Richard's clothes and shoes out of the door. Then both of them carried his body out, one by the feet and the other by the hands. I turned away as they flung him into the wagon. I was afraid that I might see his eyes. I waited until I heard the wagon stop at the gate before going back into the house.

I stirred up the fire with the tip of my sword and placed a few more splinters of wood on it. The fire immediately flamed around the dried oak, giving a bright little light for a few minutes. I placed my sword next to the wall and returned to bed and Anne's side. Her body was tense all over. She trembled from head to toe. I held her close, hoping to pass the heat from my body to hers, but she trembled still.

Mid-winter came and the river froze out from the shore for several hundred feet. Snow and sleet came and covered the ground for days at a time. All of our victuals, even the berries and grass we had gathered outside of the fort, completely exhausted. We lived, those of us who did live through that winter, from what we could scrape from the barren ground. Some boiled the leather from their shoes to make a broth. Others boiled the shavings from inside pork barrels, and others ate the flesh of other men.

The pain and madness of continuous hunger will drive men and women into the most despicable of acts. Acts that, if they were well fed and warm, would have revolted them to no small degree. Yet a hungry body has no morality, no conscience. It cries out for what it needs. It drives and pushes the mind into unreasoning delirium.

I am speaking of the time during one of the heaviest snows. One of our men surprised an Indian outside the fort and killed him with his knife. In supreme madness, he hacked away most of the flesh from the Indian's arm. In a ghoulish orgy, he ate the raw flesh as hungrily as if he were a lion stuffing himself with warm prey. The man then dragged the body back to the fort where a number of men and women fell upon the rest of it, covering the body like black winged vultures.

The Lieutenant returned from a foraging expedition in time to break this satanic feast up and, in a great rage, ordered the people back to their homes. Most of the flesh from the Indian's body, except for the head and groin, had been carved away. Blood covered the snow around him, and he lay like a butchered lamb, with his entrails spilled out onto the snow. The Lieutenant stood over him with a drawn sword, guarding the remains until his soldiers could come and dispose of them properly. I waited, looking out of my window at the naked trees which stood against the gray sky like skeletons, until the task had been completed. The wind howled through the fort like death itself was astride it.

The Lieutenant came after a while. He was extremely exhausted. His men had not even seen a trace of game. It was as though every living thing except those of us dying in Jamestown had disappeared from the earth. He sat by our small fire, shivering. Anne wrapped him in the blanket.

"It is said that once you get the taste of human flesh, you are never satisfied with any other meat. Witness the Caribs in the islands to the south. They had rather eat one of our toughest soldiers than the most fat and succulent pork roast. I fear that there will be a wave of this unspeakable cannibalism. Come the spring, there will be only one of us left alive, the one who has eaten the rest."

I put our last few sticks of wood on the fire. The Lieutenant's shivering continued. Anne was shivering also. The cold got at us from all sides; sliding under the door, seeping in from around the windows, blasting through the chinks in the walls. I went over to Richard's stack of books and took out one of them. I could not bring myself to look at it. I opened it up so that the flames could get to it and laid it on the fire. The Lieutenant looked at me with very sad eyes.

"So we are come to this, eating the flesh of our own kind and burning our knowledge in the fires, for no other reasons than to stay warm and satisfied."

The book burned poorly, but after a while it gave off a good amount of heat. I put another one on the fire. The Lieutenant stopped shivering. Warmth filled our small house.

"If there were a higher reason for what we have done, a reason that transcends mere earthly expectations, I could understand."

"Perhaps," I suggested, "it is because we want to live more than we want to die."

The Lieutenant stood up, slipped off the blanket, and laid it over Anne. Then, standing more erect, said, "Matthew, there are times when living asks too high a price and those of us who pay it, just to keep our bodies alive a few more years, will win the wrath of eternity."

I thanked him for coming and volunteered to go out on the next foraging expedition if he needed me. I went with him to the door. He shook my hand with both of his and left, trudging through the slick, icy snow toward his house. I looked around at the fort. It could have been another world on a distant planet on which I had found myself abandoned by God and men, to die in a frozen and desolate waste.

CHAPTER 21

Deliverance

The death toll reached its highest during this period. Hardly anyone had the strength to move. Even the nightly death wagon ceased to make its rounds, and the dead either lay in their houses, unburied, or were thrown out into the street by the other occupants of the house. The bodies froze there in hard, grotesque shapes and when someone finally got around to burying them, they were more like marble statues carved in a mocking pose of life.

The ground was also frozen and had to be broken up with pickaxes. The statues were then laid in these shallow holes and the frozen chunks of earth shoveled over them like heaps of stones.

The last week of February, the quality of sunlight seemed to change abruptly. The days became brighter, the sky lighter. Light once again glittered in a particular way from the river, and yet it remained bitter cold.

It was discovered that one of our men had killed his wife and had chopped her body into parts, which he attempted to preserve with salt until he could have her for his supper. He was tried and condemned to be hanged with all possible speed. Gallows were constructed. The Lieutenant read the order of execution and issued a warning against such a crime to all the people of Jamestown. There were only about seventy or eighty of us remaining alive.

The hangman then fixed the rope around the man's neck. But before he could finish, the man held out his arms, looked up to the gray sky, and, with tears streaming down his face, shouted at the top of his voice, "Alas, there is no God!"

The hangman leapt back in horror and those who had gathered around the gallows let out an anguished cry. Even the Lieutenant looked shaken. He composed himself, however, and ordered the trap to be pulled. The man dropped to his death. Many in the crowd screamed and, without waiting further, hurried back to their quarters.

The man's body swung on the gallows until well after dark, before the Lieutenant ordered it to be taken down and buried. Everyone so ordered refused. Even the men of the death patrol refused, claiming that since the man was probably cursed, they would require more payment. The Lieutenant said that there was nothing to pay them with, so he and several of his soldiers cut the body down themselves and disposed of it. A few weeks later, the Lieutenant left on a hunting expedition with those same men and never returned to the fort. Most said that it was because the Lieutenant tampered with God's justices too much. Others said that he had touched a man cursed by God.

I never discovered what happened to the Lieutenant, although I tried for many years. Probably, like most of those who ventured outside the fort for long, he and his men were ambushed and killed by the Indians and their bodies left to the wolves and vultures.

Spring came like a cruel joke. Gentle warming winds blew from the south. Life burst forth from every twig and barren spot of ground and yet, among this abundant energy of life, we died as before. We would have planted crops, but there were no seeds. We would have hunted, but our only weapons were swords and knives. Yet, even with these we did manage on occasion to capture small game. I became adept at catching frogs and snakes and was pleased to discover that the meat from these creatures made a tasty stew. I rigged noose traps and managed to catch a few rabbits and squirrels. I watched other animals that were beyond my powers of capture to see what plants they ate, and I would gather as many of these plants as I could to take home.

Once, seeing a buck grazing near an open field and driven near to madness with dreams of a great feast, I pursued the beast with a large rock, yelling like a maniac. The deer trotted off to a safe distance and stood watching me with curiosity and, no doubt, with humor. I stopped far short of the buck, gasping for breath and clutching my stone in one hand. My matted hair hung down to my shoulders. My beard was down to my chest and the clothes sagged from my bony body in rags. I must have looked to the deer like a primitive, shaggy beast. He stood so handsome in his shiny brown coat; his strong, sleek body; and bright, healthy eyes.

Despite my best efforts to gather sustenance, Anne grew steadily worse. She was now great with child and suffered from sickness so that she could hardly stand for more than a few minutes. Her eyes had sunk back into her head so that they looked more like dark caves. Her cheekbones seemed ready to push through her thin skin. Her face and head looked more like a skull, and her body was a skeleton with a tight covering of dry paper.

I would have wept, and often prayed that I could, but the tears would not come. I felt as dry as a piece of old parchment. Yet every day we managed to survive off what I thought should not keep a sparrow alive.

We moved into late spring. I wasn't sure of the month. I had lost all track of that measurement of time. I was trying to spear fish in the river with my sword, when I looked up and saw the broad white sails of two ships gliding up the river. I didn't trust myself, thinking they might be apparitions brought on by our long state of privation. I watched, unable to believe my eyes, as the sails fluttered in the wind and a long red and white pennant waved from the top mast. Above that, a large flag flying the cross of St. George seemed to sail above the treetops.

A host of Heaven's angels, led by the archangel himself, could not have been a more welcome sight. I ran back to the fort, waving my sword above my head, shouting at the top of my voice, "Ships! English ships!"

Those people who could walk or even crawl came out of their houses or stopped what they were doing and came to me. I babbled at them. The tears that I had longed for during the past terrible winter burst from my eyes in torrents. The words were all somehow coherent, as if I had been visited by the Holy Spirit. The people seemed to understand what I was saying for, in a moment, they picked me up and carried me along toward the river, all shouting and screaming. No group of lost souls could have been more joyous at seeing their salvation come. Many were so ecstatic with their deliverance that they were overcome and fainted by the river's edge.

I realized that I had forgotten about Anne. I started back for the fort and saw her struggling to walk to the river. I ran to her and, placing her arm around my neck, helped her to the water's edge where we could see this wonderful and unbelievable sight.

We watched the two small ships, in a state of almost divine ecstasy, as the sails were furled. We could hear the Captain's orders and the sailors running about the deck. The ships came up into the wind, and the anchors were lowered. We cheered as they splashed into the water. In a short while, longboats were lowered from the ships and many men entered them. They shoved away and pointed their tiny bows toward us.

The sight of these Englishmen was shocking. Then, strangely, I felt a little fearful. I looked around at the ragged, filthy, emaciated remnants of the colony's once great population, and I saw that they, too, felt as I did. The Englishmen coming toward us were so robust, so alien that I began to realize how Captain Smith's people must have felt at their first sight of us coming ashore just a year ago.

We stepped back as their boats ran up on the sand. They all stepped out and pulled the boats higher on shore. Then they gathered in front of us, each man of them with a look of horror upon his face. This frightened us further and we all took several steps backwards.

One man, with an air of command, stepped forward, asked who was in charge. There was a long silence. We looked at one another.

"There is no one in charge," I finally said, "Sir George Percy assumed presidency of the Council after Captain Smith departed, but no one has seen him in many months. He is believed to be still living, but ill.

"Who are you?" the gentleman asked.

I gave him my name and my occupation.

"I am Captain Christopher Newport, and this," he gestured to a man dressed in the fine clothes of a gentleman, "is Sir Thomas Gates, Governor of this colony."

A pitiful moan rose from our ragged people.

"Sir," I said, "I sailed with your fleet out of Plymouth a year ago. Are you come from Heaven, sir, to take us with you? Are we dead and do not know it? You were given up for lost, sir, and surely no man lost at sea for the length of a year could still be alive and be in such good health."

"My friend," Sir Thomas stepped forward and said in a gentle way, "*Sea Venture* shipwrecked on the island of Bermuda where, God be thanked, we saved most of our goods and were able over the past months to build these fine vessels that you see here. We are in good health because of the mild climate of that land and its natural bounty. Rest assured that you are not dead, and that we are not from Heaven."

Laughter rippled through his men.

"You see then, sir, that we are near death ourselves and are the remains of all those people who sailed with you, all having died a most miserable death."

Sir Thomas and Captain Newport gasped.

"You are all that is left of near five hundred people?"

"Yes, sir," I said, and staggered slightly, feeling a wave of weakness pass through me.

"Good God," Sir Thomas exclaimed. "I can't believe it."

Captain Newport turned to his men and ordered them to return to the ships and fetch as much fresh victuals as the boats would hold and return forthwith.

"You good people come with me to the fort," Sir Thomas said, "I wish to know all that has happened here."

We followed him back to the fort. Inside the fort, he stopped and looked around at our crumbling houses, our bare streets and grounds, our palisades sagging, some of which had rotted and fallen away to the ground.

I showed him the way to the vacated President's House. Every consumable object had long since been used. All of the furniture had been burned for fuel. The house was only a space enclosed by four walls.

"Tell me," he said to those present, "what happened here?"

There was a long silence, like the silence preceding a great calamity. Then everyone commenced talking at once, each accusing the other for the tragedy that befell our fort.

Sir Thomas called for quiet and, when it was restored, he asked me to speak. I told him, as briefly as I could, all that had happened after the wounding of Captain Smith and the unfortunate delegation of power to Sir George Percy. Many times during my narrative, he shook his head in disgust. When I had finished, he asked if anyone had anything they wanted to add. No one said a word.

A sailor entered the house and said to Sir Thomas that all was ready. Sir Thomas asked us to follow him to the center of the fort where all assortments of victuals had been laid out upon the ground for us. Another wave of single-mindedness seized us and we, the starving remnants of Jamestown, rushed upon the victuals with a howl and tore and grabbed everything before us.

We ate, stuffing every eatable thing we could get hold of into our mouths. Many of the people had lost their teeth and chewed with bleeding gums, often swallowing the mouthful whole, only to vomit it all up later. One of our people later died for this overindulgence.

Sir Thomas's people looked on this spectacle with amazement and fear. When we had eaten our fill, Sir Thomas ordered his men to make a place for themselves in the church and the women would occupy the storehouse. We lay where we had fallen after our orgy of eating, groaning, and holding our abdomens.

The sailors later distributed clothes for us and helped us back to our houses, when we were able to walk. Anne and I spent a most miserable night, both sick and tormented with pains and gripes. The next day we were fed in a more organized manner, the ship's quartermaster being careful to ration out small quantities and Sir Thomas entreating us to drink much water. After breakfast he called all of the people together and announced his intentions to depart Jamestown as soon as we could be restored to health.

"I came here," he said, "expecting to find a fat and prosperous colony, full of happy people laboring in their fields and vineyards, a new land flowing with milk and honey. Such were my dreams, and I was not discouraged from those dreams even after a year's sojourn in Bermuda, in all of its ugliness and horror. I see that I was a fool who sought only the counsel of flatterers and other fools.

Captain Newport stepped forward and announced his intention.

"My good people, we have only enough provisions for two or three months. But even if we had enough for an entire year, I would not risk or ask you to risk another day of hunger. In the meantime, rest and eat your fill. I will study the tides and will inform you of the day of our departure."

That day came on the seventh of June, 1610. We boarded the ships early that morning with all of our worldly possessions that we could carry, and in the quiet hours, we weighed anchors and began our slow drift down the James River to England.

I felt no remorse or regret at seeing the little island, where we had suffered so much, recede into the distance. I was more worried about Anne. Her time of delivery was coming due, and I feared that she would have to give birth at sea. Her health had improved considerably, as had the health of the rest of us, but giving birth for the first time was a rigorous ordeal and the condition of a sea voyage for many weeks made her survival even more doubtful.

She faced the future with bravery equal to that of the most

courageous soldier and, like all of us who had survived that winter of death, she was not sorry to be leaving Jamestown. It seemed, even to me, that by being one of those few who survived, all our sins had been forgiven and that we were only a chosen few.

CHAPTER 22

A Cruel Act of Fate

There was little or no wind to speed us on our journey, so we drifted with the tide all that night. The next morning, we arrived at Mulberry Point, where Captain Newport spied a longboat approaching us. He ordered the sails stricken and the anchors dropped. The longboat came alongside and hooked the sea painter that was thrown to them. The sailors shipped their oars. Sir Thomas hailed a gentleman standing in the stern sheets and asked who he was and what he wanted.

The gentleman announced himself as Captain Argall, in the service of the Baron De La Warr, newly appointed Governor of Jamestown and Virginia. Sir Thomas welcomed him aboard and spoke with him on the deck. After they had exchanged some words, the Captain requested that Sir Thomas accompany him to Lord De La Warr's ship, which Sir Thomas did after taking his leave of us.

We could see Lord De La Warr's ship in the distance coming into view, sailing slowly in the calm wind. We watched as the longboat bearing Sir Thomas plowed the water with all possible speed toward the ship. That afternoon Sir Thomas returned, and Captain Newport ordered the stops off the sails and the anchors to be weighed.

We were returning to Jamestown and the thought of it, the realization, made me sick at heart. We now seemed doomed for certain by the most cruel act of fate. Many of our people shouted against returning, begging Sir Thomas, with tears flowing from their eyes, not to go back. He tried to calm them in a gentle voice, with assurances that those of us who wanted to leave could do so in the first ship departing for England, but that he had his duty to perform and that he would do it against any man.

Thus, on the tenth of June, we once again set our feet on the shores of Virginia at Jamestown. We gathered in the ruined fort and heard a sermon by the new minister, and the Lord De La Warr read his commission. He then held a council of all the leading men while we busied ourselves unloading the ships.

When this work was completed, we again gathered to hear Lord De La Warr announce that this was to be a new beginning for Jamestown; that work and living space would be given to all and that judgements would be swift and severe for wrongdoers. He then blamed the past sufferings and failures of Jamestown on vanities and idleness but admonished those of us who had survived from those days to forget the past we had known here and to become one of his new people. As soon as the speech was ended, I went to Sir Thomas.

"Sir," I said, "it was my understanding that my Captain King of our ship, *Diamond*, would be returning with more supplies this springtime. Lord De La Warr made no mention of him. I know him from my voyage to this place, and I was hoping he could take Anne and myself safely back to England once the babe is born." Sir Thomas pressed his lips together, his blue eyes became distant as though they were looking deeply inward.

"I'm sorry to have to tell you this, lad," he said, "but the news is that Captain King perished and went down with the *Diamond* during a strong storm just as he was approaching England this last voyage."

With that unhappy news, I began to realize that my fate

was to stay in this harsh land called Virginia, and that I would somehow have to call it home. I then asked Sir Francis if I could have my former house back. He agreed, but warned that it was probably only temporary.

The next day those among us able to work were given the task of repairing the palisades. Lord De La Warr had brought a master carpenter with him, and I felt that it would be imprudent to mention my own experience in that trade. So I worked as a laborer, determined to go to the council and ask for farm land away from the fort to establish my family.

The opportunity came a few days later, after Lord De La Warr had sent Sir Somers and Captain Argall on a mission to Bermuda to obtain hogs. I approached his Lordship in the President's House.

The Lord De La Warr was a man of truly regal bearing, who dressed in the highest fashion and maintained the airs of a man of his station wherever he might be. He had brought his personal draper with him from England and, when I was given permission to enter his presence, the draper was busy cutting and fluttering about the room with his measure. His lordship had re-powdered his face against the rigors of the sun and asked, in an irritable way, what I wanted.

I introduced myself as one of those who had landed at the colony the year before. He looked aside in disgust. I said that my wife was with child and that the former Governor had promised me a parcel of land where I might establish a farm and thereby support my family. His lordship looked me up and down, his reddened lips forming a thin snarl.

"The promises of past governors is of no concern of mine, but if you are one of those rabble who wasn't fortunate enough to die in the winter, you must be a troublemaker and a thief, for I understand from scholars that such people have a way of surviving great physical adversity."

"It is true, sir. I am a thief and a scoundrel and would be only a bad influence upon your people, so please grant me this one opportunity to be an honest man, and I will forever be grateful and praise your Lordship as a noble man of mercy and generosity."

"Good Lord, don't do that. You'll have every one of you pounding at my door, begging for something. As for your request, I would be happy to have you out of the fort. Submit what you want to my secretary and I will sign it."

The draper came to his side, holding a long piece of red velvet. His Lordship dismissed us with a wave of his hand. I backed to the door, bowed, and left.

His Lordship's secretary, a small, pale man with thin lips and watery eyes, took my written request, signed it, and placed it on one side of the table he was using for a desk. I waited for some sort of answer. He looked at me angrily.

"You'll hear something in a few days," he said, and jerked another paper in front of him and pretended to read it.

I returned home and told Anne that we would have a place soon, although I doubted my own words. Still the good news, even if it was exaggerated, seemed to cheer her considerably. Our edible rations remained good and plentiful enough—more than we had had to eat since coming to Jamestown.

His Lordship sent fifty good shots to raid the village of Paspahegh where many of the Indians were killed, including the Queen and her children. All of their first harvest was taken and their fields and yehawkans burned to the ground. These men, of which I was not one, then scoured the country around Jamestown, driving the Indians out as they would wild horses, and taking all the game and corn, fruits, and other victuals that they could find, which made a considerable addition to our stores.

I continued working on repairing the palisades. Returning home late of an evening, I was met with one of the newly arrived women, the wife of a tanner. She inquired into the condition of my wife and I told her that she was well.

"She is well advanced," the woman said.

"Any time now," I said.

"When the time comes," she said, "call on me. I've had many years' work as a midwife, and there is no physician with us."

I thanked this good woman and asked what she would require as payment.

"Nothing," she said. "This new world needs strong young people born on its soil. It will be a privilege, sir."

She spoke with pride. A great feeling of affection overcame me. I seized her and kissed her repeatedly and, before I realized it, tears were flowing from my eyes. Uncontrollably, I asked her indulgence for my behavior but explained, "I thought that all human kindness had gone from the human heart."

She held me around the shoulders and walked me to the door of my house. I felt a great comfort in this woman's arms. She could have been my own mother and, in truth, after she had bid me farewell at my door, I thought about my own mother, whose face I had not seen since childhood and that I would never see again. For the first time in my life a flood of remembrance rushed into my brain, and I could not have felt more wretched than if I had been an orphan from birth.

I regained control of myself and entered the house, where I found Anne struggling to prepare our supper. I kissed her lightly on the forehead and the hands and pleaded with her not to stress herself, for I would make it a point to do whatever work needed doing at the house, and told her of meeting the tanner's wife. I instructed her to call upon the good woman if the time should come and find me away.

"So you have presented ourselves to everyone as man and wife?"

"I have. No one is the wiser among the newly arrived, and this babe that is soon to be born will be our marital bond."

A week or so later, I was summoned to the President's House where his Lordship, seated in all of the splendor of his rank and office, handed me the paper entitling me to a grant of ten acres of choice land in the eastern part of our island. I thanked him for his kindness most profusely and departed. I ran straight to our house with the grant rolled tightly in my hand, and found Anne lying on the bed, with the first of the pains. I forgot about the grant for the time being and ran for the tanner's wife.

Together we flew back to my house where the tanner's wife, a knowledgeable woman, took immediate charge of the situation. I did all that she asked without the slightest hesitation, watching this strange event and feeling like I had been a part of something far beyond my understanding. A part, perhaps, I thought, of the great divine plan that transcends human morality or conduct. I waited, almost in a state of terror, as the pains came and came and came, forcing the child into life in the world.

Anne's pains, her screams, tore into my heart. I cursed myself. I cursed the forces that brought about this agony. I cursed and I prayed. If the tanner's wife directed me to do something, I did it with superhuman strength, with lightning speed. No power on earth could have prevailed against my will.

Then, with Anne almost at the end of her endurance and I almost ready to rail against Heaven and Hell, I saw the child's head appear, then the shoulder, then the rest of the child's body, slowly emerging from the body of my wife, streaked with blood, wrinkled as dried fruit and wet as thoroughly as if it were being pulled from the edge of the sea. Born into this world amid blood and pain and destined to live that way until the end. I suddenly felt very weak. The strength flowed from out of my body in unrestrained torrents.

I braced myself against the wall to keep from falling. My head buzzed as though it was filled with a thousand bees. The scene before me took on a dreamlike quality, fluid and detached. The tanner's wife snipped the child's umbilical cord with a quick movement of her hand and a paring knife. She tied off the stump with a small thread and began washing the child from a basin of warm water. She looked over to me and said that I should begin washing my wife but, after a longer look, she knew that I was incapable of any further practical use.

Anne was very pale, her breathing shallow, her eyes closed. I was afraid that the recent ordeal of the past winter might have taken too high a toll.

"Don't worry," the tanner's wife said with a pleasant smile, and handed me the child wrapped in a blanket. Then she went about the unpleasant business of cleaning and disposing of the afterbirth, and she cleaned Anne with gentleness and care.

I stepped outside with the child in my arms. She was a perfectly formed little girl, peaceful and resting after her struggles to greet this world. I was so overwhelmed with her beauty that I started shouting for all to come and see my child of the new world.

His Lordship and the council allowed me time off to build my new farm house and to prepare my land for planting. Anne remained with our little girl whom we gave the name of Virginia, naming her after this new land. After about a month, I had the place well suited for our inhabitance. I used the timber from our own land to build the house plus provide fencing and other firewood and a store of logs to cut into planks for constructing other farm buildings. By the end of the summer, I had three acres cleared and planted. The crops would not be the best, but they would mature before the first frost and, with our rations from the fort, they would see us well through the winter.

His Lordship had sent stern reports back to the London Company, demanding that we be better supplied in the future or else he would abandon the whole colony before he would suffer one person to perish of starvation. Still, supplies were slow in coming and a good part of them often spoiled before arriving.

Yet each week we managed to have a good portion of meat, and I was able to procure a fat hen which we kept in the house during the winter. The hen supplied us with enough eggs to satisfy our needs all winter and by spring, I mated her with a neighbor's rooster and we soon enjoyed a half dozen chicks, scurrying about the yard, chirping and trying their useless wings.

I spent many happy hours watching little Virginia pursue the fleeing chicks. She would stumble and stagger about like a fawn on her unsteady legs. Like a drunken man, she would begin to run and, being unable to stop, would fall flat. She never complained with these temporary setbacks, but was soon on her feet again, trotting after the chicks, little plump arms thrown out for balance and smiling, as toothless as an octogenarian.

A new spirit had come into the Jamestown colony. Gone was the former sickness of gold and fast wealth. The people seemed more determined to survive and prevail. They seemed more helpful, more cooperative. But perhaps that was my own false view, seen from the eyes of a man with a new family and land of his own and a future that appeared predictable and prosperous.

Anne and little Virginia spent almost every waking moment together. Anne would clean and bake and Virginia would toddle after her to "help" her Momma in whatever she was doing. Anne was one of the first women to arrive and stay in Jamestown and now Virginia was one of very few children. The lack of playmates for her daughter only made Anne happier as she had the child all to herself. I whittled a top for her to spin, which sent her into peals of laughter, but her favorite toy was the doll that Anne made for her from corn husks, rags, and a dried apple for a head. My guilt and shame, though less, continued to weigh upon me, but Anne spent her days humming cheerfully and set about making a very warm and welcoming house.

———————

Sir Thomas Dale arrived in Jamestown in May of 1611 and brought with him a goodly number of new men and many heads of cattle and other provisions. I was fortunate to be able to purchase one of the cows with the production of one acre of corn. I had built a small shed to accommodate this possibility and tied the cow in it until I could fence off enough land for her grazing. I was also worried that Indians might steal her and kept a close watch on her, day and night. We saw few Indians in those two years. They would never come closer than a bow shot from any of us.

The cow would provide us with a good supply of milk, butter, and cheese. By the next winter I had added another room on to our small one-room house, which would serve as a bedroom until our daughter, Virginia, was old enough to require a separate room.

Jamestown was prospering with the export of our tobacco to England. Ships arrived all that summer with more men, hogs, cattle, and other valuable supplies, and later into the year there

was talk of a marriage between John Rolfe and the favorite
daughter of Powhatan.

CHAPTER 23

Winter 1613

I t was during this winter that my night terrors began. I dreamed often of Richard, seeing him always in the distance, usually calling to me, always naked, once appearing far out in the river. The water covered him up to his waist and his arms were extended toward me in a gesture of greeting, but also in the manner of one pleading for help. I started toward him, and suddenly I was surrounded by fire. The water had turned to fire and I could see nothing, could feel nothing but flames.

I awoke many nights with a start and found myself bathed in a cold sweat. I began staying up at night to avoid sleep and the torments that awaited me. Even in my waking hours I began to feel fearful for no clear reason. I worried over the slightest mishap.

I started drinking to try to ease my sufferings. Soon I was neglecting my work, as well as my wife and child. I took to spending days, even some nights, around the ships where I could obtain wine and brandy. Wilcox, who was becoming rich in the tobacco trade, would point me out to others and say, very piously, "There, my friends, is a fallen man. A man given over to Satan and the devil's brew."

But I did not care what he said or postured. I cared for nothing so long as I could find relief in drink. At first, Anne scolded me with a sharp tongue and seeing that that would not drive me back to my senses, she grew morose and distant, often looking at me with fear and concern. My little girl ran from my touch and treated me like a stranger.

Spring came, and the wedding of Powhatan's daughter and Master Rolfe found me drunk and searching the mass graveyard for any clues as to where Richard's remains might be buried. Unable to find it, I later cornered Wilcox and demanded to know the location. Wilcox took me to the ridge where all of the people who died in the starvation time were buried and pointed to a shallow depression in the ground.

"I think this might be it, but I cannot be certain. You see, we had to bury them together. There were often too many to give each one a personal resting place, so most of them are resting together, five, sometimes ten to a grave . . . but I think this might be the one. What are you planning on doing, mate, putting up a stone marker?"

"No," I said.

"Well then, were you planning on digging him up and raising him from the dead like a bloody Lazarus? Then you should have buried him yourself, instead of dallying with his wife, mate."

Had I been my former self, a remark like that would have brought out my sword and I would have made Wilcox apologize for it or die by my hand, but I was not my former self. I was a man who hated his present self and a man who wished for death and atonement. Wilcox knew it as he seemed to know all of the weaknesses of men and women. I endured his laughter and his scorn, would have endured a hundred strokes of the lash itself for one night of peaceful sleep.

I took to visiting the gravesite with my bottle and drinking myself into a stupor, driving myself mad thinking of the helplessness of all mankind and his miserable condition in this world.

It was on one of these visits of a Sunday in late spring that I returned, drunk as usual, to the town for more brandy. There was a great commotion outside the church. Someone said that the Indians had raided the island and had attacked several farms.

A tingling sense of horror came over me. My vitals turned to ice. My limbs would not stop shaking. I started running back to my farm, stumbling, and falling on my face many times before I reached the gate.

A twisting column of black smoke came up from my house. I listened and all was silent, not even the chirp of a bird. I ran toward the house, calling for Anne, and then I saw her. She was in back of the house, lying on her side. There were six, maybe ten, arrows pierced through her body. I held up her head. Her lovely blue eyes were open, but the light had gone out of them, the sweet breath gone. Gently, I removed the arrows and laid them to one side, then turned her so that she would lie on her back. Then, for the last time, I kissed her lips, now lifeless and breathless as stone, and brushed her hair back in place.

I knew what I would find next, although I prayed that they had taken her to raise as a captive. But she was only a short distance away where, no doubt, they had caught her trying to run away. They had smashed her little head with a war club so that her face was unrecognizable. I picked her up and took her back to where Anne lay, and that is where I buried them.

I spent the rest of the day and night building two good coffins, putting all of my woodworking skill into them. I carved their names on two sturdy wood crosses, dug the holes, and gently lowered them in, where they would remain for the rest of eternity.

When this work was finished, I returned to the house. The attackers had tried to burn the place, but the fire had not taken hold and only a small section was charred. I gathered up the title to this property and, without thinking why, picked up the leather bag containing the Indian lexicon.

I walked back to Jamestown, and it was early morning before I got there. 1 walked through the gate without acknowledging the challenge from the guard. He was on the point of stopping me when I walked up to the first man I saw and handed him the land title.

"It's yours," I said, "and everything in it. I have signed all the papers. Put your name here."

I pointed to the place below my name.

"And this good soldier can serve as a witness."

The soldier looked confused. The man took the title, read through it, noted the seal of the Lord De La Warr and looked up at me, aghast. His mouth opened but remained speechless.

"Take it, it's yours," I said again, and walked out of James- town fort forever.

———◦•◦•◦———

I became a man in search of death, not merely wishing for it but consciously seeking it. After I had walked for a while, I stripped off all of my clothes but, for reasons still unclear to me, I held on to the leather bag. I walked naked as an infant through the thick woods, not caring how I should find death. There were poisonous serpents, but they all shunned me. There were marshes and swamps, but none would swallow me up. I walked on, my body lacerated and scourged from the thorny vines that draped the trees and bushes.

Just before dark I saw a campfire and, thinking that it must be Indians, walked toward it. I stepped boldly out of the woods and into the cone of firelight. The Indians, three in all, seeing me thus naked and bleeding from my many cuts, leaped to their feet but would not come near me. I advanced toward them and, in an instant, one of them drew his bow, ready to let fly an arrow at my heart. But one of their number held up his hand.

"Wait," he said in a controlled voice. "I know this man."

The Indian moved toward me. I recognized him as Nanquoto, the Indian I had helped to escape from Sir Henry's torture.

"My friend," he said, "why have you come thus naked? Have you been attacked and robbed?"

"I have come seeking death," I said. "Let your man do his work."

"No man seeks death unless he is mad or possessed by a strong spirit."

"I am not mad," I said. "The spirit within me is stronger than madness, stronger than my former desire to live."

Nanquoto came closer to me. "What do you carry in the leather pouch?"

I held it out to him. "It is a book containing the words of your language."

Nanquoto leaped back in horror. The other Indians gasped and dropped their weapons. Nanquoto reached down and picked up a deer skin that he had used to lie upon. He came toward me, trembling slightly, and placed it around my waist.

"Here," he said. "You must clothe yourself. We will take you before the high priest, Ipataqonough. He will decide if your desire is to be granted."

We started out immediately through the woods, following paths that were unknown to me. I had no knowledge of the directions we took, and it seemed to me that we walked endlessly in a black void. Each step was like a step into eternity.

I was a man in search of death. I could have taken one of their knives and cut my own throat or disemboweled myself, but that was not the death I sought, not by my own hand, not by my own decision. I wanted death from the hand of God. I wanted a lightning bolt from Heaven to lash out and strike me to the ground, or death from God's handiwork in nature, or even from the hands of other men. I walked, not caring about the gashes that the rocks and thorns made in my feet or even feeling the pain.

It was early morning when we reached the village of Orapax. I was placed in the custody of Nanquoto's two companions, while he went to speak with the werowance and the high priest. A group of the villagers gathered around me and examined me with the utmost curiosity. Some reached out as if to touch my skin. One of them asked my guard if I was made as other men. He said yes, that I was made as other men but that I was possessed by a devil, and my maleness was not to be looked upon lest it spit fire and evil. The Indians around us retreated quickly and were careful to look away from me as they passed.

Nanquoto returned after a long time and led me to the temple where he left me in a small room with many religious signs and symbols fastened to the mat veils. In a short while, a conjurer appeared. His body was painted with the red paint made from the plant of bloodroot. He danced around me, sprinkling tobacco dust over his head. Then he stopped and sat down before me.

He dropped three grains of corn on the ground in front of us and began a short oration, straining his body so that the veins distended from his head and neck, and the red bloodroot on his face ran in small streaks down to his waist. He finished his prayers and dropped three more grains of corn onto the ground and, with a howl that deafened me, he leaped up and darted out of the room.

Nanquoto entered shortly and bid me to stand and follow him. He led me into a larger room where the high priest was seated at one end and, next to him, the figure of their god, Okee. Next to the wall, seated on a straw mat, was the werowance, Opitchapam. The high priest spoke first.

"I have been told of how you saved the life of Nanquoto when he was a captive in your town and that he has heard from others, Tatahcoope and Waahtmoca, that you are a man of mercy and strength. He has told me of how you came to him in the forest, seeking death. No man has to seek death. It will come soon enough, and any man who seeks it will find it. Yet you are alive."

"Perhaps even death spurns me," I said.

"Because of the terrible spirit within you?"

"Perhaps."

"And in that basket?"

He pointed to the leather pouch that I held at my side.

"You carry our language?"

"Yes."

Ipataqonough looked terrified for a moment.

"And you also speak our language?"

"As you have observed."

"What are you called by your people?"

"I am called Matthew, after a good man of their religion."

"It is not your religion?"

"I am not worthy of their religion or of any man's goodness or of any good man's name."

"Then we shall call you Nehiegh Righcomough, meaning he who dwells with death."

I bowed to the high priest. "It is a fitting name," I said.

"However," the high priest said, "we cannot give you what you seek. The strong evil spirit that dwells within you cannot be released upon our people."

Opitchapam nodded and held up his hand to speak.

"Let us see the thing on which you have captured our language."

The high priest leaped to his feet. "No!" he shouted. "No! Not before many days have passed and we know the power of this man's spirit."

The werowance said nothing but remained calmly seated. The priest resumed his place and summoned the guards, who took me to an empty hut where they waited outside the door. I had started to lay down upon a skin-covered bed, or tussan, when more guards came for me and led me to the yehawkan of Opitchapam.

He was eating a piece of venison and smoking his pipe. He motioned for me to sit down. He dismissed the guards and asked if I would share his pipe. It would have been considered impolite to refuse.

"Ipataqonough fears that you have the power to take away our speech now that you possess our language."

"I have no such power," I said. "Only the sounds of your language are written down in the symbols of my former people. They are only markings and have no power in themselves. It is the way men use them that gives them power."

"May I see these symbols?" he asked in a kindly manner.

I handed him the leather pouch. He smiled at me once before carefully opening the bag.

"Ipataqonough has much power over illness and is in great favor with Powhatan," he said.

"I understand."

He reached slowly into the bag and withdrew the stack of papers. He sat the papers on the mat in front of him and, after taking several long droughts on his pipe, he began leafing through them.

He laughed and said, "These markings have no meaning for me."

"Speak with Tatahcoope concerning them. He will tell you of their meanings."

Opitchapam replaced the lexicon back into the pouch.

"I will do as you say. Why do you not bring an English gun or one of their swords?"

"These are instruments to combat death. I seek it openly."

"If I acquired an English gun, will you teach me the use of it?"

"No," I said.

"Then you still love your people?"

"No, but it is my vow never to harm another man or to cause his harm as long as I am so unfortunate enough to live."

"That truly is not a vow for a man who wishes to live. You may go now," he said.

I stood up, bowed, and said, "What will you do with me?"

"Ipataqonough will keep you prisoner here until such time as he is satisfied that your evil spirit has left you. Then you will have your wish."

I bowed and walked out of the door. The guards escorted me back to my hut, where I slept very soundly until I was awakened about sunset and given a loin garment made of deerskin and trimmed with white beads, such as all of the men of Powhatan's nation wore. The hut was warm and snug, and I smelled the familiar scent of wood fires burning. Sometime later, two women came into the room and set down a great dish of corn, venison, and fish to eat. I enjoyed my meal and wondered how a man can enjoy the pleasures of this world and yet seek death.

CHAPTER 24

New Life

I lived alone, unguarded, for many weeks. Then Ipataqonough came to fetch me with many armed men and led me
to the fields where they put me to work, tending the corn
and tobacco alongside the women and children. The women
and children shunned me except for an occasional group who,
talking and giggling, would look my way.

From the fields I could look back and see the cluster of
huts nearby the river. The houses were made of long, slender
branches tied together in bundles and then woven into a frame
for the house. They were like giant baskets turned upside down,
each with a small garden and a large pile of wood by it.

I went about the work they gave me, uncomplaining, since
life and what I did with it meant absolutely nothing. The world
I found myself in was peaceful. From where I slept and worked,
it seemed the women did most of the work. They often worked
while the men lay idle and only hunted or made war. They
made mats, baskets, pots, and grinding tools to grind corn into
flour and baked bread. They did all the cooking. Some women
went out on boats for fishing.

Still, the world, whether that of the white man or the Indian,
seemed fraught with vanities and unimportance. Each day
I returned to my hut, ate my simple meal, slept, and waited.
Toward the last harvest when the earth seemed to sparkle with
every color of the rainbow, and the geese flew in from the north

in great flights of *V*'s filling the air with their honking, I was summoned once again to the presence of Opitchapam.

A handsome girl of nineteen years sat next to him, her eyes lowered, her arms crossed over her naked breasts in modesty.

"This is Arahatoka, my youngest daughter by my second wife."

I bowed to the girl and sat down on the mat prepared for me.

"She has seen you in the fields laboring with the women and children. She knows of the evil spirit that dwells within you and of your desire to be rid of this world. Yet she says to me, and to Ipataqonough, that you are a man of great loss and loneliness and that the spirit within you is good and not evil. She wishes to take you as her husband, so that you may plant your strengths and your good spirit within her body, so that her children may grow strong in both your people and ours."

I was stunned into speechlessness by this revelation. I had seen the girl in the village. She was the daughter of Opit-chapam, a great werowance, and did no labor while I was made to work with the women and children. What strange workings of the angels had brought this about?

"I am flattered by your most beautiful daughter's attention to me." I said, regaining my speech. "But she must know that a man such as I would make a poor husband and a poorer father."

"I have advised her of this," said Opitchapam. "I have pleaded with her to take a man of our own people, a man who can provide much for her and her family, but she has always been much loved by me and my wife and is, therefore, a willful child. I have never been able to refuse her anything, though in this I would happily do so if I had the strength of my younger days. Now that I am advanced in years, I cannot bear to see her tears. So I have, with an unhappy heart, consented to this."

"Do I have a voice in this?" I asked.

"No, my son," he said.

"Will you kill me if I refuse?"

"No, we will drag you to the ceremony in bondage. The daughter of a werowance will have her wish."

"Even if it's against the wishes of the high priest?"

"Yes," the werowance said, looking at me suspiciously.

"So be it then," I said. "Tell Arahatoka that I am honored and will meet her whenever she wishes."

The girl smiled happily and touched her father's hand gently. Opitchapam nodded for me to leave, which I did, after bowing to them.

It was clear that Opitchapam's wishes for his daughter's happiness were less than that of his wish to reduce the power of the high priest. By successfully overriding Ipataqonough in this matter of the marriage, the werowance's influence would be strengthened in other matters as well.

I was no longer taken to work in the fields but was given a mentor to be taught the Indian religion and customs. I was dressed as befitting a future son-in-law of the werowance and given many strings of beads to adorn my body. The hair was shaved from my body so that I would not offend anyone, and the hair on my head was shaved on the right side in the Indian manner. A cockscomb was cultivated along the crown of my head and the left side was tied in the religious knot over my left ear.

I was taught to shoot a bow by the chief hunter of the tribe and how to wield the spiked club so as to quickly dispatch a large animal. I was assured that I would never have to use this against men, only against animals taken during the hunts. I became quite proficient in the use of the bow and arrow and could place my point on target at well over fifty yards distant.

I soon brought down my first deer with this weapon and presented the skin to Arahatoka as a wedding present.

We were married in late autumn in the traditional Indian ceremony. Opitchapam, along with his two wives and a few servants, brought his daughter to my yehawkan at midday. He said a few words that I did not understand, then joined our hands together and removed a long string of shell beads from around his neck. He then broke the string of beads over our heads, and at this point we were married.

Later, after I had proved myself as a hunter, we were given a larger yehawkan with two rooms. I don't know at what point I stopped thinking about death or my past life at the fort, or of all of the sins that I was guilty of, but it was toward spring, with Arahatoka pregnant, that one morning I realized that I no longer thought about myself as Matthew James, Englishman and carpenter apprentice. My past seemed like the vague remembrance of a painted picture where the colors have long faded into dullness. The events of the past, for which I was responsible, no longer pricked my heart with the same sharpness.

My skin was as dark as an Indian's. My manner and speech became Indian. I thought in the Indian language. It is as though I had been given a second beginning, another chance at redemption. Arahatoka, through her patience and devotion slowly renewed in me a desire to live again. I began to laugh and to know joy. I felt genuine hunger and all its many pains again. Arahatoka returned heart-pounding life to me, which had fled from my soul on the last day I returned to my farm. I began to take part in the activities of the tribe and often sat in on the council meetings, supporting my father-in-law against the high priest.

My son was born in early summer, and we named him

Aranck, meaning Light of the Heavens. He was a large, healthy boy who bore the traces of our mixed blood—my blue eyes and her copper skin—and yet he was the more beautiful for it. All in the village came to look at him, mostly out of curiosity, but some, like Opitchapam and his wives, came out of affection.

Arahatoka, like most of the tribal women, was a natural mother and loved our son very much. She would wash him in the cold waters of the river every morning, as it was known throughout that that would make him strong. She would then rub him with oils and lotions to protect him from the weather. He went everywhere with her, strapped firmly to her body.

Soon, the high priest came with several conjurers and, after a long ceremony to expel any evil spirit from the child, came to me and said, "The spirit of death has left you and now you are as mortal as other men. Because you are Opitchapam's son-in-law, I cannot have you executed as I would have done. Therefore, I must ask you to give me the papers holding our language so that I can destroy it by fire, to drive away the spirits that would deprive us of our speech."

The high priest's conjurers had brought their spiked clubs with them. The men stood ready and, no doubt, anxious to use them. Resistance would have meant my instant death. Where questions of religion were concerned, there would have been little that even Opitchapam could have done.

The loss of the lexicon meant little now since I could rewrite it from my own knowledge of the language. I took the book out of the bag, being careful to not let them see the two ink bottles and quills at the bottom. Ipataqonough took the manuscript and immediately handed it to one of his men. He then stared at me for a long while, his eyes full of undisguised hate, then left for his temple.

The long period of peace that followed the marriage of Powhatan's daughter to Master John Rolfe continued for several years into my new life. It was a stable life within the settlement. I ate well and surprisingly, I was cleaner than I ever had been at Jamestown. It was Powhatan custom to bathe regularly in the river and to wash our hands before and after each meal. I happily distanced myself from my former life. Englishmen came to trade, but I saw none of them. Even fighting with the Monacans ceased for a long time.

I had heard that Nanquoto went to the fort many times and often returned with things he had traded for corn. I went to him on a day when the high priest and many of his lesser priests had gone to visit Powhatan at Werowocomoco, where the great temple was, and asked him how the situation was at the fort. He said that the people were prospering and growing tobacco at every space of open ground, even in the streets. That the present governor, Yeardly, was a good man who had even taken Indians into his army and trained them in the use of fire weapons. I asked him if he could acquire paper for me, but that it must be kept a secret from all, lest it become known by the high priest. Nanquoto said that he would do as I asked, that since I had saved his life he would bear the high cost himself. I thanked him for his kindness and gave him a string of many beads, which he liked very much.

Aranck grew stronger daily. He was an intelligent boy with bright, alert eyes. He learned fast and laughed readily. He soon became the natural leader of the other children, and it wasn't long before Ipataqonough paid us another visit, this time to demand that the boy be turned over to him upon his next birthday, to be raised in the temple as a future high priest. He saw the boy's gift for leadership and sensed that if he were raised under the influence of the family of Opitchapam, he would be a strong opponent of the priestly class. The request greatly upset Opitchapam, but such requests from the high priest cannot be refused and must be considered a great honor.

Arahatoka behaved well the day they came for him. She had adorned him in the finest pearls and copper chains. His loin covering was of the finest bear skin, and she had sown moccasins for him from the softest deer skin.

My heart swelled with love and pride as I regarded his brave composure. He knew this was a great honor, but he also knew he would be leaving his mother. As the young priests came to escort him to the great temple, Aranck looked straight ahead and walked with them without looking back.

I had instructed him to do what is just and to always do his duty and to respect the laws of the temple and of the nation of Powhatan.

After the boy had gone, Arahatoka wept for days as though her heart had been pulled from her body. My own heart felt like a great lump of stone in my breast and does to this day when I think of him.

I have kept up with Aranck, over the years. His name is now Eluwilussit, or The Holy One. I learned that he is first among the other young people who were selected for the priesthood. He now lives at Werowocomoco and serves the great temple there. I have heard, also, that he despises the English blood that is a part of him. This I expected, but it is enough for me now to know that he is alive and is still a young man bound for a great destiny.

CHAPTER 25

Bloodroot

The year came, 1618 by the English calendar, when old Powhatan died and the cement that bound the nation together seemed to soften and die with him. Our hope for his successor had been for his grandson by his daughter, Matoaka, but the child had been left in England after her death, and it is doubtful that he will ever see Virginia.

Itoyatan, Powhatan's second brother, assumed the mantle of leader and soon reestablished the old peace with the English. But Opechancanough soon replaced Itoyatan as leader of the Powhatan nation and proceeded to lay the groundwork for war. We began to hear rumors of English attacks upon our people, although none were ever proven.

As happens when a man wants to plunge his people into war, especially a war against an enemy with superior arms, he finds a mad fool to lead the way. Such a man was Jack of the Feathers. In England he would have been thrown into an institution for the insane and, had not Opechancanough and the priest devised a use for him, he could have been cast out of every village along the great Bay of the Chesapeake.

Opechancanough and his priest convinced the people that Jack of the Feathers was a man possessed with the power to see the future and that the voice of Okee spoke through him. He was revered as a holy man and his advice was sought by every man, even the high priest of Werowocomoco, who made a great show of this to the people.

Then we learned that the mad fool, Jack of the Feathers, had been killed and robbed by an Englishman with whom he had been traveling and now, owing to the work of Opechancanough and the priests, everyone called for a war of revenge on the English. The prayer on everyone's lips, led by Ipataqonough, was that they may drive the English back into the great waters from whence they came.

———◦•◦———

The final council of Opitchapam, great werowance of the Tsenacomacah and cousin to mighty Opechancanough, was held today. I was allowed to come and hear because I am his son-in-law and because my loyalty to him was proven when I handed my son over to the high priest, Ipataqonough, to be raised as Quiyoughquisock and someday to take his place as high priest of the great temple, or Quioccosan.

But I was not allowed to speak because I am a white man, and it is feared by the high priest that my words will be those of the angry sprit that is supposed to dwell within me. Ipata-qonough believes that its words, spoken through me, will have a spellbinding effect upon those present at the werowance's council, or so he told the council at the beginning. Opitchapam at once forbade me to speak until the council ended and all had left his yehawkan. I acknowledged with my hand placed over my heart.

Ipataqonough began the meeting with a passionate prayer to the Okee, entreating him not to become angry with what might be said, both in truth and falsehood. He then sprinkled an offering of tobacco powder on the floor in front of him and threw a handful into the air over his head. Opitchapam asked him to speak first. After a moment's hesitation, in which he looked straight at me, the priest raised his hand to the sun—their way of vowing to tell the truth—and spoke in a loud, passionate voice.

"The English have invaded our ancient land like a blight on our corn and have turned the whole people of Powhatan into a nation of cuckolds, offering them beads and copper for what cannot be bought at any price. They have turned the heads of our youth to their pale, bloodless god and have destroyed the temples of all who deny their religion. Every planting season they take more of our sacred land, and it is never enough for them. They steal our corn to feed their beasts. They insult us and beat us with their horse whips."

Opitchapam sat unmoved by the priest's raving.

Ipataqonough, seeing this, hesitated for a moment, looked around at me and the lesser men of the village who were there, and said in a quivering voice, "And it is believed that they hold secret ceremonies where they eat the flesh of their most beautiful children."

A muted groan rose from all those present. The priest glanced first at me, then at Opitchapam, whose face was momentarily swept with an expression of horror. He made a sign for me to maintain my silence. To speak while under the ban of silence invites death.

Opitchapam then said to the priest, "What then is the message from Opechancanough?"

"The great werowance says this: 'The English have come like a pestilence to our land. They drive all before them into hunger, disease, and death. They kill us with their gun powder and impure bodies. It is time they should be driven from the forest as the crows are driven from our fields. I will send word when the proper sign has made itself known to me.' These are the words of Opechancanough."

The priest remained standing in front of Opitchapam.

"If this is the will of Opechancanough, then so be it. We will wait for his sign and then we will do whatever he commands."

The meeting ended and all rose. They showed their proper respect to Opitchapam and the high Quiyoughquisock, and quietly left the hut. Opitchapam motioned with his hand for me to wait. Ipataqonough saw this and, knowing that I was no longer under the ban of silence, threw a threatening glance my way as he stepped through the doorway. Opitchapam and I were left alone, although I suspected Ipa-taqonough had his ear to the mat wall outside.

Opitchapam took a leaf of tobacco down from a wooden peg next to his crude bed, tore it in half and offered one half of it to me. We packed the tobacco into our clay pipes and lit them with a flaming stick from his house fire.

We sat down and smoked for a while. Then Opitchapam spoke to me in a relaxed way. He asked me if I knew what was in the minds of the English. I told him that the English were little different from his own people, despite their guns and strange manners.

I said, "Many of them want to live in peace and friendship with the nation of Powhatan while others seek nothing but continual war. There are good men and bad men among them, as with the people of Powhatan. Often a good werowance will be replaced by a bad one."

Opitchapam nodded and drew easily from his pipe.

"I understand," he said. "I have long known of Opechan-canough's desire for war with the English, and now that his brother, the great Powhatan, is dead and he knows his place as head of the nation is secure, he is ready to fight with them. I have much fear that he will lead us along the path of sorrow and bitterness. The good peace begun with the marriage of Matoaka to the Englishman Rolfe will soon be ended forever. And the English, once attacked, will come out of their town like a horde of angry bears. Opechancanough's hatred for them will devour us all—but to defy him means certain death."

A look of extreme sadness came into his eyes.

"Our only hope is that the English will be as merciful as they say their God is."

We smoked in silence for a while longer. Then Opitchapam looked at me intently.

"Why cannot the English be content to live in their own land and eat well and lie with their wives and play with their children? Why did they come here to live in hardship and want?"

"The English have a dream," I said. "They believe that a great body of saltwater lies just beyond the mountains, and across this water is a foreign land full of many riches."

"They have come here for that?" Opitchapam asked. For a dream that is not real?"

"They believe that there is a great river running through the land of Powhatan to this great salt water."

"These Englishmen who believe in such things are fools and should be cast out of the company of other men. Do not their women weep for them?"

"Their women weep for jewels and fine clothes," I said.

"And you, Nehiegh, is your heart yet with them?"

"My heart is with Opitchapam and his daughter and his people. Have I not shown this many times in the past? I have not seen an Englishman since your men found me in the forest. I have not spoken a word of their language since that day."

"Yes, yes, my son. I know that what you say is true." The old man smiled contentedly and signaled me to be silent.

"Now go to your wife, lie with her. For soon, before the first planting of corn, we will stand and face death."

Opitchapam covered his face with his hands. I left quickly, for it is shameful for them to see another man weep.

———•◦•———

My wife, Arahatoka, knows that the message Ipataqonough has delivered to our village is not good. She knows that Ipataqonough has sought nothing but war with the English for many years. She watched me gravely as I removed the bundle of paper from the deerskin covering.

There were tears in her eyes and her dark, lovely face was hot and moist. I had broken my promise to her that I would completely forsake my former life, but the time had come.

I told her what Ipataqonough said at the council meeting, and she began to weep softly. She knows what it will mean to go to war against English guns and armor.

As always in such unsettling times, when the fear is upon her, or the anger when she contemplates our lost son, she wants to make love. She back steps to the door of our hut and lowers the flap to cover it. Then, still looking at me with anxious, excited eyes, prepared the soft mat next to the fire and, standing over the mat, close to the fire, she let her deerskin slip from her body. The yellow light from the fire flickered in bright moving wavelets over her body. She was a pagan goddess and this, this mat-covered hut with its sacramental fire was her temple, her quioccosan. And I? I am her eternal worshipper.

I went to her and we melded together, our hearts and blood rushing as one, our breaths mingling into a hot, mighty wind. I felt the surge in my being like the onslaught of a great and ancient sea and, as always, I was taken back for a moment to the beginning of time.

When I awoke it was dark outside. The village was quiet. My wife was still sleeping peacefully by my side. The fire was down to a few crackling embers. I rose from our bed slowly so as not to disturb her and covered her with her deerskin. The paper was still there, waiting. I had thought, possibly in a dream, that it would not be there when I awoke, that somehow it would have vanished and relieved me of its terrible responsibility.

I put a few more sticks on the fire and quietly unfolded the covering and carefully removed the stack of paper. An ink bottle and several stripped quills were at the bottom. I had completely forgotten about them. The ink in the bottle was thick as gum, but a little warm corn oil would thin it enough to use.

This stack of old paper and bottle of dried ink and quill pens were the last personal possessions of my good friend, Richard Scott, and were bequeathed to me upon the promise that I would rewrite his translation of the Powhatan language. I have completely failed in this duty, as I have failed in all of the important tasks life has set before me.

It is for many reasons that I had decided to use my inheritance from Richard not in the way he specified, although I wish to God that I could have. In this last endeavor I must wrong him again as I wronged him so often and so cruelly in the past. Yet I believe, with all my heart, that he would understand why I have decided to not fulfill his wishes. Opechancanough and men like Ipataqonough will lead their people, singing and dancing, into a great, dark pit from which they will never emerge. Their language will be like the cry of a dying animal sounding through the forest and then never heard again.

I do this last wrong to the friend of my youth so that I may give life once again to the past and find forgiveness from all those that I have loved and wronged, and to those who fell in that wake of death I left behind.

———•◦•———

The attack will be in the spring. Our men are supposed to surprise the English in their homes while they are at breakfast. They are to go into their homes as friends and then, when the English least suspect it, they are to seize hold of their farm tools and slay them all. No one is to be spared, not even their horses and dogs.

I have told Opitchapam of our plans to escape. Five days before the attack, we will go down to our fishing weirs in the river and, so as not to create suspicion, I will take only my manuscript, on which this account is written, wrapped up in deer skin and disguised with a bundle of sticks. I will take my bow and arrows and knife so that we can provide for ourselves.

At the fish weir, Arahatoka and I will enter our canoe and paddle down river to a point several miles below, where we will meet and take with us the boy with the withered foot who lives as an outcast on the edge of our village, and who is good at hunting and scavenging. My wife has asked me to save this boy as a sad remnant of the people of Powhatan, since I cannot save our son. His mind and body now belong to the priests and he would kill me rather than go with me. However, after the war, if there are any of Powhatan's people left alive, I will come back in search of him. Opitchapam has given us his blessing but said that he is old and prefers to remain with his people to the last. We have given him our blessing and pray for his happiness in the afterlife toward the setting sun. In a few days, all of the young men of Powhatan's nation will adorn themselves with the sacred juice of the bloodroot and go into a war from which they will never emerge.

I am told that there is a planter living across the river from Jamestown. We will stop there before going the rest of the way downriver and leave this manuscript with him, along with a fair warning of the attack. I hope that he is a reasonable and prudent man.

Arahatoka, the crippled boy, and I will move into the country to the south, where the people there speak our language, and live on many protected islands that are outside the reach of the cruel hand of Opechancanough.

Epilogue

Excerpt from the account of

*"VOYAGE of Anthony Chester to VIRGINIA,
Made in the Year 1620
Narrated by a Distinguished Passenger, who
Participated in the Expedition*

———•◦•———

*RELATING A TERRIBLE AND TREACHEROUS MASSACRE
PERPETRATED IN A CRUEL MANNER BY THE
INHABITANTS OF VIRGINIA ON THE ENGLISH"*[1]

For some reasons, best known to the English government, in March 1622 the King of England had to remind King Powhatan of the articles of the treaty of peace existing between them, in answer to which King Powhatan said that he would prefer seeing the country turned upside down rather than break a single article of the treaty, but, as will be proved later on, this conduct of the savages was nothing but hypocrisy and deceit, they only awaiting a favorable opportunity to kill out the English.

Several days before this bloodthirsty people put their plan into execution, they led some of our people through very

---

1 "Two Tragical Events." *William and Mary Quarterly* 9, no. 4 (April 1901): 204–214.

dangerous woods into a place from which they could not extricate themselves without the aid of a guide, others of us who were among them to learn their language were in a friendly way persuaded to return to our colony, while new comers were treated in an exceedingly friendly manner.

On Friday before the day appointed by them for the attack they visited, entirely unarmed, some of our people in their dwellings, offering to exchange skins, fish, and other things, while our people entirely ignorant of their plans received them in a friendly manner.

When the day appointed for the massacre had arrived, a number of the savages visited many of our people in their dwellings, and while partaking with them of their meal, the savages, at a given signal, drew their weapons and fell upon us, murdering and killing everybody they could reach, sparing neither women nor children, as well inside as outside the dwellings. In this attack, 347 of the English of both sexes and all ages were killed. Simply killing our people did not satisfy their inhuman nature, they dragged the dead bodies all over the country, tearing them limb from limb, and carrying the pieces in triumph around.

Glossary

TERMS

Mamanatowick: Powhatan's title meaning Paramount or Great Chief

Werowance: Tribal Chief

Quioccosan: (Kwee-oh-koh-sahn) Temple

Quiokos: Priest or Minor Deity

Quiyoughquisock: High Priest of the Powhatan nation

Tussan: Skin-covered bed

Yehawkan: Semi-permanent Powhatan house constructed of trees and covered with tree bark and grass mats

Okee: One of the principal gods of the Powhatan Confederacy

HISTORICAL POWHATANS

Powhatan: (proper name, Wahunsenacawh) was the leader of the Powhatan, an alliance of Algonquian-speaking people living in Tsenacomacah, in the Tidewater region of Virginia.

Itopatin: Powhatan's second brother, seeker of peace, assumed the mantle of leadership after Powhatan's death

Opechancanough: Brother of Powhatan, won the title of paramount chief of the Tsenacomoco (from Itopatin) after the death of Powhatan

Ipataqonough: The High Priest of Powhatan nation.

Opitchapam: Werowance of the Pamunkeys; Brother of Opechancough, Itopan and Wahunsenacawh

Tatahcoope: Son of Powhatan and Oholase

Waahtmoca: Son of Opechancanough

Matoaka: (also known as **Pocahontas**) Daughter of Powhatan, married to John Rolfe

Thank you for reading *Bloodroot*.
I hope you enjoyed the experience.
I would appreciate it very much if you could
leave an HONEST review on
your favorite website.

— Dan Meier

About the Author

A retired Aviation Safety Inspector for the FAA, Daniel V. Meier, Jr. has always had a passion for writing. During his college years, he studied History at the University of North Carolina, Wilmington (UNCW), American Literature at The University of Maryland Graduate School. In 1980 he published an Action/Thriller with Leisure Books under the pen name of Vince Daniels.

Meier worked for the Washington Business Journal as a journalist and has been a contributing writer/editor for several aviation magazines.

In addition to *Bloodroot*, Dan is the author of the award-winning historical novel, *The Dung Beetles of Liberia*, released in September 2019, and the literary novel, *No Birds Sing Here*, released in March 2021, both by BQB Publishing.

Dan and his wife live in Owings, Maryland, about twenty miles south of Annapolis. When he's not writing, they spend their summers sailing on the Chesapeake Bay.

Other Books by Daniel V. Meier, Jr.

2019 Grand Prize Winner - Red City Review

Based on the remarkable, true account of a young American who landed in Liberia in 1961.

> ". . . The blend of fictional action and nonfiction social inspection is simply exquisite and are strengths that set this story apart from many other fictional pieces sporting African settings."
>
> —D. Donovan, *Midwest Book Review*

NOTHING COULD HAVE PREPARED HIM FOR THE EVENTS HE WAS ABOUT TO EXPERIENCE. Ken Verrier quickly realizes the moment he arrives in Liberia that he is in a place where he understand very little of what is considered normal, where the dignity of life has little meaning, and where he can trust no one.

It's 1961, and young Ken Verrier is experiencing the turbulence of Ishmael and the guilt of his brother's death. His sudden decision to drop out of college and deal with his demons shocks his family, his friends, and especially his girlfriend, soon to have been his fiancée. His destination: Liberia—the richest country in Africa both in monetary wealth and natural resources.

Author Daniel Meier describes Ken Verrier's many escapades, spanning from horrifying to whimsical, with engaging and fast-moving narrative that ultimately describe a society upon which the wealthy are feeding and in which the poor are being buried.

It's a novel that will stay with you long after the last word has been read.

Satire at its best!

In this indelible and deeply moving portrait of our time, two young people, Beckman and Malany, set out on an odyssey to find meaning and reality in the artistic life, and in doing so unleash a barrage of humorous, unintended consequences.

Beckman and Malany's journey reflects the allegorical evolution of humanity from its primal state, represented by Beckman's dismal life as a dishwasher to the crude, medieval development of mankind in a pool hall, and then to the false but erudite veneer of sophistication of the academic world.

The world these protagonists live in is a world without love. It has every other variety of drive and emotion, but not love. Do they know it? Not yet. And they won't until they figure out why no birds sing here.

Meier's writing is precise and detailed, whether the situation he describes is clear or ambiguous. Fans of Franzen and Salinger will find Meier to be another sharp, provocative writer of our time.